CARPE NOCTEM

SAMAEL OCENAR

CARPE NOCTEM

Subversive Saints Publications LLC

To everyone who has let me talk their ear off about this project, enjoy the fruits of your patience

Knock, knock, knock!

By the headache pounding in time with the door, Xinghua knew that it was far too damn early to have someone at her door. She smacked the pair of socks from on top of her alarm clock to check the time, groaning at the mocking digital blue seven flashing up at her.

Knock, Knock, Knock!

Xinghua's thin, exhausted body slumped out from under her covers like a zombie clawing its way out of its own grave, spilling herself out across the laundry laden floor. The room was spinning and her head felt like someone had poured a dick load of iron ball bearings into it, and then gifted it to a monkey as a drum set.

KNOCK. KNOCK. KNOCK.

Screw whoever the hell cop knocked at seven am.

She scooped a shirt up from beside her head without bothering to feel out whether or not it was inside out and threw it on. She didn't bother with pants, anyone willing to knock someone's door down at seven on a Saturday didn't deserve the courtesy.

Quiet, though heartfelt, Cantonese swears fell from her lips as she dizzily stumbled her way across the apartment to the door. Her head seemed to throb in time with every step.

"What?" She hissed as she threw open her door.

To her surprise, it wasn't a pair of unlucky missionaries or a gaggle of bewildered boy scouts at her door, but the *actual* cops. Several of them.

The one in front, a plain clothes detective judging by the rumpled white button down and cheap black tie, began addressing her without even looking up from the pile of papers he was holding.

"My name's Detective Richard Ransom," He said in a voice that rumbled with grit, like a stone tumbler, "We have a warrant to search the premises."

Xinghua squinted down at the apparent warrant he was fiddling with, then blinked up at him as the words settled in.

"Okay but why?"

"We have reason to believe that Thomas Airius is involved with an ongoing series of murders."

The tension in Xinghua's shoulders bled out as she released a breezy sigh. Here she'd been worried Mrs. Chen from down the hall had finally followed through on reporting her about the stench of weed coming from under her door.

"Well, can't really fight a search warrant. Just don't fucking break anything, yah?"

The detective looked up at her for the first time and seemed to freeze, his indifferent expression rupturing into wide-eyed surprise. He looked like he'd just been bitch slapped by a ghost, his dark complexion paleing as the blood drained from his face.

"You okay mister?" She cocked a brow at him.

He mouthed something that might have been a word then cleared his throat, a sharp frown slicing down his otherwise mystified face. He shifted his weight from foot to foot as he worked on schooling his expression into something more professional.

"I'm fine. Do you live here?"

"I'm not a fuckin' hooker if that's what you're asking."

"No, no," He winced, "I'm sorry, do you… do you know anything about the Snow White murders?"

She snorted, "This is an *on the books* question, detective?"

He somehow frowned even deeper, the worry lines on his forehead forming canyons.

"No, it isn't. It's just a little alarming that you'd be at the home of our top suspect. You fit the victimology of this killer nearly to a tee."

His head ticked sharply to the side as he visibly regretted his word choice, "Sorry, that was out of line."

"Probably," She shrugged, "But then I did answer the door in my underwear, so who am I *really* to bitch about being out of line?"

Two of the officers at the back gave her a once over, and the rest of them looked like they were fighting not to follow suit. She could hardly blame them, she was aware of what she looked like, which was part of why she did things like this.

They got a nice little treat and she got to watch them squirm. It was a win-win really.

The detective cleared his throat again and Xinghua struggled not to crack a smile as his ears flushed red at the tips.

"May we come in?"

She stepped aside, making a sweeping gesture to the inside of the apartment, *"Mi casa es su casa."*

The group filed in quickly, breaking into smaller teams to sweep through the area as quickly and thoroughly as possible. It wasn't an enormous apartment, but it certainly wasn't the downtown New York average. She thought it was comfortable, though Tom almost constantly bitched about the 'lack of legroom'. Trust a man who'd lived most of his life in a *mansion* in the woods to think 1400 square feet was too small for two people.

"Sooooo," She glanced up at the Detective as he walked up beside her, "The girls from this case? Do I *look* like them or do I *act* like them?"

Ooh, that struck a nerve. She watched his hands clench and unclench, his breathing pick up then manually slow back down, the veins in his neck stood out as he tried to reign himself back in.

"So far they've all been young women of east Asian descent, with short black hair and very pale skin." The detective answered ruefully, eyeing her from his peripheral, "Each was wearing white color contacts when they were found."

She perched herself up on the back of the couch, balancing like a cat on the side of one leg, careful not to flash anyone. She rested her chin on the heel of her hand, contemplating.

While Tom killing was nothing new, this was the first time she'd heard about him having a *type,* let alone one *that specific.*

She'd assumed it was arbitrary, whoever caught his eye at the time. Although, given how meticulous and borderline obsessive Tom could get, she supposed it wasn't really *that* weird for him. She did wonder how he managed to get them into contacts though.

"Well detective," She focused her attention back on him, "There's one little difference between those girls and me. My eyes, like my tits, are real."

He breathed out a little puff of air through his nose that could have been amusement or annoyance, but otherwise didn't respond, seemingly lost in his thoughts.

Now that she was *actually* looking at him, rather than just irritated that he was there at all, she noticed he was sort of handsome for an older guy. He was tall, his muscled cop physique just barely starting to transition into dad-bod. His salt-and-pepper hair was left a little long, wavy and coming to rest just short of touching his broad shoulders. He couldn't have been much over forty by the crows feet that looked to have just started by the sides of his eyes, but the bags beneath them told the story of a troubled man.

Xinghua looked away just as he glanced over at her.

"You seem awfully calm for someone who woke up to the cops."

"Not my first rodeo." She said idly, jiggling her leg, "Grew up in the shitty part of Chinatown. Cops were in and out of there so often Granny started giving them the family discount. Not half as often as they get *called* but still, ya get used to it."

Detective Ransom nodded, "I grew up in East Harlem. Big part of why I became a cop."

"Let me guess," She drawled, grabbing a hold of her leg and leaning precariously backward, "You wanted to make sure justice reached even the poorest places, yah?"

"Mmm, that and I thought I'd look good in the uniform."

A surprised laugh barked out from below her diaphragm.

"Oh yeah? And did you?"

"Definitely, right up until I lost my girlish figure."

That had her snorting so hard she lost her balance on the couch, tumbling right off the back.

"Detective!" One of the uni's called out, "I got something!"

Xinghua poked her head up from behind the sofa.

The officer was holding up a small pair of blue leggings with a distinctive brownish-red patch right on the ass of them. Xinghua nearly broke into another fit of laughter.

"Those are mine." She chimed in, resting her chin on the back of the couch, "But I don't think that's the kind of blood you're after."

The officer made a face as he reluctantly put the leggings in an evidence bag.

Xinghua resituated herself on the couch with a bag of chips she'd tossed next to it last night, resigning herself to watching them make a mess of her already messy house. It might have looked like a disaster had torn through, but it was a *carefully orchestrated* disaster. She knew where everything was, no matter how many times Trish insisted that she couldn't possibly.

She decided to at least distract herself by playing with the surprisingly personable Detective Ransom. For a cop he was pretty chill, which meant she'd need to make sure she didn't relax *too* much. Shouldn't be too hard.

"Want a chip?" She smirked a little, glancing down at the bag sitting between her legs.

He raised a brow at her, "No, thank you."

"Your loss." She shrugged, loudly crunching one between her teeth.

Half an hour later their search turned up next to nothing.

Not that she'd actually expected them to find anything, Tom had *rules.* It wasn't like he'd killed them here after all. That was rule number one; Don't piss where you sleep.

"We've got nothing." A uni whispered to Detective Ransom, "'Cept that pair of leggings, but that *could* just be the girl-friend's."

Rule number two: Don't take trophies.

"Thanks Cruz." Ransom nodded the officer away, "Alright boys, looks like we're done here. Pack it up."

"Aw, already?" Xinghua whined, pouting, "I was just starting to warm up to you."

Ransom's cheek twitched up a little like he was trying to remember how to smile. Before he could figure it out, the door clicked open.

"Xi-xi~ my little spider lily~ I have wonderful new-"

The crowd of officers turned to the mouth of the hallway where Tom now stood, his expression waxing from confused to amused.

"Xinghua, forgive my forgetfulness, but what occasion do we have for this many strippers?"

This time the force of her laughter had her hurling herself sideways off the couch.

"Thomas Airius, I presume? I'm Detective Richard Ransom. Mind if I ask you a few questions?" Ransom's tone was clipped but professional, like it had been when she'd answered the door.

Tom's lips curled up into the perfect imitation of a polite smile.

"Certainly Detective! I apologize for my assumption. Xinghua has a certain proclivity for surprising me with the most off-beat things."

"That *can't* be the first time he's been mistaken for a stripper. Not with those thighs." Xinghua whispered under her breath.

Tom's smile widened by a molar.

"Where were you on the night of November 17th?" Ransom deadpanned.

"That was last Friday, yes? Hmm, I was at the office late that day. Until around midnight. I believe I went out for a drink with my assistant, Seriah Nix, after that. Didn't make it home until one-thirty."

"And would you be willing to give us this assistant's number to confirm with?"

"Of course!" Tom beamed, "Though he did just take his annual leave, so I can't speak for how quickly he'll get back to you."

Ransom's eyes narrowed and a flat, humorless smile spanned his face.

"Thanks."

"Of course~ May I ask what it is that brings you gentlemen here? Or is that *classified?*"

"We're investigating the Snow White Murders."

"Oh dear! I remember reading about that in the papers recently. Those *poor* girls." Tom shook his head, his brows sweeping low into anguished sincerity, "Always such a tragedy when young lives are cut short like that. I do hope you find whoever is responsible. Of course Xinghua and I will cooperate with you to the *fullest."*

Tom crossed the room and sat himself down next to Xinghua, his arm wrapping around her shoulders. He kept eye contact with the detective as he pulled her closer, pecking a gentle kiss to her forehead.

Xinghua watched as the hair on Ransom's arms rose right along with his blood pressure. He exhaled a thin hiss of a breath, though it did absolutely nothing to calm him from what she could hear of his heartbeat.

"Thank you, but hopefully that won't be necessary." He said politely, though his neck was straining, "Boys, let's go."

The officers filed out of the apartment, leaving just Ransom. He and Tom looked to be locked in a staring contest that Ransom broke only to turn to Xinghua. There was a little black card held between his thick, calloused fingers that he extended to her.

"If you need anything, *do not hesitate* to call me." He said with gravity.

Xinghua took the offered card with plans to throw it out the moment the detective left.

"Thanks." She replied, flipping the thing over between her fingers.

Ransom nodded. With one last withering look at Tom, he also took his leave, slamming the door behind himself.

"He knows." Xinghua said after a beat had passed.

"Of definitely. He seems like a very astute young man." Tom slipped his lab coat off of his shoulders and stood to go hang it up.

"'Very astute young man', you sound like such a grandpa." Xinghua snorted, relaxing into her chair.

"I'm older than most people's grandfathers."

"Doesn't mean you've gotta *talk* like it."

Tom sat down and fixed her with his vividly purple eyes. Ever since she was little his eyes had transfixed her. She'd never seen another set of eyes anywhere near the same hue, a violent shade of violet that, had she not had her own peculiar eye color, she might not believe were real. Accompanied by a halo of dark, thick lashes that seemed to deepen their color, it was no wonder she occasionally got lost in them.

"Xing?"

Like that.

"Sorry, what?"

He chuckled, rolling the very eyes that had just distracted her.

"I *said* I had a major breakthrough at work."

"You did?" She sat up eagerly, turning her whole body to face him, "Aah~! Was it the *big* project that you won't tell me about because you're a big, big meanie head?"

"That'd be the one."

She bounced, excitement bursting from her in the form of a hug. He let her go on for a couple seconds before gently pushing her away.

"I'm so proud of you! I knew you could do it!" She cheered.

He winced along with her pitch, causing her to do the same. She knew better, he'd told her a million times not to be so loud, but she just sometimes forgot when she got excited.

"Sorry."

"It's alright Xing, I know this is exciting."

"Well, it's been like twelve years!" She attempted to reign in her enthusiasm with mixed results, "Now I finally get to know what's been taking up so much of your damn time."

"Not just yet." He tsked, index finger gently tapping the tip of her nose, "I made a big leap, but there's still a little bit more paperwork and red tape I've got to get through before I can show you."

She groaned, falling backward onto the couch, throwing her arms up over her head like a child.

"It's very, *very* close Xi. A couple more weeks, *max.*"

"I'm holding you to that." She threw herself back up into a sitting position, "But, like, we still get to go to Wreck, right?"

"Where else would we celebrate?"

Xinghua whooped quietly, pumping her fist in the air.

*　　　　*　　　　*　　　　*

Wreckquiem was not the sort of place most people would openly admit to knowing about.

On the surface it was little more than a hole in the wall. The building was a concrete eyesore complete with flaking paint, cracked beige tile floors with more stains than color, and a wooden bar that treated its regulars to splinters and cuts, having not been polished in the lifetime of anyone who fre- quented the bar. Plus it barely had room for twenty people.

But the beer was cheap-and it tasted like it-making it the perfect type of dive for destitutes to go to forget their suffering for a while.

But if one knew the right people, it was *so* much more.

Xinghua led the way through the back, past the sharks shouting about their cards, and through the hidden door into the small club that constituted the *real* Wreckquiem.

This bar was all pretty crushed velvet clad bartenders and plush black and red leather booths. The air was always filled with smoke from some sort of heavy incense Xinghua could never name the scent of. The stereo system, that she also could never seem to find, had a decadent playlist of hedonistic music that was in perfect keeping with the indulgent theme that stitched itself through every inch of the place. There were always people sitting too close to each other, always someone getting taken to the famed rented rooms downstairs, always a hungry eyed stranger staring from the shadows. It was dark and sensual and everything she would have expected from the number one vampire bar in town.

"Xinghua~" Her name met her ears nearly as soon as they'd slipped in the door, "Dear heart it's been *too long* since last I saw you."

The speaker crossed the room in an instant.

"Frost!" She leaned up onto her tiptoes to greet him with a kiss to his sleek cheek, coming away with a light dusting of glitter.

He was obviously dressed for work, he almost never wore makeup this dramatic in his daily life. He did well at it though, the dusting of glitter made his pale skin look especially alluring to touch, the dusky shadow making his deep brown eyes seem infinite, all consuming. Even the touch of red on his lips only drew more attention to how nicely shaped they were. His outfit matched the sensuality of the makeup, a mostly unbuttoned black lace shirt with matching leather and lace pants that flattered his thin, broad build. His silvery blonde hair had been left free of its usual ponytail, falling in loose, heavy waves to just barely cover his nipples. She'd always been just a bit jealous of that, she'd never understood how he could have so much better luck with bleach despite also being Asian himself. It was clear someone had been running their fingers through it too, lucky them.

"And what brings you to my humble establishment this fine evening?" He flicked his eyes between her and Tom.

"We're celebrating!" She flashed him a smile, "Tom killed it at work so we're out for a drink. Any recommendations?"

"Of *course,* dearest." He said, though his stare was locked onto Tom, "We recently began employing a slightly older school menu. Xinghua you still have a taste for the French vintage, yes?"

The tense stare off lasted a couple more seconds before Frost broke it by smiling down at Xinghua.

"Yeah," She replied hesitantly, nervous that things would escalate like last time.

Frost tucked a strand of her hair fondly behind her ear, as if reassuring her he'd keep himself in check. At least she hoped that's what he was going for and not 'Ayo I'm touching your girl what are you gonna do about it'.

"Thomas, I assume you still favor the Orient?"

Xinghua had a brief flashback to what that Detective had said earlier. She knew he had a flavor preference when it came to feeding, he'd always had that, but the rest just seemed like such a waste of time. And he'd never been one to waste time. Though she supposed it wasn't really her business how he chose to feed.

"While your phrasing leaves much to be desired, as you *so often* do, your supposition is correct." Tom replied blithely, the smile he'd worn earlier with Ransom making a second appearance.

Frost's own smile took on an unpleasant light, "If my phrasing offends you, I'd be more than happy to relieve you of the burden of having ears."

So much for behaving.

Tom rolled his shoulders, his fangs peeking out from the edges of his smile, "I would be absolutely *delighted* to see you attempt to make good on that threat."

Where Frost's hand had been leaning on the bar, ice began to eat up the wooden surface.

"Knock it *off!*" Xinghua hissed, her own fangs detracting as panic lanced through her chest, "We're not here to start shit, could you guys *take it down a fucking notch?*"

For a tense moment neither one of them broke their standoff.

Then Tom raised his hands in the universal signal of surrender, his fangs sliding back up into his gums where they belonged. Though if anything his smile looked all the more dangerous for it.

"I'll go get us a table."

He kissed Xinghua's hand before making his way to the farthest empty table.

"I'm sorry Xi." Frost sighed, immediately melting his ice, "I didn't mean to scare you, but I refuse to be disrespected in my own house. Least of all by *that* man."

Xinghua took a breath that did nothing to calm her nerves given that she didn't need air in the first place.

"I know you don't like him Lee, what the fuck ever, most people don't. But for my sake, could you please just pounce on him like a normal vampire? No ice, okay?"

Frost snorted, a fond smile erasing the last of the annoyance on his pretty face, "Only *you* would advocate a bare knuckle vampire fight."

"It's more fun for you anyway, though right? You're what, six...seven hundred years older than him? You could take him to church with or without powers."

"One might just think you *want* me to beat the hell out of him."

"Sometimes he could use it." She shrugged, "Not this time though, no one calls Asia 'The Orient' anymore, it's lowkey racist."

Frost rolled his eyes, tossing his arms dramatically up into the air.

"Like I can keep up with what offends who this century." He waved his hand dismissively, "Give it fifty years, it'll all change again."

She flicked at him as he waved over the bartender.

"Nonetheless," Frost sighed, "One of these days I'm going to lose my patience with him."

"I know." She leaned herself up against his arm, pouting once again, "But please, please, *please* wait at *least* until tomorrow. For me?"

That earned her a real smile.

"It's not as if I would leave you without something to *remember* him by. I'm certain one of my girls could find a way to bottle those pretty eyes of his." As he spoke Frost's own eyes lit up with little flurries of snowflakes dancing in his now blue irises.

Before Xinghua could find a reply to that, their 'drinks' arrived.

So that was what Frost had meant by 'old school menu'.

Two beautiful girls approached them, dressed in cute, *tight,* matching uniforms. One was a very European looking girl with fluffy blonde curls that she had barely restrained with a host of bobby pins, and the other was an Asian girl with her straight black hair pulled into an intimidatingly high ponytail. They were both cute, although the Asian one looked a little young to be there. Xinghua supposed she probably did too in all fairness. Still, her features were notably childlike, dissimilar to Xinghua's own sharp countenance.

"I like the on tap idea." Xinghua gave a low, impressed whistle, "When did this start?"

"A few months ago." Frost idly played with the French girl's hair, earning himself a giggle and a playful swat, "Believe it or not, these two ladies in particular were the first volunteers."

"Oh no, I believe it." Xinghua sent the other girls a knowing look, "Getting bitten is kinda addicting."

The blonde's attention drifted over to her for a moment, a little twinkle of mischief easily visible in her eyes. Xinghua was more than a little eager to find out what *that* was about.

"Plus the pay is almost as handsome as *he* is." The brunette chimed in, winking at Frost.

"Oh dear Lisa, you know flattery doesn't get you extra." He cupped her cheek.

"Will it get me a kiss?" She fluttered her falsies at him.

That got a laugh out of him as he pecked a kiss to the tip of her nose, causing her to whine out a disappointed noise.

"*I'm* not your client tonight ladies, go suck up to *her.*"

Both girls turned on Xinghua then, looking not unlike vampires themselves.

"Frost, you are the best weird vampire godfather a girl could ever ask for." Xinghua grinned as the girls each slid under one of her arms.

"And don't you ever forget it." He sipped from an actual drink he'd produced from seemingly nowhere, "Tonight is on the house, but if you take them home, cab fare is on you."

"Got it!"

From there the night passed in a blur of blood and booze and boobs. It had been a long time since Xinghua had enjoyed herself so much. Probably since the last time they'd gone to Wreckquiem she'd wager.

With Tom having been so bogged down by work, it had been *months* since she'd gotten to spend more than a couple hours with him. Even longer since they'd just gone out and had *fun*. Lately it seemed like even when he was around he wasn't really there, too caught up in whatever was going on in his head.

She'd missed seeing him smile.

Even though she may not remember every detail of the night, she'd remember the way his smile made her chest feel like her heart might just still be beating after all.

Richard had been up all night.

That in itself wasn't unusual, not in his profession. He was lucky to get more than four hours in at a time before he started to feel the past closing in on him, choking him like so many hands around his throat.

No, he wasn't surprised to be wide awake at three a.m. What was throwing him off was the *cause* of his sleeplessness.

Xinghua Li.

After their meeting during his failed search of Airius' apartment he'd made it his mission to find out as much as he could about the girl who so resembled the girls he'd been finding murdered for weeks.

He didn't find much on her. Just a birth certificate, school transcripts up until third grade, and alarmingly, a death certificate. There had been a link to the obituary, but the outdated desktop the brass insisted they let slog through its last breaths wouldn't open the damn thing.

He told himself he'd check into it when he got home, but quickly got distracted by Mrs. Silva from down the hall and her four boys.

By the time he'd helped her wrangle them back into her apartment, he'd nearly forgotten about the obit. It wasn't until he'd settled down in bed to wait the hour it would take for his mind to be quiet enough to sleep that he thought to pull the thing up, of course.

Naturally, he'd read the entire thing despite knowing it would more than likely keep him up all night.

It most certainly had.

Which is why he was currently haunting the coffee pot in the corner of the break room. If he could, he would have just shot the middle man and injected it directly into his eyes.

After the third cup he'd downed consecutively, he'd reached an adequate level of alert to try to read through the literal mountain of paperwork that had materialized on his desk overnight, more than likely all belonging to his partner.

Sighing, Richard grabbed a file and booted up his computer to get to work.

He made it through three whole reports before his eyes begged off the task. He was going to have to start using readers, though he was loath to admit it. It felt like some sort of concession his pride just wasn't quite willing to make yet.

Instead of wrestling that set of eventualities, he decided to change tasks for the moment.

He still needed to call and check Airius' alibi, and in the notes he'd uncovered at the bottom of his last report, he'd found the number for a store owner near the scene of the last kidnapping in the other case he was working.

Phone calls were usually easy, so he opted to get that out of the way first. No one wanted to be on the phone with the cops for longer than they really had to so people tended to give him short, to the point answers.

It took him about ten minutes to find out Seriah Nix had been on vacation for three months now. From what the secretary said, he'd gone visit family back home, though she couldn't tell him where that home was.

He thanked the secretary for her time and jotted down the break in Airius' story. It wouldn't be enough to get another warrant, not that he thought he'd find anything new. It was clear Airius was too meticulous to leave physical evidence, but he'd caught him lying at the very least.

Richard left a voicemail for Nix, then turned his attention to the lead on his other main case.

He'd been so busy with the Snow White case the last couple days he'd not so much as glanced at this case, not that there was much to go on. He *would* be the *babaca* to have to hunt down two serial killers, both of which seemed to be *obsessive* about not leaving evidence trails. But where the Snow White killer was never seen and never left traces, this one just made sure anyone who could be a witness didn't live to do so. Their methods were wildly different, but the result was the same.

Richard turned his attention back to his archaic computer, trying to keep his leg from bouncing as he strained his eyes to see the screen.

He should have known a few quiet hours of work would be too much to ask.

"Yo Richie!" His partner's boisterous voice boomed from across the bull pen, "We got another Snow White."

His pulse thundered in his ears for a moment before he fought the anxiety back in favor of more information. He gave himself until the count of three before he turned around.

"We know who the vic was yet, Killian?" He set down his coffee, headed towards the familiar stout redhead.

"Nah, not yet. This one just came down the line a half hour ago." Terry stopped and turned to Richard, lifting one red bushy brow in ill-concealed concern, "Last name? Really? You doin' alright Rich?"

Richard appreciated the man's concern, even as he resented the way it made him feel like he didn't have his shit well enough together.

"I'm fine, Terry." He shrugged on his jacket, "Let's go."

*   *   *   *

The first thing Richard did when they arrived on the scene was check to see if the newest victim was, as he feared, Xinghua Li.

To his immense relief, it wasn't.

He tried to ignore the cold pit that relief dragged in with it to focus on examining the body instead.

Richard had seen a half dozen girls staged just like this one. Always in long modest white dresses, arms folded over their chests as if asleep with a red bow in their hair. Always their faces were calm, happy even, and always their eyes were open, staring pale and sightless up into the sky.

Despite having been an officer for the last twenty-five years, the sight of a dead body still hit him straight in the gut.

He was happy that it did, planned on handing in his badge the day seeing people murdered stopped bothering him.

"Kid found her this morning on the way to her grand-mother's." One of the first responders told them, "M.E. puts the time of death around four thirty a.m."

"This is an ambitious place to drop a body." Terry noted, thick knuckles pressed into his thin mustache, "Public, well lit, usually a lot of foot traffic on the weekends like this. How in the hell did he have time to stage the body like this without someone seeing him?"

"He couldn't." Richard muttered, "Either he staged her somewhere else or someone would have to have seen him. Gentleman, we might just have our Big Fuck-Up."

Terry smiled at that, showing his incisors in that way that he used to intimidate suspects.

"Let's hope you're right. I'm fuckin' *sick* of this guy.

Richard and Terry spent the next four hours talking to anyone they could find who had been anywhere near that corner last night. But from the homeless all the way on up to the apartment dwellers right back down to the drug dealers, not a single person had seen or heard a damn thing.

After the fifteenth fruitless conversation in a row, Terry suggested they break for lunch.

"This is ridiculous." Richard leaned his head back onto the wall he was slumped against, "It's just not possible that not a single person on this *busy* street saw a damn thing. A dead body doesn't just *appear* like that without *someone* noticing. He's not even a part of this neighborhood, why would they be covering for him?"

"Who? Oh." Terry gave him a flat look, "Thought that Airius lead didn't pan out."

"Not in terms of physical evidence, no." Richard huffed, "But you can't tell me it's a coincidence a girl fitting Snow White's victimology to a tee *lives* with my main suspect."

"A- wait *really?*" The man's expression did a 180, blue eyes round like river stones, "What the *fuck?*"

"Yeah, she answered the door. But that's not the weirdest part."

"The fuck's weirder than that?"

"I looked into her, right? Not a thing on her after third grade but a goddamn death certificate."

Terry frowned hard, pausing in the middle of ordering a hot dog.

"This is why you oughta check your emails more often, I sent all this to you already." Richard grumbled, "I read the obit last night and apparently the kid was presumed dead after getting lost in Central Park in the middle of January back in '04. Worst part was she was probably running away from her father, who'd killed her mother and grandmother on the same day she went missing."

"Jesus Christ Rich," Terry frowned at the food he'd just been served, "You sure know how to ruin a meal."

"What I don't get is how she would have survived." Richard mused as Terry shrugged and busied his mouth with his food, "A kid, unprepared and alone wouldn't last more than a day or two outside in a winter like that one. Even if she'd gotten rescued, she should have had serious nerve and tissue damage."

"Maybe she did, it's not like you've seen her naked." Terry mumbled out of the side of his mouth.

"Close enough," Richard recalled how the girl had been brazen enough to answer the door in nothing but a shirt, "She definitely didn't."

"What?"

"Read your emails."

One very annoying lunch hour later, Terry had caught up on the details of the case so far as Richard knew them. With a couple notable exceptions, the man had mostly asked reasonable questions, which was an improvement to his usual lack of decorum.

"So you should probably go talk to that Li broad again." Terry pointed out as they made their way back to their car, "She's gotta know *something*. No way she don't."

"Me?" Richard tilted his head quizzically, "Aren't you the official people person? Somethin' about how I 'couldn't sweet talk my way into a saint's good graces'?"

Terry barked a laugh, "While that's an objective *fact*, you're a big boy now Richie, you've gotta learn to talk to people some day. Why not start now?"

"You've got a date, don't you." It wasn't remotely a question.

Terry had the good sense to try to look a little embarrassed as Richard rolled his eyes.

"That's not the *whole* reason." He insisted, "I'm looking out for you here too."

"Oh yeah?" Richard kicked his chin up at him, "How?"

"When was the last time you got laid?"

Ransom sighed and shook his head, *"Ai dios mio* not this shit again, Killian I swear-."

"Ep, pep, shut up. Don't even *start* bitching at me, you don't have to sit in a squad car with you. That leg bouncing shit shakes the whole car. The *whole car.* Besides, sounds like she was *definitely* hitting on you."

"First, no, she absolutely was *not,* she was flirting with the *whole room.* Second, that's an enormous conflict of interest, and *I* actually *care* about integrity. Third, I could be that girl's father, that's not going to happen."

"You're not *that* old."

"I'm going to go now, and I'm taking the car." He held up the keys as he walked backwards towards their squad car.

"I was *kidding!* Don't you fucking leave me here, Rich! *Ransom!"*

*　　　　*　　　　*　　　　*

Finding Li was a little tricky, given that officially she didn't exist. He had no idea how she'd gotten around that to get a job, and honestly if he looked into it he'd more than likely have to arrest her. He'd keep that in the back of his mind.

The building was nondescript, the door was a little hard to find, and he couldn't find the name of the company anywhere. Which explained how she'd managed to find work.

He really didn't want to have to arrest her.

He walked into the building, mildly surprised to find a smartly dressed, racially ambiguous secretary working in what looked like a very well maintained lobby area. There was a sign behind her proclaiming the business to be 'Click Zone Multimedia Group' in well lit black letters. There was even a small flat screen TV set to a news station he didn't recognize covering a story about some new illness going around with the group's logo in the corner.

And just like that he was confused again.

"Hello," He began as he walked up to the secretary, "Is Xinghua Li in today?"

The woman blinked for a moment before pulling on a polite smile, seeming a little dazed. She pushed her chin length red hair behind her ear as she cleared her throat.

"I believe so! Let me send for her, Mr..?"

Ransom fought to keep his expression level as a smooth deep voice met his ears. It wasn't as though he'd never met people that fell outside the norm for gender presentation, he lived in New York for crying out loud, it was just never what he was expecting.

"Oh, sorry." He gave his best charming smile, which in his opinion was far more similar to a wince than a smile as he pulled out his badge, "My name is Detective Ransom."

Their green or blue-or possibly brown-eyes widened though they kept the smile in place and got to their feet. They were quite tall, Ransom noted, and brightly dressed in a loud orange and red blouse with a matching red pencil skirt.

"I'll be back in just a moment, Detective."

He nodded and tried for one more smile as the secretary left.

While he waited he scanned around the room, more for something to do than the thought that he would actually find anything useful here. He was in the middle of trying to figure out what in the ungodly hell the statue in their lobby was supposed to be when the door the secretary had gone through opened up again.

Li was standing there looking about as ragged as he'd felt this morning. Her hair was tied in a loose, messy bun that looked like she might have done it in the dark. And either she had developed massive dark circles or she was still wearing whatever makeup she'd done last. It made her already alarmingly pale eyes all the more shocking, even if they were half shut. She was wearing a rumpled short black shirt over another with a high white collar that looked to be smeared with red lipstick. Her black skirt was pleated but looked as rumpled as the shirt. The fishnets she wore were torn in several places.

"Rough night?"

She groaned, tilting her head back like a child about to throw a tantrum.

"*Why* are you *here*, Ransom?"

So no small talk then, thank God.

"There was another murder last night."

"Oh goodie," She said without inflection, "Tom's got a... what's the name of that word? Proof? Friend excuse? No, it's *tok chi*, what the fuck is that in-- whatever, we were at a bar last night, *the whole* night. Plenty of people can cor-coror-corer- *aish! Agree* to that."

Her accent had barely been noticeable the last time they'd spoken, but this morning it seemed to be strangling her words. He wondered briefly if it worsened with fatigue like his own sometimes did.

He shook his head, "I have a witness that says they saw a man matching Tom's description leaving the scene."

She squinted at him, her expression impassive as if she knew he was lying but just didn't have the energy to call him out on it.

"In that case it, you have pr-" She stopped and sighed, rubbing her hands down her face as she restarted, "*Plenty* of evidence. So, I repeat, *why are you here?*"

He sighed heavily, the weight of the situation resting heavily on his shoulders.

"Because you're in danger." He did his best to make himself as grave as the situation called for, "How long do you think it's going to be before he gets sick of killing stand ins and goes for the real thing, huh?"

"Thanks but even if you *were* right, which you are *not*, you don't needa worry 'bout me." She said blithely waving her hand. "I can handle myself jus' *fine.*"

For the life of him he could not understand such stubborn indifference. Did she *really* believe that blindly in Airius's innocence or did she honestly think she was a match for a man nearly twice her size who'd already killed a dozen women just like her?

Whatever it was, it only made Richard all the more worried for her.

"Be that as it may, you *live* with him. You have to sleep some time, you're only human."

She looked like she was struggling not to laugh, which warped his concern into confusion and dread.

"Were *you* the one that killed those women, Li?" He asked as calmly as he could manage.

"No!" The smile immediately tagged out for a frown, "How the hell did you jump to *that?!*"

Her reaction to the accusation was genuine enough to placate his budding suspicion, though he filed the idea away for further investigation later just in case.

"You were practically laughing at my insinuation of being in danger, what was I supposed to think?"

"I don't know, maybe I know fighting? Maybe I sleep light? Maybe he's never home so I only ever see him twice a week besides Christmas and my birthday? Maybe I just know he didn't do it cause I spent *all night with him when the last one happened?* Any one of those things could have made your statement pretty funny to me."

Her hands landed on her hips, one hip jutting out as she finished her rant. With that and the one angular eyebrow that had hiked itself half way up her forehead, she looked the farthest thing from humored.

It wasn't going to do him any good to push her. As much as it felt like giving up, if he didn't back down she'd only rail harder against him. It was clear that regardless of anything else, Airius had instilled a deep sense of loyalty in her that Richard wasn't going to be able to break down with brute force.

"Fine," He relented, putting his hands up, "You're not going to listen to me. You've known him for years and you've only met me once, plus I'm a cop. I get it, I wouldn't talk to me either. But for the sake of my insomnia, please at least keep the card I gave you on you."

"If I do, will you leave me alone?"

"As much as I can from a legal standpoint."

"Seriously?"

"That's the best you're getting."

She sighed, before rolling her eyes so far back she might well have been possessed.

"*Fine*, I'll keep your stupid card on me."

That... was way too easy for how much she'd been arguing with him up until this moment. He figured she'd like him off her back but not quite that badly.

"You threw it away didn't you?"

"Yep."

Richard sighed, "Clever."

"You can't blame me for tryin'" She shrugged, that cockeyed smile of hers making a comeback.

He dug in his back pocket for a new card to give her. He didn't have a lot of them, but then he also didn't just take every case personally like this. Maybe it was because of his past but this one had struck too close to home. He knew he was too involved, but it was also far too late to start caring about that now.

In for a penny, in for a pound.

"Keep this one, yeah?" He held it out for her, faking her out when she didn't reply to his request before grabbing for it, *"Yeah?"*

This eye roll was even worse than the first somehow.

"What, do you want me to pinky promise or some shit? Jesus just give me the fuckin thing!"

"Actually that's not a bad idea. Promise me you'll keep it."

Her whole body sagged, "Are you--?"

He met her glare with a patient stare of his own, the two holding eye contact before she relented with a muffled shout of frustration.

"Fine! I promise I'll keep your stupid *fucking* card, okay?"

"On you."

"On me!"

He handed it to her, letting a sliver of a smile peek out at her.

"Thank you."

"You know I could be lying right? Like I could just *throw this away* as soon as you're gone like I did the first time." She cocked her head.

"Yeah, but you won't."

"Oh yeah? And how do *you* know?"

"Because you're a good kid, Li. I can tell." He said with all sincerity.

She froze for a moment but quickly recovered with a scoff.

"More of this gut feeling shit? You sound more and more like a made for TV cop every time you say that."

"Or maybe after twenty years on the force I'm just good at reading people." He shrugged, "Could be that."

She pursed her lips at him, "Are we done here?"

He chanced a more genuine smile, and to his surprise her expression softened a little as well. Instead of saying anything he kept it to a nod, worried the noise would break the fragile peace they'd just achieved.

He left without a word, anticipating another sleepless night.

"Okay so I have to know, who was the hottie?" Ziggy asked, perching themself on the corner of Xinghua's desk as if they owned it.

Xinghua flopped herself down into her chair, splaying out so she didn't have to focus on holding up her own weight. She flung one arm over her head to attempt to dull the headache currently trying to crack open her skull like an egg.

"His name is Detective Ransom and he's *not* a hottie, he's a pain in my ass." Xinghua muttered, the feeling of her voice bouncing around her head was making her feel sick.

"Oooh, a detective? Hot *and* problematic." They cocked their head, a sheet of red hair falling like a curtain around their face, "What was he doing here?"

"He's investigating Tom for murder."

"What?!" Ziggy screeched, making her wince, "Like your *boyfriend* Tom?!"

"Yah."

"Who does he think he killed?"

"Well, actually…. It's less one murder, and more, like, he thinks he's a serial killer?" Xinghua chanced lifting her arm to peek out at them.

Ziggy over-exaggeratedly reeled back, throwing their arms out, having to grab onto the table to keep their balance as the tirade nearly brought them to the floor.

"**Are** *you* **serious**?!" They lowered their voice even though they were the only two in this half of the office, "Did he do it?"

"He's a vampire Ziggy, what do *you* think?"

They crumpled to the floor at long last as if they had simply lost all the strength in their body.

"Oh my Gods Xing!" They cried, "Why wasn't *this* the first thing you told me this morning! You *know* I live for drama! This is like a seven course meal and you didn't think to tell me about it! Why do you *hate* me?!"

"Oh my God shut up you inconsiderate slut." She hissed, her headache lilting with Ziggy's every wailed word, "Fuuuuuck, I'm *actually* dying."

Ziggy huffed and rolled towards her on their belly, "You're immortal, asshole."

"Are we sure?"

"Well it's daytime, I could shove you outside and we could find out." They mused, examining their long red nails for non-existent flaws, "Want some of Trish's headache shit?"

"Yeahsure."

They climbed to their feet and strolled casually over to their coworker's desk like they hadn't just been throwing a fit on the floor. They picked the shitty lock on the top drawer with their pinky nail and plucked the little blue vial out of its resting place.

"Here." They tossed her the tube, though she failed miserably to catch it given that her eyes were still covered.

Xinghua made a face as she drank the minty blue liquid. Almost immediately the pain in her head began to subside and she could finally relax.

"Thanks Zig."

"Thank Trish, she was the one who donated." They sat back down in front of Xinghua, "Now, about that tea~"

*   *   *   *

"So how was your day?" Tom asked as he lowered himself down beside Xinghua on their loveseat, a glass of white wine elegantly reposed in his hand.

"Well, let's see. I woke up with the world's shittiest super-hangover, hid from the lights at work under my desk, that stupid detective from last week showed up again, I had to drink Trish's homemade hangover cure, um I got a hangnail."

"Go back a moment, what was that middle one?"

"I hid from the lights?"

"No, dearest, the other one."

"Yeah he came back." She stole a drink from his glass, cringing at the bitter taste and the look he leveled at her, "He was giving me the whole 'He's dangerous, you should be careful' spiel."

"Ah." He leaned back into the couch, drink now out of her reach, "Wouldn't it be lovely to be able to be honest in times like those?"

"*Yes!* He gave me such a good set up too, oh my God it was great." She lamented, "I could have snapped my fangs at him and everything. Such a waste of a good dramatic moment."

"Speaking of, how are those growing in? Did the second set straighten out?"

She detracted them, poking at the leftmost one. It was still a little wiggly, but not nearly as much as it had been a month ago.

"Straighter than I am." She let them pull back into her gums.

"Good, good. Does it feel like there is another set coming in?"

"Mmm, nope, doesn't itch or anything. I promise I was listening, but what's the thing about having two sets again?" Xinghua stole another sip of Tom's wine since he'd leaned in enough to be within range.

"It means you ain't no basic bitch." He deadpanned.

She snorted so hard the wine went up her nose and out her nostrils.

Tom threw his head back laughing, loud enough that it echoed through the room. It wasn't often he laughed like that, so she treasured it every time she got to hear it.

Maybe not so much *right now*, considering the stinging in her nose.

"It gives me *such* joy to do that." He sipped his wine, "Always makes me so glad that I've largely held on to my antiquated vernacular."

She was too busy blowing her nose to respond.

"Though, all joking aside, fangs are a status symbol among our kind. One set is the lower echelon, two is above average, and three is exceptional. It means you're going to be quite strong Xing."

"Thanks." She managed half sarcastically, "I'm lowkey hoping for another set. I've still got one more year before the virus finishes renovating my genes or whatever, it could happen."

"If it were going to, you would have felt them starting to come in the moment the other set finished. Trust me." He said, showing off his own three pronged set.

She made a non-commital noise.

"We're coming up on the anniversary." The words might have seemed thoughtless coming out of anyone else, but Xinghua knew Tom more than well enough to hear the excitement beneath them.

"Oh shit, it's almost January." Xinghua pursed her lips, "What's this one?"

"Six years, three months, four weeks, and eleven days." He rattled off easily.

"Vampire or not, that's freaky."

His hand cupped her cheek and a thrill raced through her at the look in his eyes, "The day I found you was one of the happiest of my life. How could I ever possibly forget a single detail?"

If she had needed air her vision would have been swimming.

"You are the very best thing I've ever been responsible for." He smiled softly, "Please know that. If I teach you nothing else, know that."

She could feel the telltale tightness in her throat at that. He did this every so often, usually after he'd been gone for a couple days but it never failed to make her tear up.

"You know, if you wanted to sleep with me all you had to do was ask."

He leaned forward and pressed a slow, lingering kiss to her lips that had shudders running up her spine.

"Li Xinghua, would you do me the great honor of going to bed with me?"

"Nothing would make me happier~"

* * * *

"Xinghua... Xing are you alright?"

Her eyes creaked open, the strain almost a tangible thing with the weight it seemed to possess. She felt so heavy all over, so tired she just wanted to go back to sleep.

"Whoa, no no, don't."

A pair of hands came up on either side of her face, both much colder than she was used to feeling. They were bony, long, and unpleasantly clammy in a way that had her wishing she were a turtle, if only to pull her entire head and neck back into the rest of her body.

Then came the face, one she distinctly did not recognize.

It was a man's face, most likely, despite the fair, delicate features. And he seemed to be smiling, his soft periwinkle eyes warm and friendly in a way she wouldn't have expected from a guy as pretty as him. His hair, blonde and curly, was left in a blown out fluffy halo around his head, making him seem to glow when the inconsistent light source in the area hit him.

"You've grown so much." The words were whispered but that did nothing to hide the tremor in them, "And yet you still know precious little."

She wanted to ask what he meant by that, what was going on, but her tongue felt like a leaden weight in her mouth.

"Just know, when it happens, it was nothing to do with you. More fate than fault."

The man began bleeding, first from his neck in two little pin pricks, then from his mouth and finally his stomach.

"None of this has ever been your fault Xinghua. Remember that and let it help you move on. You are stronger than you can know."

What little color he'd had drained from his face and the summery shade of his eyes fogged over, unseeing as a corpse.

"Don't let anything break you Xinghua."

"W-w-wh-wh-what?" She strained to whisper.

The man smiled, tight and painful as he collapsed over her.

Like a chord had snapped, she could move again, though the grief that flooded her far outweighed any relief.

"No!" She shrieked, "No, no, no, no, Fletcher please!"

As soon as she touched him, his body turned to ash, fluttering away on the breeze and into the thick woods surrounding them.

One more thing the trees had taken from her.

A pit opened up in her chest, yawning wider and wider until it felt as if there was nothing else left inside her but it's cold empty ache. And God, how she hated the cold...

Xinghua lurched awake, tears chasing screams, chasing a dream that had already begun to fade. She shook, even as she told herself it hadn't been real.

"Xing, Xing, *Xing.*" Tom called to her, taking one of her hands to get her attention, "What is it? What happened?"

She wiped away the blood-tears on the back of her free hand with a grimace. Sometimes she genuinely hated the new way that her body worked. So gross.

"I had a weird dream, or *nightmare* I guess, there was some dude that I didn't know but, like, I *did,* cause when he died I got *really* upset but I *know* I've never seen him before but then

I also like knew his *name* even though I didn't *think* I knew his name and like it was pretty much just some rando dude dying and me fucking bawling my eyes out over it, yelling his name into the distance like the protag in some old Hollywood flick or some shit."

Tom blinked several times in the face of the ceaseless onslaught. It took him a moment to sort through all of it and find something to respond to.

"You knew his name? How odd. Do you remember it still?"

"It was… Fletcher, I think..?" She squeezed her eyes closed for a moment, trying to remember his face and failing, "God it felt so real but I can't even remember what he looked like now."

"Well, you said yourself that you've never met him. It's not too surprising you wouldn't be able to recall him upon waking." He pressed a kiss to her temple, his voice deep and melodic and soothing, "It was just a bad dream my love, best not to think on it too much."

She felt the tension that had built up in her chest ease right out of her. He was right, of course. She wasn't a child anymore, there was no reason to be scared over a bad dream. Especially one she couldn't even remember.

When she thought about it, she couldn't recall the name anymore, getting Frederique the clerk from the corner store instead. And she was fairly certain she wasn't having emotional dreams about that fugly lookin' dude. Although, it *had* been a nightmare.

She sighed a little laugh at that.

"There's a good girl." Tom praised, gently pinching her chin, "Feel better?"

She nodded a little yawn and a stretch following along.

"Mmm, go back to sleep, Xi-xi, there's still four more hours until sundown." Tom pulled her close up against his chest, "I'll keep the bad dreams away for you."

Xinghua tucked her little smile up against his neck and wrapped her arms tight around his waist. Like a teddy bear, but nearly twice her size.

She knocked out in minutes, not a nightmare to be seen.

*   *   *   *

"Ayo Xi-*Xi!*"

Xinghua snapped her head up at the sound of Trish's voice.

It had been almost a week since she'd seen the girl. She'd called out of work nearly every day, which was odd. In the months that Xinghua had known her, she'd been hale and healthy, perfectly plump and rosy cheeked like a little brown spice drop. And honestly with her herbal remedy shit, she usually smelt like a spice drop too. That might have been why Xinghua had started to crave those when she was around.

"Helloooooooo? Madam Miles-Away~?" The girl tapped her forehead as if to check if she was in there.

Xinghua patted her hand away, "Stooooop, I'm fine, I'm fine!"

"One of these days you're gonna do that while we're walking somewhere and fall in a friggin manhole or something."

"I will *not.*" Xinghua wrinkled her nose at her, "I'm graceful, I'd jump over it."

"It's not that I don't believe you, it's just that I don't believe you."

She stuck her tongue out at the other, "Did you have something to say or were you just here to make fun of me?"

"Yes. I got invited to this witch thing tonight and I'm too anxious to go alone so, like, please. Be my plus one, honey bun?" She put her hands up as if in prayer, "Please."

Xinghua made like she was thinking about it, though she already knew she'd go. She had nothing better to do with Tom having already sent her a text telling her not to wait up. Plus she'd been trolling for an excuse to get to know Trish better anyhow.

"This a ' we summon demons to eat the men' type of witch group or a 'the moon is our Goddess all hail periods blessed be' witch group?"

"The second one."

"Uuuuuuuuggggggggghhhhhh."

"Please Xing!" Trish turned the puppy eyes on.

"Goddamn it." She sighed, "Fine! But there better be snacks."

"You *cannot* eat the other witches."

"I won't!" Xinghua made a face, "I meant *actual* food, Jesus."

"Oh." Trish exhaled a heavy breath, "Wait, you can eat human food?"

"*Yes.* I like the way it tastes, and chewing gives me an excuse not to talk to people."

"It's bullshit that I'm the fat one and you're not."

"Hey, you're also actually *alive.*"

"I don't think that's really a bonus."

"Trish we've talked about this."

The woman rolled her eyes, "I was kidding! Mostly. Hey, no, don't look at me like that, we both know vampires are way cooler than witches, I *get* to be jealous."

Xinghua smirked, raising a brow at her, "That mean you're finally ready for me to turn you, baby cakes?"

"No."

*   *   *   *

When she'd been teasing Trish for being the magical equivalent of a PTA mom on the drive over, she hadn't expected to actually be *right.*

But sure as shit, when they drove up to the nice upper middle class suburban house, there were no less than four PT Cruisers, two silver mini vans, and a Prius around the house. Xinghua's own blacked out sports car sticking out like a sore thumb.

On their first step inside Xinghua heard the tell tale sign of a dull gathering, at least three white ladies all fake laughing about some sort of milquetoast gossip. The house smelled like patchouli and sage. She wanted to puke already.

This was a witch gathering, there should have been more mysterious vials of glowing blue liquid for her to drink and less yoga pants. She'd expected at least *one* actual hag. That wasn't asking too much was it? A single one eyed, one toothed trouble making spitfire of an old woman? At this point she'd honestly settle for a mildly naughty milf.

"Trish!" A woman who looked very much like her name should have been 'Susan' exclaimed, heading towards them, "I'm *so glad* you could make it! Oh and you even brought a friend!"

Jesus fuck, she had a mid-western accent.

"Yes!" Trish raised a hand before seeming to remember she wanted to use it to gesture between the two of them, "Xinghua this is Suzanne, Suzanne, Xinghua. Xinghua is a friend of mine from work, Suzanne was who sent me the invite, she works at my favorite salon."

Called it.

"Nice to meet you S-s-sh-schling-"

"You can just call me Xi-xi." She interrupted what was surely going to be a painful experience for them all, "Nice to meet you too."

"Gi-gi! That's super cute, I love it!" Suzanne forced an overly enthusiastic laugh.

She reached out to tap Xinghua's wrist, but as soon as they made contact she froze.

That wasn't all that weird in itself. It happened from time to time, given that she was corpse cold no matter the environment, and it just happened to be as warm as the middle of July in this house. There were even some humans with more adept senses that could instinctively tell something was off about her. Those ones tended to steer clear of her, so she was surprised when the little witch recovered herself quickly and broke into another smile.

Nonetheless she pulled her hand back.

Maybe some of them were worth their salt after all.

"Ladies!" Another dark haired woman began before the mind-numbing small talk could, "Welcome and thank you for your participation in my little group."

The ladies all golf clapped and cheered at an acceptable volume.

"Thank you. Now, during our last few sessions we went over herbal medicines and how to use the natural flow of energy in the body to help it heal. Today's lesson is an outward expansion of that idea."

In spite of herself, Xinghua found herself paying attention. The woman had a manner of speaking that reminded her of Tom when he explained some of his research to her.

"Like the body, the world around us is a system. That system is made up of many different parts that function as a whole, and in order for that system to work at all, it needs energy." She explained, "That energy is something that, in the right hands, can be harnessed."

Xinghua's sixth sense, the one that nearly always knew when there was trouble to get in, was going nuts. The more this woman talked, the more Xinghua became certain she was the genuine article. How on Earth had Trish even *found* her?

"Today we will be working with one of the most abundant sources of energy. Each other. So as not to do anything too intense with our energy, we will start with divination."

A woman with blonde hair in a messy bun raised her hand. "Yes Monica?"

"I'm sorry Miss Florence, but divination seems *really* intense energy wise."

Florence smiled, nodding, "If we were to take the traditional route, you are absolutely correct, it would be. My method however is much more passive. If you would, turn to the person on your immediate left."

Xinghua was more than a little glad she'd sat down at the end of a row, next to Trish, making them partners. She wagged her eyebrows at Trish who lightly slapped the top of her hand, trying to focus on Florence instead.

"Now, take their hands and close your eyes. Focus your senses on them, try to feel the little bubble of energy that's surrounding them. Picture it like a soap bubble made of static electricity." She instructed, "Once you've locked onto it, I want you to follow it as it extends out in front of them. Open your mind to it and let it carry you off into the future."

"Do you even *have* energy?" Trish whispered, peeking an eye open, "I mean you're *technically* dead."

"Fuck around and find out." Xinghua smirked.

"You are such a- you know what, I *will*."

Trish took both of Xinghua's long, cold hands in her small warm ones and let her eyes close. She slowed her breathing and began to focus. Honestly she just looked like she was incredibly determined to force sleep to come to her.

Xinghua would have sniggered and poked fun at her, but the chanting caught her ear.

It was soft at first, not even loud enough that a human would have heard it as a whisper. Then it grew louder and Xinghua noted with slight horror that it was coming from *Trish.*

It sounded *old.* Something deep and heavy and powerful that Xinghua had never had the audacity to try to learn before. The type of words that scraped their way across the inside of the skulls of their victims, kept them tangled up in paranoid delusions for weeks.

"Um, Trish?

Three things happened at once.

The first being Trish squeezing Xinghua's hands hard enough to break several of the bones. She heard the crunch of them and just barely managed to keep herself from trying to throw her friend. The second was Trish's eyes flying open, now a cloudy white very close to the shade of her own. And the third, and undoubtedly most concerning, thing, was Trish beginning to scream.

It was the kind of guttural, animal scream that people only made when they were on the edge of death or a pain so intense it was worse. Xinghua felt every hair on her body rise as terror clenched her stomach tight.

"Calm yourself child," Another, more powerful voice intoned from the front of the room, "Speak, then leave us in peace."

"It's so dark," Trish gaped out in a voice that both was and was not her own, *"They're everywhere, oh God they're **everywhere!**"*

"Who is everywhere?" The speaker appeared beside them, the older woman who'd been addressing the group earlier, Florence, Xing thought her name was, "What can you see?"

*"They took my arm! I can't- I can't! It hurts so much, please **please** just leave me alone!"*

Florence grimaced, visibly disturbed, but her voice didn't falter, "That's enough, come back now Trish. Follow my voice back to this time. Follow my energy, let it guide you."

She put her hand on Trish's shoulder and her death grip on Xinghua's hands relaxed ever so slightly.

"That's it, just like that. Ground yourself with my energy. Very good."

It took a moment but slowly Trish's eyes unclouded, their normal dark brown leaking out into the iris from the pupil. The fear however, did not leave her face. She dropped Xinghua's hands like they'd burned her, panting and gasping like she'd just run a mile.

Xinghua cradled her broken hands to her chest, breathing through her clenched teeth as the bones began to knit themselves back together. The room was so silent she could hear them popping back into place.

"What-" Suzanne peeped nervously, "What just ha-happened?"

Xinghua could feel every single eye in the room trained on them. She hated being stared at like that, it made her itchy.

"What you have just witnessed is something very rare." Florence began slowly, "Genuine, real, *magic.*"

Trish's eyes nearly bugged out of her head as the room burst into whispers.

"I don't know about you ladies but that's plenty enough excitement for me for one night. We should leave this session here." Florence addressed the room, though her attention was on Trish, "I will see you all next week. Patrica, a word, if you would be so kind."

Trish's hand flashed out to grab Xinghua's shirt, just as she was making to leave.

"Don't you fucking dare. That was *your* future I saw."

"Trish-"

"No."

"But-"

"No."

Xinghua let her cheeks fill up with air as her shoulders rose along with her distaste for the situation. Trish was right, she knew she was, but that didn't mean she couldn't throw a little fit.

Fifteen minutes later saw them sitting around Florence's dining table. She'd brewed them all a cup of tea, though the ingredients she'd used for each of them was different. She'd selected the herbs individually as she went, humming something to herself Xinghua couldn't quite place.

As she took a sip of the tea, she noted that it tasted nostalgic, though she couldn't remember where she knew the flavor from.

"As I'm sure you ladies well know, there are a great many things in this world that do not coincide with humanity's general world view." Florence said, setting her tea aside.

"Yeah," Xinghua sighed, "I mean I would hope I knew that. I'm a fucking vampire for Christ sakes."

Florence nodded slowly, "I suspected you weren't human, though I'll admit I wasn't sure of what sort you were."

"Was it the eyes? I bet it was the eyes."

"Among other things." The woman sipped her tea.

"Excuse me," Trish chirupped, "I'm still really sketch about the whole 'real magic' thing. Like I get vampires and stuff, cause that's a virus. A really weird, aggressive one, but like it's still a virus. I just straight *saw the future* fam, that doesn't just *happen.*"

"You most certainly did, uh, fam." Florence cleared her throat, "But believe it or not, that's not any more difficult to explain than your friend here."

"Then please please explain because I'm pretty sure I'm panicking."

Florence took Trish's hands into her own and made sure she was looking her in the eye as she gave her a reassuring smile.

"Do not be afraid of your own magic, young woman. It is the best friend you will *ever* have, and as you learn to harness it, you will realize how much it has to give you." She said with conviction, "Magic is only energy, it is neither good nor evil."

"Okay, that would be fine but I just watched myself get torn apart by like- undead zombies."

"Zombies are undead already, that's what makes them zombies." Xinghua muttered.

Both Florence and Trish sent her twin withering looks. She sipped her tea noisily.

"I *know*- but they-! They *acted* like zombies but like I guess they weren't really dead, or missing skin or anything? They just... hunted. Their eyes were so blank... even when they were tearing me to pieces it was like they didn't even know *why.* They just... *did."*

Trish shuddered, her shoulders hunching up towards her ears as Florence squeezed her hands.

"I'm sorry your first foray into magic was something like this." She said, "But try to remember, the future you looked into was that of an immortal. Those events could happen thousands of years from now."

Trish nodded though she didn't seem all that comforted.

"Yeah, you're right. But I- as far as I know, *I'm* not immortal. And I definitely saw myself there."

Florence's expression folded in on itself, "There is that."

Trish's heart rate spiked.

The woman cleared her throat, adjusting in her chair.

"That's a bit more urgent then." She said, the slightest of tremors in her voice that likely only Xinghua heard, "Would you tell me more about what you saw?"

"I- yeah." Trish took her hands back and shook them out, clearing her own throat, "I think I was seeing from Xinghua's perspective, because I saw me, one of our other friends, Ziggy, and at least three other guys I've never met before. We were all running away from a literal *horde* of not-zombies. There had to have been *hundreds* of them. They were so fast it was fucking insane, even Xinghua was having trouble outrunning them."

Xinghua frowned, "*I* was?"

Trish nodded, "You also had a sword and you were trying to keep them away from us too. But they were crazy strong. You lost an arm and then I screamed and then they were on me too. The guys we were with tried to help, and I- I think one of them was a werewolf because he turned into a big ol black wolf and one of the other ones turned into like a *panther I fucking think?* I didn't see what happened after that, that's when Florence dragged me back out."

Xinghua gave a low whistle, "You sure you saw the future? No funny mushrooms in the hors d'oeuvres?"

Trish laughed nervously and Florence sent her another flat look.

"I wish it were that." Trish let herself slump against the table, "But wait..."

The other two gave her their attention as she sat back up.

"Just because I saw it doesn't mean that it's going to come true right? The future changes all the time!"

"That's very true." Florence nodded sagely.

"Is there... like... a magical way we can, uh, *check* or something?" Trish winced, "Is that a thing?"

Florence breathed in deep and slow and for a moment Xinghua could have sworn she saw her eyes flicker darker. They probably had, but Xinghua wasn't about to ask why.

"There is one way we can be certain. But it is very, *very* risky."

"Now we're talkin'." Xinghua grinned, "I'm the riskiest kid in town, what's good?"

Florence laughed for the first time since they'd met her, "I appreciate your spirit, young vampire. Though summoning the Witch of Time is hardly an average risk."

"The what of who? I thought you guys were witches."

"No, no, dear. We are *mages*. A Witch is something very different, and leagues more powerful."

"How much more powerful are we talking?" Xinghua raised her eyebrow.

Florence looked as though she were weighing her words, "If a mage is like a lightbulb, then a Witch is like the sun."

"Oh. *Fuck.*" Trish breathed, "And we're *summoning* one of those? I'm concerned."

"You absolutely should be."

*　　　　*　　　　*　　　　*

It had been a long time since Xinghua had felt genuine fear. Generally there was nothing that could actually do any damage to her, not really, and even fewer things that could stop her. She didn't *need* to be afraid.

But watching as Florence and Trish set up their black and white candles, nervousness crept up her neck. It was *exhilarating.*

"So what's this Witch bitch like?" Xinghua asked idly.

"Time is one of the most fickle beings in existence. Older than your maker, and incredibly unpredictable."

"Oh nice." Xinghua nodded, "And when you say 'Time' do you mean like, time the concept?"

"What else would I mean, dear?"

"Just checking."

When they finished prepping, Florence turned back to the two, hands sternly placed on her hips.

"Given Time's disposition, it's much safer for you to avoid drawing his attention to you at all costs. Do not speak to him, and do not move from your place. Is that understood?"

"Clear as crystal."

"Got it."

"Good." Florence nodded, reaching her hands out to them.

Xinghua took both her and Trish's hands, closing the circle. Almost immediately she could feel the hum of magic flowing through her, like a circuit. As the elder mage began to chant, the feeling grew stronger until Xinghua was nearly vibrating with it.

"Lord Juno, Witch of Time, I humbly entreat you to enter this place, bring your wisdom into this sacred space."

Out of the corner of her eye Xinghua swore she could see a vase aging to dust and rebuilding itself again.

"Share the insight we hope to gain, even that which would be called profane, guide us in our search for knowledge, bless this, our humble three person college."

In no time at all, or maybe a hundred years later, Xinghua began to hear the soft piano notes of a hauntingly placid melody.

In the middle of their circle, a silhouette began to form.

As the music became clearer, so too did the form before them. It was very obviously not human, far too thin and tall to be.

First came the smile, composed of unsettlingly large, impossibly white teeth like sun bleached tombstones. Next was the hair, blonde and slicked back like an old-timey reporter. Then came the hands, one set steepled together, with another pair resting lightly on hips that rippled into being as they did. Then the legs, rail thin and nearly eight feet long. Last to appear were the eyes, although Xinghua would be hard-pressed to actually call them that. Where his eyes *should* have been was melted, scarred skin that looked as though acid had been thrown at it.

He was still as the grave, silent too as his music faded away.

Xinghua had never been so horrified in all her life than she felt looking at this 'Witch'.

"So I see that you've called me to quite the
Grim timeline, although I know you'd hardly
Go through the trouble of calling me up,
If things here but blossoms and buttercups." He intoned, his voice seeming to echo endlessly back to them.

He reminded her of a poet, with his inflection pitching into a lilting upper class affectation even as each of his sentences rhymed. She wanted to ask what the fuck was up with that, but remembered what Florence had said.

"You are correct, Lord Juno, we called you to ask you what *you* know."

His smile widened by a molar, looking genuinely painful now. Xinghua could have sworn she heard skin tearing.

*"This and that, oh yes, I know **many** things.*
I could tell you all, I could sing and sing
But it's moot without specificity
Ask what you wish to know, explicitly."

Florence opened her mouth to speak but before she could, Trish's voice cut in.

"I saw a vision of the end and I am desperate to know! Is it set in stone or can I change the way that things will go?"

For an gratingly long moment, no one moved. Xinghua couldn't even hear anyone breathing. Time himself didn't move even so much as a muscle, like he hadn't even heard her. The taste of fear soured the air as the seconds slouched by.

After seconds or days of him standing stock still, he whipped his head in Trish's direction, irrespective of the way it caused his neck to crack sickeningly. The angle was so unnatural, and the sound so unsettling, Xinghua almost didn't notice how his smile ticked impossibly wider.

He had *far* too many teeth. And were they…moving? They were! Ticking by like the second hand of a clock.

"*Who are you, little bug, to speak to me,*

And put your little life in jeopardy?" His voice rolled into a much lower tone, like someone had put a distortion effect on it.

"*Do you know the risks or the benefits,*

Of what it is that you have lately done?

It's not my concern, you'll soon learn, daft chit

*I do hope that your final year is **fun**.*"

His body walked itself around slowly, his neck cracking once again as his head settled on straight. He loomed over Trish like an obelisk, his eyes glowing intensely yellow. Xinghua could feel the power radiating off of him and the desire to put herself between them was mounting, though it felt delayed, like she had to *load* the desire fully before her body could move.

While she was preoccupied, his second set of hands lifted off his waist, swirling idly around the air in front of him. Xinghua noticed that if she stared hard enough she could see people, buildings, and places in the haze between his hands.

"*The answer you are seeking is quite bleak*

Are you certain that you'd like to know it?

Not everyone can handle their sneak peek

Can you presume to be so devoted?" His voice had returned to 'normal' and Xinghua couldn't believe she was happy to hear the unsettling echo again.

He unfurled one of his unreasonably long arms towards Trish, cocking his head towards her as if telling her to speak.

"Y-yes My Lord, if you'd be so kind. I... know the truth would e-e-ease my mind."

He waited until she took his hand, not moving so much as a hair until she did. Trish hissed when their hands made contact, jerking her arm back as though burned. An hour glass was now etched into her skin, like a tattoo, aside from the fact that it was moving. Trish stared at it in horror while Time took a low bow. When he came back up, part of his cheek was disintegrating like the sand in her hourglass.

"*The future you've seen, while wild and obscene*
Will most certainly come into being.
Try that which you must, try that which you may,
It stops nothing at the end of the day." Time flourished his hands, all four of them.

Xinghua glanced at Trish as she smacked her hand over her mouth to cover the sob trying to break out from between her teeth.

"*Despair not, young mage, this is not the end.*
There is hope yet, for both you and your friend.
Fight and fight, with your considerable might,
Do not go quietly into the night.
Stand strong and fast against the coming storm,
And a hopeful future your hands will form."

"T-thank you Lord Time." Trish stuttered.

His head cracked aggressively to the side and one of his teeth shattered, the splinters of it lodging into Trish's cheek. Xinghua was nearly vibrating with how badly she wanted to run to her, but her body just *would not* move.

"I'm s-sorry that I forgot to rhyme!"

The tooth shimmered back into existence and Time's neck once again cracked back to its original angle. Jesus fuck Xinghua was going to have nightmares about that.

"Now that I've given my thoughts on your plight,
*I return my attention to **my** fight.*
Once they return what is rightfully mine,
My day shall improve by Seven and Nine,
Good day ladies, though I'll see you again,
But for your sakes I hope not 'till year's end."

Xinghua blinked and he was gone as though he'd never been in the first place.

"Holy *fuck.*" Trish fell to her hands and knees, tears already streaming down her cheeks, *"Oh my actual God."*

Xinghua finally felt able to move! She was at Trish's side half a second later, beginning the work of plucking the shards of Time's tooth from her cheek.

"What did I tell you about talking to him!" Florence hissed, *"Stupid* girl!"

"I didn't mean to! My mouth just started going! I didn't even notice I was talking until his fuckin' head did that *thing,* and then he *looked* at me in and I *couldn't stop.* Oh my God I feel like I've been alive for hundreds of years... and dead for thousands. *What the fuck was that?!"*

"I told you, a Witch." Florence's shoulders slumped and she turned around to the bar, grabbing a large bottle of wine, "You may as well have looked a God in the eyes."

She poured three incredibly tall glasses and drained hers without pause, pouring another one without hesitation.

"He didn't even *have* eyes." Xinghua muttered too quietly for human ears.

"I told you not to talk to him, not just to keep you from getting hurt like that." She said, handing them each a glass, "But because getting his attention like that buys you membership to the worst club in existence."

Trish's hand flew to the hour glass now staining the skin of her wrist.

"What....what club?"

She pulled up her sleeve, showing an identical hourglass, save that hers was much lower on sand, "Welcome to the Minute Men, Memento Mori."

*   *   *   *

The drive back to Trish's apartment was starkly silent.

Xinghua couldn't think of a single thing to say that would come close to touching anything about the night, and Trish seemed lost in thought. Not that Xinghua could blame her.

When she pulled the car to a stop in front of Trish's place, for a moment both of them simply sat in the silence created in the wake of Xinghua killing the engine.

"So, how are you enjoying the supernatural world tour? Been fun?" Xinghua anxiously asked after a few seconds had passed.

Trish barked a laugh which quickly slid into a watery cry.

Xinghua winced as she slumped forward, her forearms bracing against the console as she wept. She reached out to her, awkwardly patting her back. It took a bit but eventually she condensed her tears down into sniffles.

"I *just* moved to this goddamn city, I feel like the protag of a fucking isekai." Trish muttered, sounding half drowned, "My black ass does *not* have the cardio to make it through the plot of one of those bitches, I will *actually die.* Oh my fucking God I'm gonna *die.*"

Trish clutched at her hair, hunching nervously into herself.

"You're *not* gonna die."

"How do you know? The big, spooky Witch dude seemed pretty damn sure!"

"Okay but he *also* said not to give up. Which to me says okay yeah so we couldn't change *getting* to that vision, but we sure can change the survivability of it!" Xinghua tossed her hands up into the air, "This seems exactly like the time to let me turn you."

"I've only known about vampires for like *two months,* I cannot just *become* one!"

"Sure you can!"

Trish leaned back in her seat and scrubbed her hands over her cheeks.

"I need to be able to die *someday,* Xing. I don't have the emotional stamina for immortality." She looked back over her way, "Doesn't mean I want to die *soon,* so like I still need to figure *that* the fuck out, but vampire is not the winning answer here, sorry."

Xinghua folded her arms and let herself lean back into the seat.

"Fine."

The silence slid back into the cab of the car, but this time Trish was the one to break it.

"Thank you. For being willing to be my vampire sugar mama, though." She muttered.

"Yeah, course."

"You...want to come in for a drink or something?"

Xinghua considered it for a moment, before ultimately deciding the night had been long enough already.

"Normally I'd be down, but I think I'm gonna take a raincheck this time." She gave Trish an apologetic smile, "Are you gonna be cool on your own?"

Trish picked at her nails but nodded.

"Yeah, totally! It's not like I can summon the spooky Witch dude back on my own. And I kinda want to get a jump start on researching this whole 'Minute Men' thing." She breathed out, long and heavy, "Yeah, actually that's a good first step. Just gotta keep asking myself WWSD."

"WWSD?"

"What would Shiro do?"

"Who's Shiro..?"

"You don'-- okay, after this whole lot of bullshit blows over, we're sitting you down for an anime marathon."

Trish opened the passenger side door and began climbing out of the car.

"If you can get me to sit still for more than ten minutes, then you'll have earned your place as a mage." Xinghua chuckled.

"Aha! A metric!" Trish smiled back a little, "Night Xing, despite...well *everything* thanks for coming."

"Despite everything, thanks for inviting me."

Trish shut the door with a wave and turned to head into her place. Xinghua let herself release a long, tired breath before turning the car back on to head back home.

Richard had a headache, the same one he had from the night before in fact. A day spent staring at a screen, trying to trace the pattern of abductions in the second case he'd been working hadn't helped. Getting stonewalled by the absolute dearth of usable leads was just insult to injury.

It had been a long day, even as long days go. Richard was coasting on fumes, ready to finally let himself take the eighteen-hour nap he'd earned now that Friday night had finally come around.

If he was smart about how he spaced out his alcohol to water ratio, he might even wake up feeling refreshed.

As he stepped down the last stair of the station, he tugged on his tie. It was tight today, or maybe he'd just been smoking too much again. He couldn't be certain either way but it hardly mattered. When he eventually woke up, he'd go lighter on both of those things. Maybe. If he remembered.

The detective was so far lost in his thoughts, plans for dinner-another brilliant collaboration between his microwave and freezer-and maybe a shower, that he didn't notice the tail he'd picked up.

He ducked into the ally he always took to cut that extra minute off his walk to the parking lot he used, idly wondering if he should light up a cigarette before he got in the car. It sounded good, but he knew he was supposed to cut down on that, he'd literally just been thinking about it and-

A scratch on the pavement caught his ear.

Richard glanced behind himself, expecting a civie, maybe another cop, or a mugger if he was unlucky, but apparently he was *real unlucky.*

Standing at the mouth of the alley was a dog, except that it most certainly was *not* a dog because it was the size of a *van.* Its eyes, trained steadily on him were gold, so bright he could have sworn they were glowing in their sockets, although that was probably the adrenaline spiking through his ribs directly into his heart.

He didn't move a muscle, as badly as every inch of him wanted to bolt. He was fairly certain that would only cause it to chase him and he'd be hard pressed to outrun that thing in a *car,* forget on foot.

The creature sniffed the air, a growl like the roar of a jet rumbling through the ground.

"Hey," Richard's mouth began without his permission, "None of that now, I'm gettin' out of your space big fella, don't be mad."

The growling grew in volume as its ears laid back and Richard couldn't fight the urge to run anymore.

The parking garage wasn't that far away, it wasn't that far, he could make it if he put everything into it, he could, he wasn't *that* out of shape, it was only twenty feet, fifteen, ten-

Pain tore through his left ankle, far too reminiscent of the bullet he'd taken in nearly the same place during his second tour. He tried to cry out, but rending agony erupted through his right side and stole his breath away before he got much more than a hiss out.

The monster was on top of him, its jaw clamped around his waist and its claws piercing his ankle. It squeezed its jaw down and he felt something crack, pain burning through his torso. He needed out of this thing's mouth but if he moved to get away, its grip alone would take a chunk out of him and he'd be no closer to escaping.

Richard reached for his sidearm, glad for once he'd forgotten to leave it at work. His hands were shaking and the pain was making him sick, but he wasn't dizzy yet.

He aimed at the thing and fired without hesitation. The noise, as it always did, made his ears ring, but the not-dog seemed to have an even worse reaction to the sound. It let go of him, thankfully, shaking its head hard enough to smack into the wall nearby, further disorienting it.

Richard fired two more shots, these two into its head, dropping the thing.

He didn't bother sticking around to check if it was dead or not, because if it wasn't he *would* be.

Limping towards the nearest building was the most he could manage, now dizzy and feeling feverish he suspected by how hot he was and how hard it was beginning to get to focus. There was no way he'd be able to drive in this condition, he'd more than likely injure someone, if not kill.

But he needed to get to a hospital, he knew that at least even if he couldn't remember where one was. He groped his pockets for his phone, slumping against the building as his body began to feel like too much to hold up. How much blood had he lost?

His phone was shattered, had probably happened when that thing had taken him down. He tried pushing every button on it, but the screen was nothing but primary colors and black spots blooming between cracks. Dead. Like he was going to be if he didn't get help.

The concrete seemed to be tunneling, stretching down infinitely beneath him, warping into dark hallways and heavily lit corridors even as he felt as if he had stayed planted where he was. The sensation of being on a boat rose up to meet him. God he hated boats, even more than planes.

"Ransom?" A distantly familiar voice called his name, "What are *you* doing here?"

Richard blinked, finding Li in front of him. Standing. In a door frame. *Her* door frame, he recognized even though the thing seemed so far away from him. What *was* he doing there? And how the hell had he gotten there?

"Listen if you're here to tell me about how dangerous Tom is, save it. I've had a really long day and--"

She sniffed at the air a little, before her peculiar eyes zeroed in on something, on *him.*

"You're bleeding." She stated, rather superfluously since he was pretty sure the wound on his side was dripping over the hand that had at some point began clutching it, "What happened?"

He must have said something, because she nodded, even though he hadn't heard himself speak, hadn't even thought about making words happen. She stepped aside and waved him into her house.

"I'm not the best nurse but I can at least wrap that for you and call an ambulance." She said, though her voice was echoing like she was speaking to him through a cave.

She steered him to a chair, thank God, and the instant he sat down, it was easier to breathe. The world stopped rocking quite so violently back and forth, but the ringing in his ears worsened for a moment, leaving him dizzy and all but deaf. He leaned his head back, feeling like someone was using the damn thing as a tuning fork.

"Let me see it." Li said, from twenty miles away.

Richard couldn't move, not right now, he'd either throw up or die.

"Can't." He heard himself this time, though it was hard to recognize as his own voice, maybe that was why he hadn't heard himself earlier.

"Fine," She huffed, "Just don't get hyphy about this later, yeah?"

He felt a pair of hands so cold they might just belong to Death himself pawing at his abdomen and gasped, though he could do very little else. It felt good once he relaxed, the coolness pleasant on his feverish skin.

"You're burning up," She stated once again rather redundantly, "Jesus, it almost burns to touch you, what the hell- *oh.*"

That was about the last thing anyone wanted to hear in the situation he was in right now.

"Oof," Li breathed out as if the sound had been punched from her, "I'm sorry to be the one to tell you this, but you're gonna die dude."

Richard cracked open an eye and nearly threw up with the way it immediately shot pain from his head all the way through the rest of his body. He was still dizzy, even sitting down. The wound had begun throbbing, he could feel his pulse through it, and it was slowing down.

He let his eyes shut again.

"I know."

"You- you *know?*" She sounded alarmed.

"C'n feel it."

And he could. He'd nearly died more than enough times to know what it felt like. The sensation slowly draining from his limbs, the heaviness in his body but the lightness in his head. The cold that would have been eating him up if it weren't for the damn fever. He'd felt his heart stop before, and in the wee hours of the night when it was just him and his empty walls, he could admit he'd enjoyed the feeling. It felt freeing, the struggle that life embodied even in its calmest moments was gone. On more than one occasion, he'd prayed for it.

"If you know that, why the hell are you here instead of in a hospital? Or like, with your family or some shit?"

The little ping of pain that normally went through him at the mention of his family was like a faint pin prick. He didn't have the energy for angst at the moment, which was one more thing he was grateful for about dying.

"Don't.... have any." It was getting hard to force words out around the heaviness centering in his lungs, had they been punctured?

"Oh *God* that's so depressing." She groaned, and for a moment it felt like her forehead pressed against his leg but when he peeled his eyes open to check she was sitting up straight,

"You know what, that's *too* depressing. I've just decided you're not gonna die. Not tonight at least."

He tried to laugh, but it was a wet affair full of pain and coughing that told him something had most *definitely* punctured at least one of his lungs. He suspected a rib to be the culprit behind that, though he couldn't see the injury well enough to check.

"Don't fucking laugh, you sound like a vacuum filled with jello. But I'm gonna get you through this, okay?"

"How?"

She wiggled her nose back and forth as if deciding whether or not to be honest.

"Because I know what bit you, and I know you *can* survive it. But you've got to work with me here, so no more of this 'I know I'm dying'. You gotta think like a survivor."

He let his head slump forward, too tired to bring it around properly.

"I've had...plenty of... adventures. I think... this one... can.... be my last."

That's what he wanted. That's what he'd wanted for *years.* It had been enough to outlive his brother and mother, but outliving his-- he just wanted to be done. He'd done a lot of good in his life, surely he'd earned that mercy.

Li's face pinched up, whether due to the idea of watching someone die, or watching him *want* to die, he couldn't have said. It felt like hours, *decades,* before her expression changed.

"Well if you die, then who's gonna stop Tom?"

The fire that had been raging through his whole body seemed to calm for a moment. It concentrated in his belly as the question leached into his skin, breaking down the weariness in his body until he felt much more lucid than he had been since he'd been attacked.

He could see the room in perfect clarity, which was more than he'd been able to say for at least the last five years without readers. Li was staring down at him with something like shock etched onto her sharp features, or maybe it was worry.

"How far are we from a hospital?" He asked, his voice stronger than it had been seconds ago, his chest feeling looser too.

"That's the spirit!" She replied, the faint flicker of a smile lighting up the corner of her mouth, "But I'mma tell you right now, a hospital ain't gonna cut it with that. The virus is a will power thing."

"Virus?"

She reeled back like she hadn't meant to say that, wincing before she finally relented with a sigh.

"Yeah, virus. The thing that bit you probably *looked* like a dog, but I can tell you right now, *that* was a werewolf." She gestured to his wound.

"A what?"

She hissed, ticking her head to the side, "I know it sounds fuckin' crazy but just bear with me here for a second."

She pulled her upper lip up, showing her teeth which he thought were oddly straight for someone with a background as poor as hers. As he watched though, a second pair of incisors, no, *fangs,* slid out from her gum line like a snake.

She let her lip go, but didn't tuck away the teeth.

"Vampires, werewolves, faeries, and Witches apparently, all that shit is for real." She explained indelicately, "Probably Santa too, but I've never met him."

Richard stared for a solid minute, convinced that the fever had him hallucinating. He blinked hard but the fangs stayed right where they were resting gently against her thin bottom lip. He'd stopped swaying minutes ago.

"I know," She continued when he still hadn't spoken, "It's a lot. But if you're gonna make it through this, you should at least know what's on the other side."

"Becoming a...a *werewolf?*"

She shrugged and finally sucked her fangs back up into wherever it was they came from, "Not as cool as a vampire by a long shot, but yeah. If you can manage to last through the fever, you'll be a werewolf."

Richard rested his face in his hands for a moment, trying to reconcile the 360° shift his world view had just taken in the last thirty seconds. When he tried to contemplate it in any sort of way past recognizing that the words had been spoken and proven, his head filled with radio static.

"Okay," He said, trying his best not to let it come out like a thirteen year old mid puberty, "Fuck it. Werewolves. *Why not?* So the fever is the big danger here?"

Li looked concerned, but nodded, "Uh, yeah, your body will heal up the rest of the damage. Werewolves don't heal as well as vamps do, but still way better than a human. The fever though, that's some real shit. I don't remember *everything* I read about this, but we're gonna need to cool you down or like, your brain will boil like minute rice in a bag and that'll be that. You're still gonna trip out, probably, but that's part of where the will power comes in. And me of course, I'll keep you from doing anything *physically* dangerous."

Richard nodded, he was fairly certain the healing had already started since breathing had gotten significantly easier.

He didn't feel like he was dying anymore so much as he felt like he was standing naked in Nevada at high noon in July.

"Right." He forced himself to breathe slowly despite his body panicking, "How do we cool me down?"

At that she stood up. He blinked and suddenly she was in the kitchen, having evidently decided that now that the cat was out of the bag, there was no reason to act like a human.

"Ice bath." She called from the bathroom next, "I'll run downstairs for more when you melt through this."

She was back in front of him in the space between heart-beats. It was eerie, and honestly doing very little to help his grip on what was real.

"So do you want me with you or do you wanna veg out on your own?" She asked, hands on her hips.

He didn't think being alone with the snarled mess his thoughts had become was necessarily the *best* idea.

"I'd rather have you with me." He admitted, softly.

In the next instant he was in her arms, to his complete surprise. She wasn't straining a bit under his significant weight as she zipped into the bathroom. It was disorienting, but efficient.

"If you wanna strip, I can turn around." She said as she sat him down on the edge of the bath, "Or you can go in clothes and all, your choice."

"Turn around."

"Boooo." She rolled her eyes but turned around anyway.

Richard stripped down to his undershirt and boxers, happy to have the extra layers off but alarmed by the amount of blood staining them. Nervously he looked down to where the wound on his side was.

It was bloody and ragged certainly, but it was nowhere as deep or as wide as it had been when he'd gotten there. It hurt when he grazed it with trembling fingers, but the bleeding had stopped which had been one of his biggest concerns.

"You done, madam?" Li spoke up, reminding him that she was still there.

"Yeah, I-" He swallowed hard, "I was checking the wound."

"How's it looking?"

"Better." He huffed, trying to ignore the panic still niggling at the back of his mind, "It looks much better."

"That's a good sign," She turned back around, her brows raising as she looked him over, "You definitely look…. healthier."

He climbed into the water, shuddering before the relief settled in. It felt even better than he'd imagined, he immediately sunk all the way up to his chin.

"Aahh, siento muy bien." He sighed heavily as the cold fought against his fever.

"I understood one and a half of those words but 'good' was in there so it sounds like we're five by five." She gave him a thumbs up, crouching down next to the tub.

"Feels good." Richard translated, "I feel much more lucid now. Hardly even nauseous."

Li nodded, "Good. I remember in Tom's notes it said something about three main fever spikes. I think you just finished the first one."

Richard breathed out heavy, before something occurred to him.

"Wait, *who's* notes? *Airius* knows about all this?"

Li pulled that face from earlier, but with the urge to kick herself doubled.

"Yeeeeeeeeeaaaaaaaaah."

"...He's a vampire isn't he?"

"Well I mean, I had to come from *somewhere*, right?"

That was... it made sense in the way that none of this made sense. If he really accepted that as reality, it would account for why all of Snow White's victims had been exsanguinated. It would also explain how he'd accomplished things that should have been impossible, like staging a body faster than a security camera could follow. Really, it would explain a lot of things, but it would also make him *extraordinarily* harder to stop.

It also raised a myriad of other questions.

"So if you're both vampires... do *you* kill people too? Is *this* why you didn't seem phased about me insisting you were in danger?"

"One at a time Holmes. I haven't killed anyone, or well I *haven't* since my first feed. Which, in my defense, I wasn't really *conscious* for that. I normally can't drink a whole human honestly, makes me feel all sloshy and bloated and gross. Second, I wasn't afraid because I'm fucking immortal. He couldn't kill me even if he wanted to so I have nothing to worry about." She replied with a little smirk, "Dude you have no idea how hard it was to keep quiet during that, I wanted to show you my fangs *so* bad."

"Wait, if you don't-" He frowned, "Is there a limit to how much you can drink?"

"Well yeah," She rolled her eyes like it was obvious, "I'm still in a human shaped body, there's only so much room in here."

"So you don't *need* to kill people to survive?"

"I mean, *no* but-"

"So he's been killing and drinking more than he needs and you didn't think that was suspicious or cruel in any way?" Richard frowned hard at her.

"Look it's *not my goddamn business* how much he drinks! Do *you* police other people's eating habits?" She threw her hands, "That's just fucking rude!"

"I would if they were eating *other people!*"

"Humans have been food for vampires since for-fucking-ever, so what if a few die, there's *millions* of them!"

Richard reeled back and Li did too, like she'd only just realized what she'd said.

For a long uncomfortable moment they were silent, neither making eye contact as they both tried to think of something to say.

"I know you're not... human, but there was a time when you were." Richard finally broke the silence, "You're friends with humans, I'm sure, plenty of them. You *know* we're not cattle."

"I know." She said so softly he almost wasn't sure if he'd heard her or not.

"Then why are you okay with him doing this? And to humans that look so much like you no less."

She stared at her feet for a long moment as if they might give her the answers.

"Mortal lives are so short it doesn't really matter when they end. It would never be the right time, so how *can* it matter? Especially if that death feeds a predator higher on the food chain? Isn't that just how it works?" She shrugged, "And as for his type, I mean, I was basically dead when he found me, practically, maybe it reminds him of when we first met. Morbid? Probably, but it's also kinda... cute."

Richard wanted to be sick.

He'd run into plenty of victims who'd been brainwashed by their abusers, but this was a whole other level. The way she spoke sounded much less like a genuine thought and more like a script she was reciting. If Airius had been with her since she'd *become* a vampire, he'd had plenty of time to condition her. And even worse, given that *he* turned her he might have even *more* control over her. Richard wasn't sure how that worked, but it had to mean something significant.

Things were getting more and more complicated by the second. This would have to be a conversation for a time when a supernatural virus wasn't affecting his cognitive skills.

"So how about we pass the time until the next spike playing a little vampire 'Fact or Fiction'?" He deftly switched topics.

Li gave him a look that matched the hesitant way she said, "Sure."

"So sunlight, does it set you on fire?"

She snorted, "No, it's much grosser than that. I don't really know why other than something about photo-activeness and rapid growth, but when the sun hits us we get all...lumpy. Like a whole bunch of tumors grow in that spot and it gets worse and worse the longer we're in the sun. It's, like, one of the only things that won't smooth out on its own too, we've gotta cut off the growths and let it heal up. Super nasty."

Richard winced at that, picturing it far too graphically in his mind's eye.

"What about mirrors? They a no-go?"

"How is it that even when we're playing around you *still* sound like a cop when you ask me shit?" Li shook her head, "I think someone was fucking around when they said that. I show up in mirrors and cameras just fine."

"I read somewhere it was a common belief back in the day because mirrors were backed with silver and silver is supposedly a holy metal so the undead couldn't touch it, not even in a reflection."

"Oh, that makes sense in a very ye Old Catholic church kind of way. Silver doesn't bother me at all, garlic either before you ask. I'd be fucking livid if I had to give up Italian food for eternity. Mint, and like citrus fruits though? Fuck those, they're way too strong, makes my nose hurt."

"You... can still eat human food?"

"Yup! I mean I don't *need* to, I just like the taste. So long as I drink enough blood my body will handle it just like it always did. Honestly I think it makes me a little jittery-hyper if anything. Like a sugar high." She shrugged.

"That's- uh, unexpected." Richard shifted so that his back had a slightly less ridiculous incline to rest against, "Is everything like that? Unnecessary I mean."

"Mostly." She pursed her lips, walking her fingertips over his knee, "I don't need food or water or air. I don't have anywhere near as good a grasp on what the virus does as, like, *Tom* does, but the way I understand it, the virus will continue to run my body as usual without any of those things. The only human-ish thing I really *have* to do is sleep every so often, and honestly I can even wait that out for about a week without feeling it too bad."

"What happens if you don't sleep?"

"About the same thing that happens to anyone else. I get pissy as all hell, and I can't concentrate. I can't really remember how to speak anything except Cantonese and I start seein' shit." She made a face, "Not a fan."

"Huh." Richard said as the information sank in past the dissociative disbelief coloring the entirety of this experience, "Honestly not as crazy as I expected."

"That's because you haven't asked anything *interesting* yet." She replied, "Don't you wanna know if I'm super strong or have, like, magical powers or if I can turn into a bat?"

"Well I know you're disproportionately strong already because you carried me in here without a problem and I am literally more than twice your size. With the muscle mass you have, you should have shook at least a little if you were a normal human."

She stuck her tongue out at him, "Clever *detective.*"

"And I know you're incredibly fast for the same reason." He continued on as if he hadn't noticed, "The rest though, I didn't even think of."

"The powers are a thing," She grinned mischievously, "Or okay, *I* don't have any powers outside of the usual vampire toolkit. But some vampires do, it's just really rare. The bat thing is a myth so far that I've seen."

"What's the usual tool kit? And when you say powers, are we talking like... one of those mutant-y guys from those, uh, comics?"

She sniggered and he was well aware that it was most likely because he sounded his age when he tried to talk about things outside of his range of expertise.

"The standard stuff is like, the speed and the strength, and being able to talk humans into wanting you. That's all easy, even a newborn can do any of that. Anything else? That's where we start getting into the comic book shit. I know a vampire that everyone calls 'Frost' because he can create ice. I have no fucking idea how that works honestly, like *no* idea, but he can. It's trippy, his eyes look like a snowstorm when he does it." She shivered, rubbing at her arms.

"That's quite a talent." Richard agreed, "Must be quite a sight to behold."

" Oh it *is.*"

They kept talking like that for quite a while. Richard was almost beginning to think that maybe the bath had sufficiently kept the next fever spike at bay when it hit him with a *vengeance.*

He couldn't remember ever having been so insufferably, suffocatingly *hot* in his entire life. It felt like his muscles were melting, his eyes were burning against his eyelids when he blinked, and no matter how hard he panted he couldn't quite get enough air.

"Second wave." He managed past the desire to drink the entire bath he was laid in.

Li cut off the story she'd been telling, immediately becoming serious.

"Okay Ransom, I need you to listen to me, okay?" She began, though it was already starting to sound like she was talking to him from down a tunnel, "Whatever you see, it isn't real. Remember that and *don't* chase the rabbit, okay?'

He didn't know what she meant by that, but he also wasn't paying as much attention as he had been a few minutes ago. The walls were leaning in towards him and he could have sworn he heard something, like a breeze or...

A whisper.

The closer he listened to it, the easier it got to understand until he could make out the voice plain as day. It would have made his blood run cold if he weren't on fire.

"Daddy?"

Richard sat up faster than he should have, his head spinning, though it hardly stopped him. Frantically his eyes scanned the room until they found her, standing in the corner of the room in her little peach colored dress.

"Fiona?" He breathed, his voice barely supporting the fragile hope carried in the name, "Baby, is that you?"

The little girl nodded, her long dark pigtails bobbing on either side of her head. She smiled at him, showing off the gap between her teeth that he'd grown unfairly attached to.

"It's me Daddy." She bounced over to him, swinging her arms wide just like he'd told her not to a hundred times or more, "Where have you been? I missed you a lot."

"Daddy's been-" His voice broke, "Daddy's been at work a lot. Been trying to help people."

She rocked back and forth on her heels and he tried to count her freckles. She'd gotten her mother's fair skin, almost every summer new freckles popped up on her cheeks and arms until there were too many to count. When she'd gone through her astronomy phase he told her they were like little constellations on her skin and helped her map them out with one of her favorite scented markers.

"'Course you have. It helps you forget, right?"

"Forget-?"

"That you didn't save *me.*" She said, casual as anything, "Like maybe if you help enough people you can make up for not being there. Well you *can't.*"

Richard felt like someone had ripped his chest open, just like when he'd gotten that goddamn phone call.

"You were so busy protecting everyone else, you didn't protect me." Her eyes flooded with tears, the green of them that was so like his own washing out, "I wasn't scared, because I thought you would come save me, Daddy. Even after a week I kept thinking you'd find me and everything would be okay. But you didn't!"

The force of her shout was a physical thing that pushed him back, the raw pain sucking the air from his lungs.

"He had me for *weeks* and you didn't find him! I died crying for you to save me!"

He gripped his head as her shouts made his ears start to ring, the painful truth in them too much to hear. Not from her.

"Please-" He gasped, *"I'm sorry."*

"You're sorry?! They raped me and stabbed me to *death* and you're *sorry?!* I was only nine years old!"

Richard curled in on himself, sobs racking his chest as the memories played behind his eyes. He'd felt like someone had ripped his lungs from his chest when they'd found her. The agony had threatened to kill him on the spot, and had only grown when the M.E. had told them what had happened to her. She'd had skin under her nails, telling him she'd fought the entire way, and it was because of that that they'd been able to convict her killer. But it hadn't felt like enough, not nearly enough.

For years he had dragged his heart over the broken glass of grief. He refused to forgive himself, he couldn't think of a reason to. He'd failed to do the *one thing* that mattered most, how *could* he forgive himself?

"When you die, Daddy, I want you to know I'll be waiting for you." Fiona's voice whispered right beside his ear, "And with how your temperature is rising, I won't be waiting long."

He had forgotten how hot he had gotten until she mentioned it. It felt like swimming through mud, but he remembered there was a reason for that. Something he was supposed to be doing.

"Ransom!"

He snapped his eyes open, not knowing when he'd closed them. He was panting again, and when he looked around, Fiona was nowhere to be seen.

Instead in front of him was an incredibly concerned looking Xinghua.

"Dude you stopped fucking breathing." She said in a rush, "I thought you *actually* died on me. *Don't* scare me like that, oh my God."

He squeezed his eyes shut for a moment, trying to push back the impending emotional breakdown with very little success. He knew it was only a hallucination, and one borne of his own guilt at that, but that's exactly what made it stick.

"Are...you okay?" Xinghua asked with surprising gentleness.

He considered lying but immediately dismissed it. It wouldn't have been remotely convincing. So instead he shook his head, curling back in on himself.

"I-" Her voice caught and she swore before she continued, "I'm sorry. It's not the same but when I was little, before I was turned, my mother was killed. Losing a loved one like that... it's not something I would wish on anyone and I'm so sorry you-"

"Can we please not talk about this?" He snapped, an apology rising up to his tongue the moment after, "I just-- I'm sorry."

"No," She said, slowly, "That's fair."

They sat quietly for a long moment, long enough for Richard to feel like his skin was itching under the swell of his fever, before Xinghua spoke again.

"So you were a DILF?"

Richard snorted so hard it hurt, having not expected the pass in the slightest. Xinghua had a peculiar way of making him feel better, but somehow he appreciated it much more than the sympathy.

"If you find dark circles and premature grays sexy."

"Did you have the beer gut to match? Because that's what really does it for me."

An exhausted laugh whistled out of him and he let himself slump back down into the bathtub. The night was far from over, he knew, but he'd take the little moment of peace while he could.

Richard tried fitting in a little nap while Xinghua went to get more ice for the bath. He'd hardly been prepared for how much energy this would take out of him, and he'd skipped dinner...and lunch.

His dreams had been inconsistent, thready, muddled things full of faces that he'd missed for years and feelings he'd been trying to keep hidden for even longer. But between the guilt and the heartache, he noticed he'd started seeing visions he didn't recognize. A forest he'd never been to, red fur, and the moon seen from somewhere else by the way the surface was just a little different looking than he was used to.

He noticed, the more he focused on the moon, the more his body began to ache.

It wasn't until nearly midnight that things started to escalate again.

The images he'd been seeing kept racing through his mind until he couldn't stand to keep his eyes shut any longer. He sat up, slower this time with the heaviness that had begun weighing on his chest. The ache had come on so gradually he hardly even noticed how bad it was until he tried to move and he felt as if he were far, *far* older than he knew he was.

"It's almost over."

Richard's eyes closed, his heart beat jumping a little at the sound of that voice.

He turned to where the voice had come from, letting himself prepare before he opened his eyes again.

It had been years since he'd seen her, but she still looked exactly the way he remembered her. Of course, that was because she wasn't *really* there with him, but that hardly mattered at this point.

"Claire." He said her name with a softness he'd tried for years to smother in vain, "I wondered how long it would be before I saw you."

She walked slowly across the room to him, her movements graceful, measured, restrained the way he knew she spent years perfecting. She was a willowy woman, so slender he'd been worried she didn't eat enough until he'd watched her take down half a pizza by herself on their fourth date. When she'd gotten pregnant he'd been hopeful some of the extra weight would stick to her ribs, though it hadn't.

She reached her hand out to cup his cheek, her expression impassive as ever.

"You know you're dying, right Rich?" She asked without the right inflection, "You can feel it."

He nodded, swallowing thickly, "I'm fighting it."

"No you're not." She responded, the corner of her lip twitching up just the slightest bit, "If you were, I wouldn't be here. You still want to let this kill you so you don't have to keep living with everything you've done."

He hung his head.

Her fingers threaded into his hair-he'd been meaning to cut it for months but just couldn't ever seem to find the time and the motivation at the same moment-and she pulled so that he was forced to look her in the eyes again.

"You don't get to take the easy way out this time." She snarled, "Pull your shit together Richard."

"Claire-"

"Don't." She snapped, "Whatever you're going to say is going to be an excuse and I frankly don't give half a fuck what *you* have to say. You got our daughter *murdered* and by rights I should let you die here too, but I'm not feeling that merciful."

She pushed him back into the tub, climbing into it, on top of him seemingly heedless to how the water soaked through her slacks. Her nails dug into his chest and all of the pain in his body seemed to all focus to the points where she was touching him.

"You're going to *live*, you goddamn coward." Her voice was so cold and harsh, just like the night she'd left him, "And you're going to do what's needed of you. I don't give a damn how you *feel* about it, that's the man you've chosen to be and you're not going to get out of it by dying now."

She pulled her hand back and Richard cried out as it felt like his ribs began to tug themselves toward her. The smile she wore as he screamed was nothing short of sadistic.

"See that?" She tilted her head, her dark hair spilling down over her shoulder, "That's the start of a really, *really* painful metamorphosis."

Her hands came down and cupped his ribs, pressing against them hard enough to make his bones obey her orders. His chest had warped outward into a protruding barrel shape as her hands molded him like clay.

"I'm going to enjoy this." She said acidically, reaching her hand down to his stomach, "Do me a favor and be noisy, hm?"

The touch of her hand snapped his hip bone in half, causing a strangled scream to claw its way out of him. She pulled, merciless as she rearranged his body to suit whatever agenda she had. Or maybe she didn't have an agenda at all and was just interested in torturing him. The way she reached her hand into his belly and hauled his guts lower suggested the latter.

He wanted to beg her to stop but the pain had stolen his voice. He could barely breathe past it, couldn't much tell where his lungs were besides.

"Did you know that when you're pregnant, your body rearranges itself to make room for the baby?" She said idly as she broke his leg, "Not this quickly, but it still hurts. Not something a lot of people talk about. It hurts so much to carry a little one, even before labor."

He couldn't see, his vision had clouded over with black dots, and he wasn't even sure his eyes were open any more. He couldn't think, he couldn't focus on anything but the overwhelming agony ripping him apart.

"But you take on that pain, knowing that a life will be created from it. A life that will matter far more than any of the pain you suffered for it." Her voice was soft for the first time since she'd appeared.

She flicked his shoulder and shattered it.

"You took that from me." She said evenly, as if his screams were nothing more than background noise, "And in the place of that precious little girl we made, you gave me more pain instead."

Her hand pressed through his skin, grabbing onto his spine and pulling it into a shape it had never been designed to make.

This one was by far the worst, causing him to black out for a few seconds.

"Wake! Up!" Claire's voice lost its calm, collected disposition as she shrieked, "You don't *get* to hide from this! You deserve every single second of this you bastard! It was *your* fault that fucking psycho took *my daughter!* If you hadn't taken that goddamn case, if you had listened to me even fucking *once,* she would still be here! *Wake up, Richard!"*

His heart was beating out of his chest, even as he tried to cling to unconsciousness, it wasn't working. He couldn't take any more pain, he *couldn't,* he'd die, he knew he would. He felt his mouth moving but he couldn't hear his voice over Claire's shrieking, over the roar of his own pulse in his ears.

He hoped he was begging for it to stop, he wanted it to stop so badly he could almost use the ferocity of that need to drown out all else.

Slowly a ringing replaced the litany of cursing in his ears. It hadn't *stopped,* but rather the ringing was gradually drowning it out. He took the lifeline, forcing his focus to hone onto that. It took an amount of time he wouldn't hazard to put a metric to before he noticed the ringing wasn't ringing at all.

It was singing.

'Arrorró mi niño,

arrorró mi sol,

arrorró pedazo,

de mi corazón'

Tears stung his eyes, his next scream breaking on a sob. He knew that voice, he'd know it anywhere.

It took far more willpower than he'd imagined he'd use for something as simple as opening his eyes, but he did it. He hoped against hope she'd be there, one good thing in all this madness for him to hold onto.

It took a moment for his eyes to focus, but when they did he broke down.

Sitting in the corner of the room, in the rocking chair his father had made for her years and years ago, was his mother.

She wasn't small and hunched over and sickly, she hadn't been like that long enough for that to be how he remembered her. Instead, he saw the long wavy hair, so like his own, that he and Aarón used to hide in when they were boys. The kind, dark eyes that had only ever seen the best in him. She was holding the beat up little guitar she'd had ever since he could remember, strumming it lightly as she sang.

'Este niño lindo
ya quiere dormir;
háganle la cuna
de rosa y jazmín.'

It had been years since he'd heard her sing, but he still remembered it clearly. He hoped he always would, she had such a beautiful, strong voice, like rain rolling down their windows on a warm summer afternoon. It felt like it wrapped itself around him, protective and comforting the same way she herself had always been.

Though the pain continued, it was far more bearable. He could forge through it, if only he could keep hearing her sing.

'Háganle la cama
en el toronjil,
y en la cabecera
pónganle un jazmín
que con su fragancia
me lo haga dormir.'

He wanted to close his eyes and go back to sleep, but he couldn't stand the idea of missing a single moment of a memory he held so dear. She swayed back and forth with the music, a soft little smile on her lips as she nodded to him.

But soon, sooner than he could bear, she finished her song. He didn't want her to go, who knew what else would replace her, he couldn't take- he *couldn't-*

She stood up from her rocker, placing her guitar in the spot she'd just vacated, and padded her way over to him. He'd forgotten how small she was regardless of age. He'd grown to be at least a foot taller than her, though she was so spirited it was easy to forget.

"Mi niño," She said gently, her accent gentle and warm against the familiar words, "You have been *so hard on yourself.* You have suffered so much all these years, tried to carry such heavy burdens all on your own. You are a strong boy, but you are no island. No man is. It is time to forgive yourself and let love have a place to bloom in your heart again."

He bit his lip, trying unsuccessfully to stop the tears that were rolling down his cheeks.

"Mamá," He began, the tightness in his throat stopping whatever he might've said, *"Mamá-"*

She cupped his cheeks, calling his attention to their changed shape for a half a moment before she pressed a kiss to his forehead.

"You have nothing to explain to me." She said, "Nothing to apologize for. You have done the best you can and that is all that can be asked of you. You do not deserve the things you are doing to yourself, you are *not* evil. Your demons may say so, but they do not love you like I do."

He made the effort to lean his misshapen body forward as best as he could figure out how to, leaning into her embrace as much as he could.

"How?" He whispered with a tongue barely fit to form the words, "How can I-- I don't have anyone to... You-- you've been gone for *so* long. Aarón too. And t-then Fi and everything with Claire-"

"I know, *niño*." She pressed her forehead to his, "It always seems bleak when you walk in the dark, but don't close your eyes and mistake that for darkness. There will always be a light, if you remember to look."

She pulled away then and he began to panic.

"No! No, Mamá come back, please don't go! Don't leave me here alone, *please!*"

She smiled back at him, tears in her own eyes.

"I am always with you, Ricardo." She said softly, "I miss you very much, but we will see each other again someday. But for now, you still have work yet to do."

He reached out to her, confusion meeting panic as he found that his hand was no longer a hand at all.

He tried to call out to her but the sounds that came out instead weren't pleas, but rather something much more akin to a howl.

Before he could scramble to get himself together, she was gone.

Instead his vision was finally clear, far clearer than it had been in years if he were honest. He could see the little cracks in the grout of the tiles from across the room, could easily make out the fine print on the toothpaste tube even from where he was. It was peculiar, especially taken with the lower viewpoint he was seeing it all from.

"Ransom?" Came a nervous whisper.

That drew his attention immediately back to Xinghua whom he'd *entirely* forgotten was still there.

She didn't look *at all* the same as she had before all this had started. Or she did, but he could see *more* of her, it felt. Her eyes had a faint glow to them, like the white of them came from a low powered flashlight. Her skin was also much more even and smooth, pore-less like the airbrushed faces of models in magazines. It was practically see through, like a crystal in the sun. When she moved, even just the slight adjustment of her head as she sized him up, it was fluid and without the little tremble a human would have. She was *too* perfect, didn't pass for human in the least and he wondered how he'd ever thought she did.

"You still in there big guy?" Her voice too was unsettlingly harmonic, like there were multiple pitches of the same voice all speaking at once, like a song.

He growled as the strangeness of her alarmed him.

She took a step back, raising up a hand that had a syringe clenched in it. It wouldn't be an effective weapon, normally, but then Ransom had no idea what to expect from her at this point.

"Easy buddy," She said like one would to a very large animal, "It's just me, I'm not gonna hurt you unless you try to hurt me. I don't know if you can hear me in there, but it's okay. It's okay."

Ransom was baffled less by the tone, even though it still made his skin prickle nervously, and more by what she was saying. Why would he hurt her? Yeah she was freaking him out, but honestly he'd been freaked out for the last, what, four hours?

He took a step closer to her and the answer was almost immediately obvious.

He looked down and found a paw in place of a foot, like he'd thought he'd seen in his last hallucination. He shouted in panic, though the shout was a bark and that caused him to panic even further.

Clumsily he took another step forward, trying to make his way out of the bath. He made an enormous miscalculation.

In his panic, Richard forgot two key things. First being that paws meant claws, and second that he was in a bathroom with tile flooring. The combination of the two things resulted in him skittering across the floor, trying to find his balance in a body he was not used to.

It was like trying to ice skate on all fours while very, very drunk.

He smashed into a wall snout first.

It didn't hurt much, just his pride really. Which wasn't helped by Xinghua's immediate heartfelt belly laugh filling the room.

"Oh my *God!*" She roared, "You look like *a little baby deer!*"

He threw what he hoped as an annoyed look back at her, sitting himself very carefully down to avoid any more embarrassing antics.

"I'm sorry dude but that was the best thing I've ever seen, thanks for that. So from the lack of attacking I'm gonna guess you're still in there?"

He nodded.

She let her shoulders relax, the tension that had been present in her since he'd gotten there finally easing.

"Oh thank God." She set her syringe down, "I really did not want this to go like the last werewolf I met."

She took a couple steps closer to him and he couldn't get over how unnatural her movements were. Was it only the difference between his eyes that let him notice now or had he always been able to see that and had just ignored it? It just seemed like such an enormous thing to overlook.

Also, she appeared to be *soaking* wet.

"So congrats on the whole 'not dying' thing. Good job." She gave him a thumbs up, "But now we've got to get you out of here before you get any bigger."

He cocked his head, hoping she'd understand his confusion.

"You started out the size of like a German Shepherd when you first finished shifting, but now you're like, Tibettan mastiff sized and I'm pretty sure you're going to keep getting bigger since werewolves are, like, *huge.*"

That made sense, mostly. The werewolf that had attacked him was the size of a car at least.

"First, though, how do you feel? You good to, like, move around and stuff?"

He nodded again. He felt fine, considering. The pain was gone and as odd as it was to be in a body that felt nothing like his own, he didn't feel sick or anything. Just confused, and a little nervous to deal with the floors again.

"Cool, in that case I think I know where we can take you for the time being." She grinned.

He barely made it out of the door to the apartment, both due to the hardwood flooring, and because at this point he was easily larger than he was as a human. His shoulders touched the door frame, and he had to crawl out.

"Holy--." Xinghua had said, dwarfed at his side, "You're *ginormous*. And fluffy. Can- this is gonna be weird, can I pet you?"

That *was* weird, but he owed her a lot more than letting her pet him after tonight. He lowered his head and butted it into her shoulder gently.

She smiled wide, sliding her cold fingers into his thick black fur. She immediately went for his ears and suddenly Richard understood why dogs could be so insistent about that. It felt almost like a massage, combined with the most satisfying back scratching session he'd ever had. His tail had started wagging and as much as he wanted to stop it, he couldn't focus hard enough.

"You're so *soft*," She marveled, "I seriously just wanna put my whole face in your fur. Like I'm not gonna because it's *you* but dude I wish you could pet you."

Richard laughed and the sound came out somewhere between a little growl and a heavy gust of air.

"You're right, we gotta move." She pulled her hands back and he immediately missed the feeling, "Follow me."

Luckily it was fairly late and there was no one in the hallways or the elevator. Wedging them both inside was tricky, considering Richard alone took up nearly the entire thing. He was definitely still getting bigger and he was slightly worried about how much larger he'd become. How was he going to get into *his* apartment later? How long would this last?

The elevator door dinged open.

"Shit. The building manager is here. That jackass is *never* here, which God did *I* piss off today?" She pointedly asked the ceiling.

Richard glanced over at the desk where a greasy looking balding man sat in his white wife-beater, reading a newspaper with his stubby legs propped up on his desk. His resting expression screamed *"I'm going to be a dick because I think mine isn't big enough"*.

"Welp, here goes nothing."

She turned and walked backwards into the lobby, her hands raised as if she were trying to guide him.

The building manager lazily looked up at them, panic striking across his face like lightning.

"What the hell is *that?!*"

"Dude, your guess is as good as mine." Xinghua said, her own voice tremoring in a way that Richard now knew it didn't.

So there *was* a difference. Could she do that on purpose? Did she stop because he already knew? Did *she* know she was doing that?

"I found him wandering in front of my place, barking at the walls." She explained, glancing nervously over at Richard, "He's pretty friendly, but I've never seen a dog this size."

"That's not a fucking dog!"

"Then-" She took her hand back, taking a little step away, "A *wolf?*"

"Lady that's a fucking government secret is what that is! Get it the hell out of my building! Like *now!*"

She nodded, "Yeah, that's probably the best idea. Is Animal Control still over on 4th?"

"Yeah..!"

She nodded and turned back to Richard, seeming a little more cautious now. He never would have thought she was a decent actress, although he supposed she'd been lying about quite a lot of things to likely everyone she knew for quite some time now.

"Uh, h-here boy?"

Richard barked, making the chandelier rattle and the manager jump.

"Jesus! Get that damn thing *out of here!*"

There was no harm in playing his role as well as Xinghua was, right? At least that's what Richard told himself as he crouched down and playfully jumped from side to side, barking again and again.

"Alright, let's go!" Xinghua clapped her hands, "Come on boy! Er, I think it's a boy, but I'm not checking so we're going with that. Come on boy, come on, follow me!"

One more giant bark and they were trotting out of the building, easy as anything.

Xinghua made it around the corner before she doubled over to laugh. Richard could hardly blame her, he couldn't believe that had even worked. He hadn't thought things like that even happened outside of the movies. Although a few hours ago he would have said the same about werewolves.

"This has been too much fun." She said, holding her ribs as she came back up, "Ransom you should look into hiring yourself out as a canine actor."

He nosed her shoulder again.

"Yeah, I know. Let's go before he *actually* calls animal control."

*   *   *   *

Richard hadn't been out to the woods in years. Not since he'd first moved here in fact. He and some of his work buddies used to go camping on the weekends. He didn't quite remember why they'd stopped but he missed it.

Glancing out the corner of his eyes he saw Xinghua with her arms wrapped around herself. She was shivering, but that didn't make sense. She shouldn't be able to feel the temperature.

He bumped her with his side, now *very* much larger than her, and she jumped. Her eyes were wild, though she quickly took back control of herself. He nosed at her arm, letting her pet him again as her other hand came to rest over her heart.

"I'm fine. I'm just not a fan of the woods."

She was fine with living with a guy who killed girls that looked like her, but the woods scared her? That made absolutely no sense to him, made clear by the way his head cocked to the side.

She licked her teeth, looking away from him for a moment as her jaw clenched. She didn't stop petting him though.

"This is where I died." She explained, "I was eight years old at the time, running away from my Dad who'd just killed my mom *and* grandma right in front of me... I ran in there, in the middle of fucking *January* with nothing but a light jacket and pj pants on. I froze to death in two days."

Richard's eyes went wide as a million things raced through his head, tackling each other to get to the forefront of his thoughts.

She pressed herself into his side as the wind blew towards the trees.

"I don't like the woods and honestly snow and ice and slush can all go fuck themselves. It's stupid, I *know* I can't die anymore, and I can't even *feel* the cold really, but apparently my stupid brain doesn't know that."

He shook off his shock and wrapped himself around her a little more securely. It wasn't much, it was markedly difficult to comfort someone without a voice, but she seemed to appreciate it.

"I haven't actually told anyone that." She whispered, "It's been years and I've never really told anyone. I think I'm starting to get the appeal behind therapy dogs."

She cleared her throat, taking a step backward, seeming to remember herself.

"Sorry, it's been a *really* long day." She slid her hands down her cheeks, "But there's a reason I brought you here, despite how much I fucking hate the woods. There's a pack that roams around here, friendly from what I've heard. Hopefully if we wander around a bit, we'll run into one of them and they can give you a crash course on 'How to Werewolf'."

Richard couldn't decide between gratitude that she was once again hurling herself outside of her comfort zone to help him with this, and nervousness at the idea of meeting other werewolves. But at this point, he trusted her, for better or worse.

He laid himself down on the ground, though he was still the height of a draft horse.

"What are you doing?" She frowned.

He flicked his head up, trying to suggest that she climb onto his back. It wouldn't be much, but she seemed to be re-assured by contact. If they were going to go somewhere that made her so uncomfortable for his sake, this was the least he could offer her.

"Are you-?" She squinted, "Are you telling me to *ride you?*"

Well that made it sound bad but he nodded.

She smiled and patted his head, "Thank you but I can keep up just fine."

She thought- Jesus he missed being able to talk.

He nodded her onto his back again.

"Nah, nah, nah son. You've seen how fast I can go." She bounced on her toes, "I've got this. You wanna race?"

She wasn't going to understand what he meant. Might as well go with the next best thing; a distraction.

He got to his feet, crouching down like he was ready to run.

"There we go." She grinned, the hint of a fang glittering in the moonlight, "This'll be fun. On the count of three."

"One, two, thr-"

Richard took off.

"You cheatin' ass hoe!"

She was on his heels, though it was quickly apparent his longer stride was going to give him the advantage.

It was funny, he normally hated running. His knees ached and the motion was just so repetitive he couldn't help but get bored after a few minutes. But running like *this* was exhilarating. He could feel every muscle group in his new body all working together like a well oiled machine. There was no pain, no strain, just the earth connecting with his paws as he pushed himself faster and faster.

He was ahead of Xinghua by a few hundred feet when he finally came to a stop in a little clearing between the trees .

"Okay, first of all you cheated." She said as he trotted around her like a show pony, "Second, you're the size of a fucking school bus, that alone should be cheating."

He made a wheezing sound that was remarkably close to his actual laugh.

She looked like she was going to continue but before she could a twig snapping across the clearing caught their attention. Not seconds after, a howl caught the air in the distance.

Richard's instincts took over, instincts he hadn't realized were there until he was sniffing the air with his hackles raised. A growl was building in his chest as the smell of unfamiliar wolves registered to him. Wolves, but also people.

"Easy, Ransom." Xinghua reached out to pet him again as the bushes across the way parted, "They're friendly."

The first person to emerge was a very small red headed woman. Even if Ransom hadn't currently been the size of a bus, she would have been tiny, no more than five foot tall. Her hair was a curly cloud around her freckled face and her hands were held peaceably up in the air. She was smiling and she looked friendly enough, though the two wolves that followed her out of the bushes still made Ransom nervous.

"Hiya," The woman greeted, "Name's Charlotte, but you can call me Lottie. Smelled someone new, figured we should come say hi."

She had a very light accent, Irish if he had to guess though it wasn't quite clear. Something about her bright attitude and the way she spoke had Richard feeling less nervous, though he still stayed on guard.

"Hi, I'm Xinghua, and this is my, uh, *friend... * Richard." She hesitated to say, "He just got turned earlier tonight and I figured the best idea was to find him a pack to help sort him out. Heard you guys were friendly, so here we are."

"Oh a *baby!*" Charlotte cooed, her eyes all but sparkling, "I mean, I know in human terms you're probably a full grown man but it's been so long since we've had a *pup!*"

One of the wolves, the silver one at her left side head butted her.

"Sorry, I get really excited." She apologized even as her voice leapt back up at the end of her sentence.

She took a step forward and when Richard didn't growl at her, a few more until she was only a few feet away from them. She smelt stronger up close, earthy and musky the way Richard remembered his childhood dog had been, with an overtone of perfume and female and human that made his head spin a little. He didn't know how he was putting a name to all these things, but his brain just seemed to be filling in the blanks for him.

"You're doing *really* well for a pup." She leaned closer to him, "Your eyes are clear, no missing fur, no blood on you, you haven't tried to attack any of us. Impressive."

He was fairly certain all that was due to Xinghua. If she hadn't helped him, even if he had somehow survived regardless, he didn't think he'd be in anywhere near the same state of mind. He leaned his head towards her to indicate that.

"Ah," Charlotte smiled, glancing at the girl, "That makes sense. You got lucky, it's really rare to know another supe before the change. Even weirder for a *vampire* of all the supes to be the one to help out. No offense."

"None taken, we've got history. Sorta." Xinghua explained with a shrug, "And I figured, hey, if he bites me in half it's not like it's gonna kill me."

Charlotte laughed at that, a full body laugh that made her jiggle just enough to be distracting.

"Yeah I mean, I guess not!" She wiped the tears from her eyes, "Well he's lucky to have such a good friend. Speaking of, you look like a nice young wolf. If you'd like, you're welcome to join my pack. We're not very big or strong, but I like to think we're like a little family."

That was a lot to think about, he knew this was ultimately what they'd come for, it still felt like a big thing. It had been so long since he'd been close with *anyone*, even in just a minor capacity. The closest thing to a friend he had was his partner, and even that was still tenuous sometimes.

Charlotte seemed to pick up on his hesitance, a little smile catching on her lips, turning her expression into something softer, gentler.

"It's okay, you don't have to make up your mind right away. It's a lot, and you've had a crazy day already." She idly waved her hand, "First things first! You want us to show you how to shift back?"

Richard couldn't help the excitement at the prospect of being back in his body again, barking what would have been a loud 'Yes!' could he have managed it.

Charlotte laughed again, casually reaching out to sift her fingers through his fur. It was odd, as unaccustomed to being touched as he was, but it felt so good to have someone pet him. He found himself leaning into her touch.

"It's been forever since I've met a barker. That's so cute!" She giggled up at him, "You're really adorable for a man with a voice that gravelly."

"Can you hear him?" Xinghua cocked her head.

"Yeah, course." Charlotte pulled her hand back to Richard's dismay, "Not like I can hear my pack members, but I hear words when he barks."

Richard blinked in confusion, having not even thought about the potential of her actually understanding him. He barked twice more and watched a shit eating grin take over Charlotte's face.

"What did he say?" Xinghua glanced between them.

"'Testing' then he said 'Don't call me Richard'." Charlotte translated.

Richard was absolutely floored that she'd been telling the truth. He almost missed Xinghua throwing up her hands dramatically towards the sky.

"What, are we not *close enough* for first names?" She glared at him, "The hell was I supposed to call you?"

He barked again.

"He says to just call him Ransom, everybody does. Richard was also his father's name."

"You're Richard Junior?" Xinghua made the rapid shift back into laughter, *"Junior."*

This time Charlotte stepped in for him before he could start barking up a storm.

"We're getting a little off topic, I bet your buddy here would like to be able to yell at you himself."

Richard barked in affirmation.

"I thought so." She grinned at him, "It's gonna be hard to shift back the first time, especially with the moon still out, so we're going to need to get you somewhere a little more comfortable. Do you mind following us back to our place?"

Ransom glanced at Xinghua who shrugged, being of about as much help as she normally was.

"You're welcome to come along," Charlotte chirped to Xinghua, "It's a ways away though so you might wanna, uh, *carpool* for time's sake."

The vampire snorted, her expression morphing into something mischievous.

"You're suggesting I ride him?" She waggled her eyebrows at Richard faux flirtatiously.

Images flooded his mind unbidden, though he stopped them before it got too far. He growled low in his throat, more like a grumble than anything truly threatening. Charlotte barked out a surprised laugh of her own.

"Ooooh I like him." She grinned, "So sassy."

"What'd he say?"

"Ya know, I think I'm gonna keep that to myself."

Riding a werewolf, Xinghua quickly found, was very different to riding a horse.

For one, Ransom's shoulders were more narrow which meant she'd have to work harder to keep herself perched on him. As well, his bones were closer to the surface and his muscles rolled more easily over them, giving her even less purchase.

Secondly, and most notably, he was *significantly faster.*

At best, at *best,* she'd gotten a horse up to about twenty-five miles an hour. She'd still been little, new to Tom and his penchant for 'the finer things in life', which included horse-back riding. She hadn't been terribly confident in her ability to ride fast, but still, she'd given it a go and gotten her horse, Silk, to her top speed. Ransom was *easily* twice as fast.

She was grateful for her strength because that was the only thing keeping her anchored to Ransom's back.

He streaked through the trees after Charlotte like it was nothing. Xinghua couldn't even see her, despite her wolf form being a bright red ball of fur. Ransom however seemed to have a pretty good lock on her, dashing after her with alarming surefootedness.

Before long the trees began to thin out, revealing the mouth of... a cave?

It wasn't exactly what she'd been expecting, but then again she had no idea what she was expecting. It was kind of fitting though for a group of werewolves she supposed.

As they slowed down she slid off of Ransom's back, gazing up at the impressively sized cave in wonder. They were pretty far outside of the city, but she hadn't thought the caves out this way got this big. When she looked closer, into the gloom of the cave she could see rudimentary buildings.

"Welcome to our clubhouse!" Charlotte said, now back in her human form, draped in a pink robe.

"Some clubhouse." Xinghua noted the sound of opening doors and could see no less than six pairs of eyes reflecting back at them from the shadows.

"You like it?" Charlotte grinned, spreading her arms wide, "It's very 'Whatever the fuck we could find' chic."

Xinghua laughed.

"So, first things first, I told you I'd help you change back." Charlotte cantered over to them, "It's pretty hard the first time, so don't get disheartened if it takes a second. It won't hurt like human to wolf did either, don't worry."

Ransom visibly shivered.

"Okay, so try to focus on your body, your human body. Remember what you look like, what you sound like, and *will* yourself back into being. I know it's vague but that's the hard part."

Ransom grumbled something that made Charlotte fake a scandalized gasp and shut his eyes.

Xinghua started to get antsy after the first minute of them all standing there, but after two she couldn't keep herself from shifting around.

"You're really easily bored for an immortal." Charlotte commented.

"I'm a millennial." Xinghua replied.

"Really?! You've got to be the youngest vampire I've ever met."

"Not helping the concentration." Ransom butted in.

Xinghua's attention flew to him though she forced herself to look away when she noticed he was completely naked.

"That was fast." Charlotte chirped, "Henry, would you bring us a robe please?"

Ransom turned so he wasn't facing them straight, awkwardness in every furtive movement to cover himself.

"Thank you, for…everything." Ransom muttered, shrugging on the robe another red headed man brought him.

"No problem! Gotta say though, you're as handsome as your wolf makes you out to be." Charlotte winked.

"Uh, thanks..?"

"Course! So how'd you get wolfed up anyway? Usually anyone who knows a vampire picks that route." Charlotte turned and made her way into the cave, clearly expecting them to follow.

Xinghua's eyes flicked to Ransom only to find him already staring back at her. A silent question passed between them, the answer following after as they too followed after their host.

"I was- I was on my way home from the station when a giant dog came out of nowhere and attacked me." Ransom replied, his eyes distractingly reflective in the low lighting of the cave.

"You a cop?" Charlotte bounced when Ransom nodded, "Oh that is so cool! It's shitty that you got bit by a rando and all, but I think this might actually help you. Being a werewolf has a few perks."

She walked them backwards into a larger area hidden by a screen of moss growing from the pool on the little ledge above the entry. Xinghua blinked as her eyes adjusted to the sudden light in the area, and once she did she was surprised to find what looked like a community.

Charlotte had said that their pack wasn't very large.

There were easily enough people there to constitute a pack and then some. The space had clearly been lived in for quite a while, with clothes lines strewn above their heads like a spider's web. The floors were compressed, well worn paths cut through the dirt. The air smelled heavily of cooking meat and soap and there were even children running around.

Though when Xinghua sniffed the air, she found that not everyone in the room was a werewolf. Most of them in fact were human, which had her an even deeper shade of confused.

"I thought you said there weren't a lot of you." Ransom asked for them both.

"Hm?" Charlotte glanced around as if only just noticing the collection of people around her, "Oh! I guess this does seem like a lot. Most of the people here aren't technically part of the pack, but they're under our protection."

"Protection?"

For the first time since they'd met her, Charlotte frowned, her expression darkening.

"Yeah. You'd be surprised at the amount of people who run out here trying to get away from someone. Usually women and kids. It's easy enough to find them when you can smell fear." Her hands clenched at her sides, "We find them and take them in, keep them safe from whatever drove them to us."

She looked out into the bustling room, both wistful and tired, "It happens a lot."

Ransom shifted at her side and Xinghua didn't have to look at him to know what his expression was right then.

"And the people you're protecting them *from?* What happens to them?"

Charlotte smiled again and this time the expression is far from comforting.

But it was gone almost as soon as it came, the same smile from earlier taking its place.

"Looks like dinner is ready!"

She trotted over to the nearest campfire where the red headed man from earlier was carving up a large piece of meat to divide between everyone.

"You know, I like her." Xinghua assessed.

"Of course you do, she probably kills people." Ransom muttered.

"That deserve it!" Xinghua argued, "It's just community service if you think about it."

"Taking lives is wrong no matter the circumstance." Ransom said with gravity, "Even if they're creeps. That's what prison is there for."

"No, prison is there to exploit vulnerable minorities so that the people that *own* those prisons can profit off of the money given to them by the government for their incarceration and the free labor they provide." She corrected, "Your ideals, however well intended, are based in a world of absolutes that does not exist, and as such are intrinsically flawed enough that your ideology could even be considered harmful in its naivety."

The look of shock on Ransom's face was worth the hour and a half she'd spent struggling through an article on the subject.

"Don't look so shocked Richie-Rich, I'm not just a pretty face you know. I can *read* too."

"You just... keep surprising me, Li."

"It's not very hard apparently."

Whatever comment he might have said was interrupted by Charlotte bopping back up to them, a plate made up for Ransom in her hands.

"You gonna sit down and eat or are you just gonna loom in the background?"

Xinghua barked out a sharp laugh.

"Thank you, but I think I should be going."

The look of hurt that flashed across Charlotte's face was enough to nearly cause Xinghua to swat at him. God for a detective he was fucking dense.

"I understand. It's probably been a long and crazy night for you." She nodded, "If you need anything, support, cool werewolf facts, someone to talk to, you know where we are. Don't be a stranger."

Ransom hesitated for a moment before nodding, "I won't. Thank you, Charlotte."

"Please, we're friends, call me Lottie."

"Lottie." He corrected and Xinghua could feel the woman's blood pressure spike and did her best to bite back a smile, "Thank you for your help and hospitality. I'll see you again."

Charlotte nodded, her smile softening at the edges, her rich green eyes as comforting as a dewy meadow.

"I'll hold you to it, Detective."

*   *   *   *

Xinghua refused to get out of bed until hours after the sun had set. She'd been way late getting to bed, having made sure Ransom was alright before going back to her apartment. She'd *earned* the rest.

There wasn't much of a point to getting up anyway.

She didn't have to work, which was one of the only two things she left her bed for anyway. She hated how in the empty house all she could hear was her own footsteps.

Tom had been gone for three days now. While it wasn't anywhere *near* the longest work bender he'd gone on, she'd been hoping that since he seemed to be wrapping up his big project he might be home more often. She should have known better, she supposed.

The last few days had actually given her something to talk about, instead of the usual boring office gossip she could tell he wasn't interested in. Hell, she wasn't even interested in it most of the time, making up little details to make her day seem more interesting than it had been and still meeting a wall made of 'Uh huh's and 'That's great honey's.

Sometimes she didn't know why she bothered talking at all.

She forced herself into a sitting position, groggy from dreams she couldn't remember and already sad before she'd even been up for ten minutes. It was going to be one of *those* nights then.

What she needed was a distraction, something to keep her from tumbling too far into the rabbit hole of her own misery.

Misery? Since when had she started thinking of herself as miserable?

Though when she poked at the sluggish, heavy feeling wrapped around her lungs, she supposed that was what it should be called. She'd never been the best at telling what she was feeling at any given moment, trauma and all that, she was confident she knew what that one was at least.

"Ugh," She cradled her head in her hands, letting her fingers sink into her hair, lightly pulling and scratching, "What the fuck is wrong with me tonight?"

Fighting the temptation to let herself fall right back into bed and wallow for the rest of the night, she pushed herself up to her feet. If nothing else, she really needed that distraction.

She snatched her phone from her bedside table, texting Ziggy and Trish to see if either of them would come out with her.

Ziggy didn't reply, which wasn't surprising considering they almost never actually had their phone on them, and Trish was neck deep in research. With everything else that had happened last night, Xinghua had nearly forgotten about Trish's situation. For a moment guilt flirted at the edge of her ribs, threatening to burrow itself in deep and join Misery in crushing her, but she almost immediately quashed the rebellious little thing.

It wasn't like she'd *purposely* forgotten about the girl, she'd had other problems.

She asked if she could help, though a flashing ellipses greeted her time and again for a long enough moment she wondered if the girl was typing a novel. The reply however, was a flat, to the point 'No, but thanks'.

Well, that idea had been shot in the face.

She flicked on the TV, but quickly grew bored with it. She tried playing games but sitting still was making her bones ache as the ringing silence of the apartment echoed back to her even over the sound of the game.

She threw down her controller and paced, nearly tripping over an errant pair of shoes.

Cleaning! She could clean!

Ordinarily Xinghua hated cleaning with a passion. It always reminded her of her father's strictness, how he required that every little thing be put in its proper place or else a smack would soon follow. But the activity would give her something to *do*, a goal, and as much as she hated to admit it, it was kind of needed anyway.

Darting over to the music dock on the counter, she plugged her phone into it, selecting one of her favorite sad day comfort bands. The music helped ease the knot of tension in her chest as the familiar aggressive distorted guitar riff bled into the bubbly Japanese of the first verse.

She then set about cleaning the apartment, starting from her own disaster of a bedroom, expanding outward from there.

It wasn't that she was the *only* one who made a mess, Tom was nearly as messy as she was, he just wasn't home as often. And when he was, his time was mostly spent at his desk meaning his mess was confined to that area. Which, when she finally made her way to it, looked like a mad pigeon had nested on it.

Firstly, the thing was huge, taking up nearly an entire wall to itself. It was one of the few things Tom had kept from his human life, an enormous heirloom that Xinghua suspected was likely even older than he was. She didn't know much about woodworking or craftsmanship, but even without that knowledge she could tell the thing was nice, probably super expensive too, even back in the day. It looked vaguely presidential, or it would if not for the cabinet built onto it that was overflowing papers in a display so akin to her current mental state she had to stop to laugh.

Cleaning it was something of a daunting task, one that she wasn't sure she should actually undertake. More than likely Tom had the thing in some sort of chaotic, unseen "order" that she'd disturb by trying to tidy. She knew better than to touch his things, but *everything else was so clean it would drive her insane if she just left it like that...*

If the pattern held, she might even have a couple days to enjoy her nice clean house before Tom came home to scold her. Maybe she could even organize everything so that it wasn't just a random nest of bullshit so he might not be quite so pissed?

Deciding on her course of action, Xinghua got to work.

Mostly the files were half written ideas for things that didn't make a whole lot of sense to her, but then she also didn't have three separate doctorates in genetics. Even still though, she couldn't imagine a way to make 'cyber-lizards' work. That had to have been written during one of the times he'd woken up in the middle of the day to jot down something he'd dreamed of.

She was making decent progress until a file with a photo of a girl attached caught her attention.

That one looked a whole lot more like something Tom would miss if she misplaced it, though she didn't remember him working on anything involving actual people. Ooooh, maybe it had to do with the secret project he'd been working on!

Unable to resist her curiosity, Xinghua found herself reading the file.

Mostly, she didn't understand it, too many big technical words used in place of simple ones that would have worked just fine. Plus Tom had the handwriting to back up his doctorates. But what she *could* make out had her blood running cold.

She read, re-read, and re-re-read the file just to be sure she wasn't misinterpreting the confusing text.

Within the next ten seconds she was in motion, though she had no idea what she was doing or what her goal was. For a moment she spun around uselessly before deciding she needed someone else to help her deal with this.

There was only one person she could think of.

She was out the door and down the stairs before the timer on the lights clicked off.

*   *   *   *

Twenty minutes later she was pounding down Ransom's door.

She'd been surprised he'd been awake when she called, though in hindsight she supposed that could just have been because she had woken him up.

The fluffy, tired, half dressed mess of a man that answered the door certainly made that seem more likely.

Regardless, she didn't hesitate to rush into the apartment.

"Yeah, absolutely come in." He said, his voice so low and rumbly had she been human she likely wouldn't have been able to hear it.

"I'm freaking out." She started pacing, gesturing emphatically with the file she had yet to stop clutching onto, "I don't know what- I mean I *do,* but it doesn't make *any* sense! I mean it does, *kind of* but it *doesn't* you know-!?"

"Li," Ransom took her by the shoulders, stopping the rut she was wearing in his floor, "What are you talking about?"

She thrust the file out at him, but pulled it back before he could take it.

"You have to swear to me, right now, that after you read this you're not gonna just burst out of here and go full five-oh."

He frowned, the sleep apparent in his eyes slowing down his thoughts.

"I... promise?"

"Gonna need you to mean it, Rich."

"I *promise.*"

She breathed through her teeth, nervously handing him the thing. It felt like a physical weight had been taken from her.

"Subject 0813, Isabeau Heathrow," He read out loud, "Second clinical trial of HSV1-Necroactive Polyphage..... batch number two... subject shows no signs of genetic instability... the subject appears to be experiencing notable improvement of both cognitive function and motor function though further data is needed to determine-- Xinghua what is this?"

"It's a file I found while I was cleaning Tom's desk today." She replied, "Keep reading."

Ransom's eyes flicked back down to the file, "Subject has displayed an unusual increase in both mental and physical capacity. The effects of HSV1 appear to be not only counteracting the subject's Huntington's disease, but actively erasing its presence in the host's cells to replace it with.... it-self. Full effects unknown and will require further testing and subsequent experimentation to properly gauge."

He continued reading on in silence, the line between his eyebrows furrowing deeper and deeper until it was more a canyon than a dip. By the time he finished a haunted look had taken over his eyes.

"He's conducting human experimentation." He concluded, just as she had, "With the vampire virus."

She nodded slowly, the fear in her gut churning slowly at the confirmation of her fears.

"I don't know a whole lot about vampire laws, but I'm pretty sure that's illegal." She managed around the knot in her throat.

"Well I know a lot about human ones, and it most certainly is." Ransom handed her back the file.

She took it with all the enthusiasm of someone being handed a handful of gutter sludge.

"From the sound of those files, he's been at this for a while."

She sagged against the wall behind her, feeling the words as a physical blow. How had she not *known?*

"I think-" She swallowed hard, "I think this is the project he's been working on. If- fucking *fuck,* if it is then he's been working on this for the last five years. At least. Fuck what are we gonna *do?*"

"*I* am going to take this information to my superiors and start an investigation. *You* are going to find a friend to stay with until we get a handle on things."

"But-"

"This is *not* a negotiation Li." Ransom's voice left no room for argument, "That man is dangerous, and he's more dangerous to you than anyone. You are *not* going back there."

Her chest tightened and for once she couldn't tell if it was from anger or appreciation. She still didn't like the insinuation that Tom would hurt her, but after what she had just learned she wasn't sure she knew him quite as well as she had thought she did.

So instead of fighting, she sighed, all the tension bleeding out of her shoulders.

"Fine."

Ransom too appeared to relax, like he'd been anticipating having to fight her. He slid his hand up into his hair, scratching at his head and for the first time she realized he wasn't wearing a shirt, just pajama pants with little rockets on them, leaving the litter of new, angry red scars on display all over his abdomen.

The strangeness of the situation dawned on her then.

She was in his apartment. And he was only about half dressed and probably even less awake. She'd pretty much just barged in, which, while she'd had a good reason, it made things significantly weirder now that they'd gotten through it.

"You want some coffee?" He asked, stretching out his neck, "I know it probably doesn't do anything for you, but I could use some."

"Yeah, sure."

Ransom shuffled into the kitchen blearily, cracking one of his shoulders loudly as he went.

She sat on her hands for a moment before growing antsy and deciding to be nosy.

There wasn't a lot to go on in the room, not even a blanket out of place. It barely even felt like someone lived here, which from what she'd seen of Ransom, she couldn't imagine he was home that often. The decoration was done in an impersonal black and white modern style, she half thought he'd just hired someone to do it for him. The walls were sanitary white and there were only two pictures hung on them, one on either side of the doorway to the kitchen.

The one on the left was a picture of what she suspected was Ransom when he was younger, with maybe... a brother? He looked a lot like Ransom, though a little taller with a giant smile plastered to his face. There was an older woman with them too, with a kind smile and long brown hair, her dark skin just beginning to wrinkle. They had their arms around each other and though Ransom was in the middle of rolling his eyes, he looked the happiest Xinghua had ever seen him.

On the other side was a picture with a man who looked a lot more like the Ransom she was familiar with. He had less grays but he had the eyebags and the seriousness down pat. This one also starred a pretty brunette woman who looked almost as enthused as Ransom, and a little girl with a smile like the sun. She was missing a couple teeth but it did nothing to dim the wattage of that grin. Her short black hair was done up in pigtails, and her cheeks were bunched up so hard her eyes nearly disappeared. If she was honest, she reminded Xinghua a bit of herself when she was younger, before...everything.

Xinghua thought back to Ransom's hallucinations when he'd been turning, a sad sort of understanding rising up from somewhere in her chest.

She'd known there had to be a reason he was so determined to save her, but she hadn't been prepared for it to be *that*.

Luckily, Ransom came out of the kitchen, giving her something else to focus on.

He'd thrown on a T-shirt, which startled a laugh out of her.

"Fuck the Police? Really Ransom?" She snorted, gesturing at the graffiti print shirt he was wearing.

"It was a gag gift from my partner." He grumbled, setting her coffee down in front of her, "I didn't look, I just grabbed the first shirt I pulled out of the dryer."

"Uh huh." She grinned.

He took a long drink of his coffee, ignoring her entirely.

"Richard?"

He glanced over his cup at her.

"Thank you." She murmured, "For helping even though, like, you kinda told me so."

"I told you to call me if you ever needed anything," He caught her eyes, "I'm just glad that you aren't hurt."

"Physically." She huffed, folding herself over her knees as though to hug herself, "Emotionally I feel like a fish that just got scaled."

"That's vivid." He sat down with his coffee cup, "Do you want to talk about it?"

"No…. Yes? I'm just-! I'm confused. I don't get why the hell he'd want to *do* this. Like what the fuck does any of this get him?"

"Recognition?" Ransom suggested, frowning, "He seems the type to want the whole world to tell him how smart he is."

She shook her head, "He *would* but he wouldn't go through this much effort *just* for that, there's got to be more to it. Did you see the notes scribbled on the left hand margin?"

"I couldn't read those."

"Fair enough, if I wasn't so used to his weird ass cyphers I wouldn't have been able to either. That's how he writes *grocery lists* too, it took me like six years just to be able to go to the store without him because of that shit. It's *technically* in German in the same way Floridians are *technically* speaking English. But the notes talk about how the virus has 'a wide variation between its intended purpose and it's *usual* effects' and how he 'needs to refine the margin somehow.'" She said in air quotes, "It's mostly jargon, but what I want to know is what the hell the intended purpose is for this."

"Yeah. I admit, I have no idea what he'd need this for either. It seems counterintuitive for a serial killer to look into curing disease."

"Exactly! Like all this is gonna do is get him some serious heat! I don't know how a coven elder hasn't *already* snatched his ass up." She frowned, "Unless none of them know."

"Or all of them do."

She stared up at him.

"Corruption happens everywhere." He spread his hands non-aggressively, "You'd be surprised."

"Not on this." She shook her head, "This is like the *one* vampire rule no one fucks with. Don't tell mortals. Even *I* know that one, and I barely remember the whole rules run down. This... this would *definitely* out us."

"I would say so." Ransom took another long drink from his mug.

"What a fucking mess." She leaned back, pressing the heels of her hands into her eyes and rubbing at them, "I feel like such a fucking idiot. I can't believe I didn't know-"

"It's not your fault, Li." Ransom put a hand on her knee, scorching but still comforting somehow, "I'm sure he's not exactly been up front with you on a lot of things. You're as much a victim of his as anyone else."

"I don't *feel* like a victim, I *feel* like a goddamn moron." She gesticulated wildly into the air, "I really thought- I thought it was just that no one understood him like I did....*how fucking naïve is that?*"

Ransom's hands gently wrapped themselves around her forearms and pulled her hands down from where they'd lodged in her hair. He waited until she looked at him to begin speaking, but he left his hands right where they were. Focusing on the warmth and the weight of them around her own hands made her head feel a little less like it was filled with wasps. She squeezed her eyes shut.

"It's hard to be objective while you're standing right on top of a problem. He *raised* you, Xinghua, he's more or less been responsible for molding a lot of how you think of him. Sure, some of the warning signs were more overt than others, but like I said, he more or less conditioned you to think those things were normal."

He squeezed her arms and she could swear she felt her chest squeeze along with it.

She felt like she was out to sea, a storm churning the waves below her and the farther out she got the more she desperately wished for a life line.

Logically she knew that Ransom was right, but that really didn't make her feel any less stupid. She couldn't help wondering if she'd missed him doing something like this under her nose, what else had she missed?

"Can-" Her voice was so soft *she* almost didn't hear it so she cleared her throat, "Can I hug you? It's okay if not, I just-"

He was pulling her into his arms before she finished her sentence.

It had been a long time since someone had hugged her for more than a couple seconds. She hadn't realized how desperately she missed the contact until Ransom was shifting her and she panicked that he was letting go already. She clutched at Ransom's shirt, pulling herself closer to him, until she was practically cradled in his lap.

She held on up until he began rubbing her back, but the sob that had been encircling her throat since she found that stupid fucking file erupted from her.

"It's okay," Ransom murmured, "I'm not going to judge you for crying."

She couldn't help it. Like an ugly whiplash, the tidal wave of emotion welled up from her throat in what she suspected was about far more than just the file. She couldn't place why, strictly speaking, but there was something achy and hollow in the pit of her stomach that felt...familiar. Like the after image of a dream she couldn't remember upon waking, or the quiet of a room echoing with only her own footsteps.

It didn't take her long to cry herself out, she'd never been a big crier. She felt better in the sense that she was more or less numb for now. However she'd definitely ruined Ransom's shirt.

"Blood tears?" He asked, vague alarm nesting in the gravel of his voice.

"It's one of two fluids in my body." She wiped at her cheeks, "Sorry."

"Been looking for a reason to throw out this damn thing anyway." Ransom shrugged, "You okay?"

"No," She answered honestly, "Probably gonna do this again later tonight, but I do feel better for now."

"That's a close second."

She climbed out of his lap but hesitated for a moment, deciding to peck a quick kiss to his cheek.

"Thanks Ransom."

He blinked, surprise evident on his face, "Any time."

*   *   *   *

After she'd gotten herself cleaned up enough to be seen in public without causing panic, Xinghua slammed her coffee and talked her way out of Ransom's place. Given that it was eleven thirty at night, Ransom didn't put up much of a fight. Poor bastard probably still had to work in the morning.

When Ransom had told her to go stay with a friend, she'd thought of Trish and Ziggy first. Normally she would have picked one of the two of them, but in this case she had someone else in mind.

By the time she got to Wreckquiem it was nearing midnight, meaning the club's activities would more than likely be in full swing already. It was going to be hard to pull Frost away from things, but she figured he'd be pretty accommodating given the circumstances.

It felt weird to make her way into the club without being decked to the nines. She felt like she stood out like a sore thumb, dozens of reflective eyes roaming over her from the darkness to check for some sort of defect. She did her level best to ignore it, but the feeling had the back of her neck tingling.

"Xinghua?" Frost's voice greeted her from behind, "I almost didn't recognize you without the come-fuck-me eyes and the leather. *And* you're without your lesser half, is it my birthday already?"

She turned around and she must have looked as upset as she thought she did because his expression changed immediately.

"I need to talk to you. Alone."

He turned to the bartender without hesitation, making some sort of signal with his hand that she assumed was code for 'Hold down the fort'.

"Right. We can talk in my office."

She followed him towards the actual back of the club, around a corner and down the black hallway the 'private rooms' were located in.

She'd never been in Frost's office before, hadn't really had a need to. It was surprisingly modest for the gaudy style of the rest of the club. It was still easily one of the nicest rooms she'd been in, with its doubtlessly expensive handcrafted wooden furniture and antique executive desk. Taken alongside the deep maroon walls and stark black curtains, it matched Frost's personal aesthetic nicely.

He took a seat at the desk and gestured for her to do the same.

"What brings you to me this evening, little one?"

Xinghua took a breath before launching into the story of what she'd found. She decided to omit a couple details, like crying into Ransom's chest like a baby. For time's sake, of course.

After she'd finished Frost steepled his fingers together, his sharp elbows resting on the desk. Ostensibly he looked calm, but Xinghua had known him for nearly as long as she'd known Tom.

He was *furious.*

"I'm very glad that you came to me, Xinghua." He said, little flurries of snow flakes fluttering from between his teeth, "This is troubling, to say the least. I was aware that Thomas had a certain... *proclivity* for knowledge he shouldn't pursue, but I had thought it little more than that."

She bit her lip, trying not to interrupt while he digested the information fully.

It took a few minutes but eventually Frost blinked back to the present.

"Well!" He huffed, "Obviously, you are more than welcome to stay here with me while we sort things out. Is there any-thing you need, darling?"

"A shot?"

Frost smiled, his brows pulling together like they did when-ever she did something that made him feel an actual emotion, "I can do that."

He opened one of the desk drawers and produced a rather large decanter of expensive brandy and two crystal glasses. Filling them both up rather generously, he stood and walked around the desk to hand her hers. Leaning back against his desk he took a sip and sighed.

"For what it's worth, I didn't want to be right."

She swirled the liquor in her glass before slamming the entire thing, making a face at the bitter burn of it.

"For what it's worth, I didn't want you to be either." She flicked her eyes up at him.

He caught her chin, frowning hard enough to almost make creases in his foundation.

"Do that again."

"Do what?"

"Look away and back to me."

She frowned but flicked her eyes down and back up at him.

He tilted her head around, his own eyes focused on hers clinically.

"Jesus."

"I don't like it when you curse with other people's deities, what is it?"

He frowned once again, setting his glass down as he let go of her chin.

"Your eyes caught my attention. Well, more than they *usually* do." He adjusted so he was closer to sitting on her level, "It's much harder to notice since your eye color is so light and generally you're wearing something that does not encourage *eye contact.* I might never have noticed if I hadn't seen this before."

"What is it?" She asked again from between gritted teeth.

"When I was younger I knew a vampire with an odd gift. She was able to add, alter, and erase memories from people. Honestly she's a very large part of why I have such an expansive fortune, the two of us liberated Europe of *quite* a few treasures and made a killing selling them back to their rightful owners. What a fun few decades! Why there was this time-"

"Lee."

"But I digress! The point I intended to make was that her gift left a very distinctive silver ring around the iris of the afflicted since her ability was largely mesmeric. Your eyes, my dearest, have that same silver ring in them."

"....Come again?"

"It's very difficult to see because your eyes are white and the silver looks quite natural, but it's there, just a few centimeters away from your pupils." Frost continued, "Troubling."

"So you think someone has just been Patty Pasta-ing my memories?"

"I haven't the slightest fucking idea what that means, Xinghua darling *do* try to remember I'm over a thousand years old." She opened her mouth to explain, though Frost didn't so much as pause, "I also haven't spoken with Celeste for nearly a century now. But the proof is there, sure as anything. The question is what has been altered and why?"

"Is there a way to... fix it?"

"Time." Frost shrugged, taking his drink up once again, "Gifts only cause temporary effects, it will fade on its own. Ordinarily Celeste's gift would only last a week or so at most."

She nodded, sighing heavily as yet another worry crowded into her already infested head.

"I....feel as though I owe you an apology."

It took a moment to puzzle out the words past all the clutter in her mind, and a few seconds after that to try to reconcile why *Frost* of all people would be apologizing to her.

"For what?"

He took a moment to refill his drink, and hers, which she was thankful for the moment he answered.

"I've...known for years Tom is hardly innocent. It's part of why I dislike him so damn much."

"What...do you mean by that?"

He took his seat back at his desk, folding his long legs neatly at the knee, his mouth digging a canyon down his sharp chin.

"As you may know, there are certain rules that, coven or no, all vampires are expected to follow. There are a few, but there are three that we hold above all others. You do not tell humans the Truth, you do not kill your donors, and you do *not* turn children."

Frost's stare on her was weighty and loaded with meaning.

"Oh." Xinghua replied mildly, as if her head weren't spinning like a wheel ready to fly off a car.

"Thomas has always thought of himself as above these laws, and frankly every other. I suppose, given his overall arrogance, he likely thought he was more clever than the reasoning behind them. In your case, however, he was fortunately correct in that."

"I- why the kid one? I mean I get that telling humans would be like inviting a shit storm nobody needs, and I don't really want to touch the whole donor thing..."

Frost's expression hardened in an instant.

"Has he killed donors? Have you...?"

"No! I mean-- I haven't-- *I asked you first.*"

Frost's grim expression remained steadfastly in place for a long moment before he managed to pack the ire away for later.

"Because it's considered cruel to trap an immortal in the body of a child. To this day I haven't the slightest clue of how Tom managed what he did with you, but I assure you, you are the *only* such being in existence. Ordinarily, something like that would have resulted in the Sire being quartered and buried."

Xinghua flinched back, almost as if physically struck.

"Quartered?"

Frost looked a little happier about that image than he really needed to, taking a long pull from his glass, subsequently causing her to remember her own drink and do the same.

"Yes. As I'm certain you're aware, we're incredibly difficult to dispatch. Impossible, more like. So in lieu of a lethal option, a vampire caught violating any of the three essential laws is subject to quartering, and then a few centuries spent in a box at the bottom of the ocean. Generally the decision isn't over-turned for five hundred or so years."

Xinghua felt herself grow colder.

Sure, Tom had done some fucked up things but did she really wish *that* on him? In the file it sounded like he'd been *curing* things. Even if he's been experimenting on people to do it.... That was how science worked right? Terrible things that made major progress? Sure he'd broken other laws apparently too, and he wasn't exactly in the right for doing what he did, but he didn't deserve--

"Xinghua."

Xing blinked back into the real world outside the increasingly loud turmoil in her mind, to find snowflakes falling from her eyelashes. In fact her entire body was covered in a thin layer of frost.

"What the hell Lee?!" She snapped, frantically dusting the powder off of her as if it were smoldering ashes instead.

He raised his hands in the universal signal of "don't shoot".

"I didn't do that, darling."

"Today is *really* not the day to fuck with me."

"Devil's honest, Xing, I would *never* fuck with you like that."

"Then--" She caught the look he was giving her and reeled back so hard she stood up from the table, *"No. No."*

"I had always had my suspicions of whether or not you truly were his." He cocked his head like Xinghua's entire understanding of the world wasn't being turned upside-down, *again,* "I suppose not."

"That doesn't make any sense! I remember--"

She stopped abruptly, recalling what Frost had just told her about her memories being tampered with.

For the second time today, she felt like a kid bumbling obliviously through life and it nearly brought her to tears again. Just how little did she really know?

"Then if- if not him then *who?*"

"I've got a guess myself, though I think maybe you've had enough world shattering revelations for the day, hm?"

She wanted to argue, push for the answer, insist that she was fine and could take it, but she knew Frost was right. Her head hurt and her eyes still felt swollen and itchy from crying. If she could throw up, she likely would have already and every new realization felt like falling further into a hole she already couldn't see the bottom of.

"Right, no, yeah, you're right." She pressed the heel of her hand to her eye, "I should...I should go to bed. It's been a long, *shitty* couple days."

Frost nodded and offered her a hug that she immediately took him up on. She held on for longer than she usually would, the reassuring presence of such an old friend helping even more than Ransom hugging her earlier had.

"Get some rest, Xi-xi, we can talk about it more tomorrow, hm?"

"I mean this in the nicest, most "Thank you for letting me stay with you" way possible, but fuck no. I am done talking for the whole week."

Frost breathed a laugh, really more just the suggestion that he *could* laugh than anything.

"We'll see about that in the pm. Now, to bed with you."

*   *   *   *

Xinghua couldn't sleep, which surprised her about as much as it surprised her to find out that yet another celebrity had been arrested for some sort of sex crime.

She was prone to sleepless days anyway, more so when she was stressed. So when she left Frost's office to bed herself down in one of the guest rooms, it wasn't like she was really expecting anything else.

Still, it was irritating with how physically tired she felt. Not to mention being emotionally exhausted. While her head chased questions she didn't have the answers for, she tried to distract herself by researching what she could from the Clinestra Pharmaceuticals website.

What she found was nominal at best. Really the only thing she *hadn't* already known was that Tom was evidently not just a researcher as she'd assumed, but the CEO. No wonder he was never home…

Ding!

Xinghua squinted at a text from an unknown number, but a line in was she was pretty sure it was Ransom. She spared a second to wonder how and when he'd gotten her number while she saved him into her contacts, but she quickly set aside the worry.

[Ransom 2:55AM] *I followed up with my Captain and hit a wall. Airius has connections, we won't be able to go at this legally.*

Of course he did. Xinghua wasn't even surprised. If any-thing, it would explain how he'd gotten away with so much for so long.

Before she had time to thank Ransom for what he'd already done, another message pinged in.

[Ransom 2:55AM] *But if it's to bring down Airius, I don't really give much of a fuck about legality.*

She was genuinely growing to appreciate this man.

Ding!

[Ransom 2:56AM] *So here's what I'm thinking...*

*   *   *   *

"So then you broke up with him, right?" Ziggy asked from their little window in the group chat Xinghua had created be-tween them and Trish in a desperate attempt to hold onto the last of her sanity that had survived the night.

Xinghua winced.

"Technically no.... He hasn't been home in, like, four days now?"

"Baby girl, that was *already* enough reason to drop his ass right there." Ziggy snapped their fingers.

"But...human experimentation...? Murder...? Seriously?" Tr-ish shook her head, still processing though the call had started an hour ago, "That's like...really *really* bad."

"For *humans.* I thought that was just how vampires *worked.* I mean the other part of the murder thing is still weird and a fuckload more concerning now."

"Other part?" Trish clutched her pillow while Ziggy set down their nail polish to squint at the screen.

"What *other part?*"

Xinghua bit her lip, tugging at it as she prepared for the inevitable tide of yelling about to crash down on her.

"He was dressing them up to look like me..."

She could have heard a pin drop in the resulting silence. And then-

"What?!" Ziggy shrieked, dropping their brush altogether.

"Xinghua what the--" Trish shouted into her pillow.

"--hell?! Why didn't you--"

"--Tell someone?!"

"How long has it--?!"

"Are you safe?!"

"Oh my God I can't-"

They continued to talk over and over each other like an entire flock of worried seagulls.

"Guys! Chill out just a little, the lag is real here." Xinghua butted in.

"Bitch you can't just drop that your man practiced killing you and expect us to chill!!" Ziggy yelled.

"Please, *please* tell me you're not still living with him." Trish asked, dragging her hands down her cheeks with a stressed out expression that promised any wrong answers would result in more screaming.

"No! No, I'm staying with Frost for now."

"Oh thank Oberon." Ziggy slouched forward.

"Okay, good, good. Still wish you'd left sooner, but that's *good.*" Trish visibly forced herself to take a deep breath.

"In my defense I didn't actually know about the dress up thing until a few days ago when that detective came to talk to me."

"That's still-- That makes me feel negative amounts of soothed, actually."

"ThAt wAS WHy he shOwED uP at wORk?!"

Xinghua hugged onto her knees. Now, away from Tom, knowing what she knew, her reasoning felt even more naive and stupid than it had before.

"I thought it was kind of romantic, in a vampire kind of way…"

"Oh honey no." Ziggy's expression became drawn, like they genuinely felt bad for her rather than judging her for her *obvious* stupidity, "You know better than anyone 'vampire' is *not* a synonym for 'serial killing weirdo'. Nothing about that is romantic."

"Yeah, I get that *now* but…. he was….he was my first *everything*. And I-- he's been--"

She felt her eyes tearing up for what felt like the twentieth time that night and made herself take a step back from the edge of self flagellation before she could throw herself over it.

"He groomed you." Trish said with a certain cautiousness that Xinghua immediately did not care for, "So that you *wouldn't* know any better. It's….more common than it should be."

Xinghua somehow managed to frown deeper.

"There's a w-word for that?"

Trish breathed in through her teeth, "Yeah…. There's like a whole thing about the six steps of it and everything and all told it's a lot like a cult, except you don't *decide* to join. Usually victims of this kind of thing *don't* know there's anything wrong until so much later the damage is more than done."

It felt almost unreal, next to everything else she'd learned recently. It shouldn't have been as much of a shock as it was, but the part of her that wanted to defend Tom, to find a way to explain things that wasn't...wasn't *that*, was nearly screaming as she asked her next question.

"What...are the steps?"

"Maybe we should come down there and see you?" Ziggy suggested before Trish could start, "I can already tell this is gonna be a *lot,* and this isn't the kind of chat you start without chocolate and friends.*"*

Trish looked gratefully at Ziggy's window and nodded.

"Yeah, actually that's probably a good idea. Where did you say you were staying?"

Xinghua wanted to argue but honestly that probably *was* a good idea.

"I'm staying with Frost, at Wreckquiem. There's a few guest rooms in the back and he's letting me use one. I'm pretty sure he's had one reserved for me, since he's been hoping I'd break up with Tom for years."

"Wait, you don't mean *the* Frost, do you? As in Leland McKnight?" Ziggy bent over their screen.

"Uh, yeah, you know him?"

"Do I--? Of course I *know* him! Or, I know *of* him. He's only the heir apparent to one of the biggest covens in the city, owner of one of the best supernatural bars in the city, and you know *drop dead sexy.* How the hell are you just *friends* with a guy like that?"

Xinghua had wondered that a few times herself.

"I'm not sure why he decided to be so ride or die about it, but I met him once by accident when I first moved back here with Tom. I stuck out like a sore thumbs since I was still little back then, but we were out in one of the vamp heavy parts of town. I guess he and Tom have a bit of a history, but neither one will tell me what the deal is. Anyway, Frost came up to chat, saw me, chatted a bit and we've been friends ever since." She paused, "Actually... knowing what I do now about the whole turning kids thing, he was probably trying to investigate what Tom was doing with me."

"Oh. Well that's... not what I was expecting but honestly it just makes me want to hug you both. Maybe a little more groping for Frost--"

"Okay, okay, whoa, whoa." Trish interrupted before Ziggy could get any more out of hand, "We're on our way, Ziggy go grab yo' thirsty ass a bottle of water."

"Mmmm, yas, one tall drink of water~"

"Ziggy."

"So this is a *vampire club?*" Richard asked, his trademark frown already astride his lips, "I'm pretty sure I've seen narco getting ready to bust this place."

Xinghua had come outside to meet Richard and usher him into the club, likely to keep him from looking too closely if he had to guess. The place hardly seemed above board.

"Probably." She shrugged, nodding to the 'bartender', "You see the part of town we're in? Everywhere around here gets the shake down once a week."

Richard made a non-committal grunting noise, still looking around to make sure there weren't any *obvious* laws being broken. Every time he breathed in, there was something harsh in the air, a sharp, chemical smell like bleach or something...

"What is--"

"I'm not gonna answer anything you ask me, Ransom. All you need to know is that it's a safe place run by a good friend of mine." Xinghua interrupted breezily.

He stared at her for a whole twenty seconds though she appeared not to mind, "Fine."

"Thank you." She sing-songed back.

Richard managed to keep his mouth shut up until the stained backrooms opened up into the velvety opulence of Wreckquiem proper.

"What are the chances this place files taxes?"

Xinghua rolled her eyes, opening her mouth probably to tell him to shut his, but another voice beat her to it.

"Excellent! I would *never* skirt the ill concealed thievery that qualifies as the American government's taxation system! I'm rich as hell, the little mosquitoes hardly come knocking at my door at all." Frost replied as he strode out from the backroom where his office was, "But next time, when you make an entrance, compliment the decor before you question business practices, it's so *gauche.*"

Xinghua didn't bother to hold back her laughter while the speaker came into Richard's line of sight. He was also *definitively* a vampire. Too pale, vaguely see through, uncannily perfect, and prettier than Richard had previously thought a man capable of.

"Right. Sorry. Richard Ransom, nice to meet you, uh....?"

"Leland McKnight ." McKnight extended his well manicured hand, *"Charmed."*

"Right. Nice, uh....drapes." He shook the offered hand.

"Thank you, they do match the carpet, if you're curious." McKnight winked.

He'd walked *right* into that one.

Xinghua stepped in to save Richard's ass just as he was sure he was about to sputter out something genuinely embarrassing in reply to that.

"Have Trish and Zig gotten here yet?"

Before McKnight could respond, the answer came in the form of a screech, one Richard would have swore wasn't human had he not smelled the very human girl who crashed into Xinghua seconds later.

"Xing! Oh my lawd girl *fuck* this week. I don't know if it's the stars or what, but I'm *over it.* I've been driving Zig nuts all morning worrying myself in circles about all this noise."

Behind her came the redheaded secretary from Xinghua's workplace, or at least he *thought* it was them since that image appeared to be superimposed on top of something... *else.*

They'd been confusing to him the first time he'd met them but now he was having a significantly worse time. The harder he focused, though the more he was sure they weren't human. Unless they'd decided to don an incredibly elaborate costume to comfort their friend, which seemed unlikely and wouldn't explain much.

The image below the redheaded secretary he recognized had skin that was a light pink color, dotted with dark pink freckles across their shoulders and down their paper-white throat. Their hair was different as well, it looked less like hair and more like red and white striped lily petals. Two long pointed ears stuck up from either side of their head, extending far above where Ransom would have expected an ear to end. Their eyes however struck Richard the most. They were bright, vivid red without a pupil or sclera to be seen.

"I've tried to drug her, what? Four times? Trish and her 'that smells like valerian and poppy seed, that's not Starbucks'"

They rolled their eyes, though Ransom could only tell because their entire head moved, "Ooooh, hello again Detective~"

"Hey." He said, unable to blink or look away.

"Right, Ransom, this is Patricia Arcana, and Ziggy Vega-Polvo." Xinghua gestured between the two like a gameshow host.

Vega-Polvo's attention left him and immediately zoned in on McKnight, a salacious smile curling their bright blue lips.

"And *hello* Mr. McKnight~ Big fan." They held out a delicately jointed hand.

"Xinghua, you never told me you were friends with such a gorgeous creature~" McKnight smirked, kissing their knuckles as if nothing were amiss.

Vega-Polvo giggled, showing off a pair of fangs that could rival Xinghua's, hiding behind their shimmering lips.

"Table that, I don't have the *anything* to listen to that conversation right now." Xinghua stepped in, unintentionally saving Richard's sanity as well as her own.

McKnight chuckled and Vega-Polvo gave her the long suffering look of someone who'd been cockblocked for the umpteenth time.

"Right, niece first, flirting later."

Xinghua frowned, "Niece?"

"We're of the same bloodline dear, that makes us family." McKnight's expression softened, "It's one of the many reasons I've made it a point to get close to you."

"Here I thought you just liked me."

"That came later. I could smell the ice on you when we first met, though up until yesterday I'd never really been able to tell if it was from *you* per say. There was a chance it was from

Tom, though I was sure he was of a different bloodline and I have next to no desire to claim *him* as kin."

Evidently the looks of collective confusion were enough for McKnight to decide to explain.

"Each bloodline is unique, and some are far more rare than others. Generally vampires of the same bloodline can more or less *sense* the presence of others of their same bloodline. Since you were never without him, it muddied my ability to tell which of you I was sensing. Did he teach you *nothing* about what it is to be a vampire?"

"I know what the fangs mean."

"He *would.* Well, we'll just have to add that to our list of things to talk about. For now I believe we have other matters to attend to."

His attention slid back over to Richard who was honest to God relieved to be being addressed for business this time. He squared his shoulders and cleared his throat.

"As I'm sure Li has told you, Thomas Airius has taken steps to enact a plan that will cause chaos should it be allowed to come to fruition."

"Sweetie," Vega-Polvo said in what sounded like their approximation of the 'old southern white lady' voice, which was beyond odd coming out of a creature like themself, "We ain't cops here, no need to talk all fancy like."

Richard sagged a little.

"Force of habit. Short version: Tom fucked up and made a virus that will not only reveal the existence of all of this to humans, but also likely cause a class war. It's going to be a giant clusterfuck if we don't do something about it."

Vega-Polvo reached over to squeeze Richard's arm, though he jerked it back anxiously they didn't seem to mind, "Good job hon."

He noticed something fluttering behind their back and had to force himself to just say 'Thank you' and not fall into his habit of interrogating anything that made him nervous.

Arcana raised her hand to speak and with amusement McKnight pointed to her, "You, with the glasses in the back."

"Thanks, uh, I feel like I should also mention I had a really *really* bad vision of the future a few days ago. It was some real Romero *ish*. I, um, saw it when I was looking into Xinghua's future."

"You're a mage?" McKnight looked surprised, "*Xinghua* we *really* have to have a talk about you hiding all of these interesting people from me."

"It wasn't on purpose but now I'm sticking by that, down boy."

"Excuse me, sorry, can we back up just a second here?" Richard spoke over the beginnings of din, "I'm sure I'm the newest to the supernatural tea party, so would you mind explaining how and why you can see the future, and maybe include how accurate it is?"

"Honestly? I would if I could but doing *real* magic is new to me too." Arcana played with a strand of her curly brown hair.

"You've always done *real* magic, babe." Vega-Polvo gave her a funny look.

"Making tea is not anywhere near the same league as seeing the actual future, Zig." Arcana frowned back.

"Yeah, healing is *way* harder."

Arcana's expression ran the gamut from confusion all the way up to vague disbelief. Richard could relate.

"Have you... are *you* a mage?"

Vega-Polvo laughed but when Arcana's expression stayed the same they switched to squinting instead.

"I thought you already knew what I am."

"Uh.... gay?"

Vega-Polvo snorted so hard Richard was surprised they managed to stay standing.

"Please tell me you haven't thought that's what I've meant....when I said I was a faerie." They managed to laugh the words out.

"*Was it not?*"

Vega-Polvo laughed themself onto the ground.

"I'm wildly confused." Richard deadpanned, "Does being a fairy make you pink?"

"Me too." Arcana agreed, then, "Wait, what do you mean pink?"

"What do *you* mean? Their skin is pink."

"*What?*"

"Are you telling me you can't see that?"

"Whoa, whoa whoa, time out." Vega-Polvo stepped in, miming the action, "Gimme-- gimme a sec, *whew* I can't fucking *breathe.*"

"Uh, I'm not *super* familiar with faeries, honestly Zig is the only one I know personally, but wasn't your interior designer a faerie? That's what's with the resin cast candelabras right?" Xinghua looked to McKnight.

McKnight seemed more than a little distracted by Vega-Polvo's hysterics, but nodded anyway.

"Mhmm, for those of you who don't know, Fair Folk, The People, or Fae, whatever you want to call them, are among the oldest denizens of this planet. If the legends are to be believed their ancestors made a pact with a God to use their power to mind the planet and tend nature in exchange for eternal youth and longevity. They live by a set of rules that they consider more sacred than any mortal law, and most of them have quite the nasty allergy to iron, thus the resin cast candelabras, yes."

Vega-Polvo finally made it back to their feet, leaning into McKnight's side despite distinctly not *needing* to.

"That laugh made me feel about six hundred years younger, thanks for that."

"Okay, but in my defense you are a *giant* Queen, that was a fair assumption. Whoa, whoa, rewind that back, *six hundred?!* How old are you?!"

Another giggle bubbled up to their lips, "You shouldn't ask a lady her age."

"Are you?" Richard chimed in, feeling suddenly like he'd just stepped into enemy territory without a blind, "A lady, I mean."

Vega-Polvo only winked back.

"Not to be the fun police, but I think we've gotten a bit off track yet again." McKnight cleared his throat, though his voice was still filled with amusement, "You were saying about your vision, dear?"

"Right! Yeah, uh, I saw some definitely-not-zombies in Xinghua's future while we were at this suburban witch club I go to. Or no, sorry *mages* because apparently Witches are *different.* We learned *that* since we needed to know more about the not-zombie thing, so we sorta summoned the Witch of Time. Let me tell you, spookiest bitch I have *ever* met."

Richard glanced around to find Vega-Polvo looking shocked, Xinghua staring into the middle distance as though she were hardly present, and McKnight looking *incredibly alarmed.*

"You what?"

Arcana bit her lips, tugging them into her mouth with her teeth.

"We, uh, summoned Time and asked him a couple questions and I...kindasortajoinedacultIthink."

"I don't get the supernatural mumbo-jumbo but cults are bad news." Richard said firmly, turning her way, "Do you need help getting out of there?"

Arcana looked over at him like she would be hugging him if they knew each other even slightly better.

"Thanks but I'm pretty sure it's a magic thing." Ransom noticed her thumb slide across a little hourglass tattooed to her inner wrist, "Like mama always said I was gonna, I ran my mouth at the *worst* time and got my ass auto-enrolled to this weird time wizard club. So, uh, yeah I'm pretty sure what I saw was legit, the Witch of Time himself told me so."

"Anyone else need a drink? I'd like a drink." McKnight said, darting back behind the bar.

"It's 11 am." Ransom frowned.

"And I'm nocturnal, drink?"

"Yes, please, God yes." Xinghua answered instead, letting vampire speed carry her to the bar in milliseconds.

"There's uh, one other thing I oughta mention about that vision. And please could I get a *really* strong double-shot?"

"Do you have a preference?"

"Nah just fuck me up."

Xinghua winced, "That good?"

Arcana glanced over at her fleetingly and Richard would have sworn he saw a brief flash of guilt.

"Okay, so I didn't tell you about this because I was still kinda hoping I was going to be able to change things and then everything with Time happened and I've been *freaking the fuck out-*"

Xinghua bounced off the bar and took Arcana's hand in hers, giving it a little squeeze. Arcana took a long, deep breath and visibly relaxed some.

"It's okay. I'm not gonna, like, take away your birthday or some shit."

"Alright, okay so the thing is...when I saw myself in that vision, I, uh, I didn't look that much older than I am now. If at all." She stared down at her shoes, the rest of the words coming out quiet enough that if he weren't now a werewolf, Richard was sure he would not have heard them, "And I didn't know this until *now*, but I saw everyone in this room there."

The room fell silent.

"Trish-"

"I know."

"Trish."

"I'm sorry! I didn't mean to hide important shit but- I was *scared as hell okay!"* Arcana broke the uncomfortable silence by shouting, "I ain't indestructible like you, Xing! I ain't a vampire, o-or-- a *faerie* or *anything!* I ain't even a good mage! I can't just vibe with seein' people getting *ripped to pieces* in front of me, 'specially not when I'm *pretty damn sure* my ass is next! I pussed out like a bitch but it's *easy* to be brave when you ain't a big squishy bag of meat!"

Xinghua looked a little taken aback. From what he'd seen and heard from her so far it was entirely possible that she'd forgotten just how terrifying mortality could be.

Xinghua pulled her into a hug, giving her a firm squeeze.

"Sorry Trish, I... wasn't thinking."

"Shot?" McKnight interceded, walking over to hand Arcana her alcohol.

She took it and slammed it without letting go of Xinghua. She hissed and bemoaned the taste of it, but settled back in to continue hugging her friend.

"I get the hype now, you're like...*so* much cooler than Airi-asshole." Arcana muttered.

A surprised laugh burst from McKnight, evidently prompting him to pat Arcana's head gently.

"I'll be calling him that, *quite literally* forever now."

It was Xinghua's turn to laugh, while Richard cleared his throat.

"So, what I'm getting out of all of this is we need a game plan."

"You sound like you've got something, Rich." Xinghua pointed out, "Lay it on us?"

"The first step has to be recon. If we're going to stop him we're going to need to know exactly what he's up to."

"Ooooh, my specialty~" Vega-Polvo grinned.

Arcana frowned from over Xinghua's shoulder.

"You stick out like a sore thumb Zig. No offense."

They arched an eyebrow at her, "Do you really think this is what I actually look like?"

"Well *now* I don't know. Apparently you're *pink.*"

"Fae are shapeshifters by nature. The strongest of us can look however we like." They shrugged, "What you're seeing is called a glamour, sweetie. I could hardly walk around in my true form. Well, given the average New Yorker, I probably *could,* I just don't like the feeling of the human world on my bare skin, plus all the weird looks I'd get. Mmm, not worth it. "

Richard had to physically bite his tongue to keep himself from asking the questions burning in the back of his tongue.

"Right, so you can get in?"

Vega-Polvo grinned, and then between blinks the secretary look superimposed on top of their pink self changed into an almost entirely different person. They were still a redhead, but less on the David Bowie side of the spectrum, leaning more towards Nicole Kidman. Their features were softer and more feminine, their body curvy and voluptuous. Their eyes had even changed to a deep, whiskey brown.

"I can get in."

"Yes you can." McKnight said, in a sultry tone that had Vega-Polvo waltzing back his way.

"Before that finds its way to a table, I think that's a good place to call this meeting." Richard said, eyeing the two, "Thank you for your hospitality, I'll see myself out."

McKnight snapped his attention away from Vega-Polvo.

"Oh no, my dear wolf faced Detective, I'm afraid you'll be joining us until this little coup is finished."

Richard frowned, "And why is that?"

"Because if I know Tom, and I unfortunately *do,* he'll have been keeping tabs on you for some time now. I can protect you here, but if you step back out there without me and mine, you'll be a rather open target. And believe it or not, Thomas does have a rather *nasty* temper."

Xinghua fished her phone out of her pocket, grimacing as she scrolled through it.

"I've got six texts from him, last one says 'Where are you and why does the house smell like dog and detective?'"

"Point proven."

Richard wanted to argue but decided to swallow the protests instead. There was no real point in it. He didn't know enough about what he was up against to know for sure whether or not McKnight's claims were founded. And it wasn't as if he had any real *need* to return to his apartment, he didn't have even so much as a goldfish waiting for him.

"...Thank you for your generosity."

McKnight nodded minutely and turned his attention to Arcana.

"That goes for you two too, you're close with Xi-xi, I'm sure you'd be his logical next step." McKnight zoned in on Vega-Polvo, *"You're* more than welcome to follow me~"

"Oh *hell yes~*"

*   *   *   *

Three hours later found Xinghua on the right side of a shower and a snack, coming back to the main lobby to see if she couldn't find someone to chat with.

She was in luck, as it seemed the others had all had more or less the same idea. Trish was seated at a booth, making what appeared to be a pentagram out of toothpicks. Ransom was perched at the bar with a notebook, listening intently to Frost who seemed to be giving him a supernatural rundown. Ziggy, God love them, was laying draped across the stage, crooning some low 50's number she didn't recognize.

"Xing!" Frost perked up as she approached, "Lovely of you to join us, I was just filling in your *incredibly curious* wolf pup here in a little bit better on the way our world works. It astounds me how many immortals are just letting their brood wander around uninformed these days!"

Frost touched the tip of his finger to the bourbon he had finished pouring Ransom, his trademark frost blooming over the surface of the glass.

"You have magic?" Ransom cocked his head.

"See!" Frost tossed his arms up in exasperation, "Vampires call them 'gifts', but they're a form of magic, if significantly more limited than what our little mage friend over there could do."

Trish placed the final match stick across her pile and to her surprise, and Xinghua's, a small purple fire erupted from the center of the creation. She squeaked in panic and began beating it with a napkin to try to put it out.

"See?" Frost grinned at Trish's frantic efforts, "More magical potential in her little toe than the three of us put together."

Frost noticed the looks he was receiving from Ransom, and to a degree Xinghua as well.

"Very well, gather around kiddies, let me tell you a story."

Within about twenty seconds they were all sat at the bar, including Trish who had managed to get her supernatural fire put out.

"I am by *no* means the oldest of us, but I do remember hearing the stories the elders passed down from the beginning." As Frost spoke, little icy figures began to form on the bar, acting out his story as he told it, "All vampires hail from one True Bloodline touched by the Witch of Death herself."

Ransom frowned hard at that, "There's a Witch of Death?"

Frost hummed, "The only Witches I have heard of are that of Death and Time. I don't know if there are more, but I certainly hope not. Those two are frightening enough in their power."

"*A Witch* made vampires?" Xinghua frowned, suddenly understanding with greater depth the level of jeopardy they had been in to have just casually summoned Time. What the hell had that lady been *thinking?*

Frost nodded, "Some stories say she cursed the first of us, some say it was a reward for valor in battle. No one is really sure, the originals have been lost for so long it's anyone's guess really."

"But we...all came from one dude?" Xinghua frowned, "That's pretty biblical."

"Lucious VanHaven," Frost nodded as if that were a name they should all know, "At the time, he was an old King, dying of a lung disease modern medicine has all but erased. But after Death took from him the ability to die, he became the first of us. He turned two of his lesser known children shortly thereafter, Godric 'Lionhart' VanHaven, and Marcine VanHaven. Thomas believes that the cause of our condition stems from a virus, and while he's not *wrong,* he's also not entirely right. There is another component, something a bit more magical in nature that the VanHaven siblings managed to tap into far before their father did.

"You see, the three originals each possessed a gift. Lucious VanHaven gave rise to The Conflagration, Lionhart created The Voidwatchers, and Marcine sired the first of the Children of the Ice. Our lineage, Xinghua, can be traced back to her. Your fangs can tell you how many generations you are removed from her."

Xinghua frowned and watched Richard do the same.

"You mean the power level thing?"

"Ugh, Thomas *would* only think of it that way. Yes, vampires who are closer to the original source tend to be stronger than others further down the line, but generally age will level that playing field so it really doesn't matter to anyone who isn't either an original or a direct descendant." Frost rolled his eyes.

"Right... that's okay, great. So, what, we're extra special because we're from the original three bloodlines?"

"But of course dear. I myself was lucky enough to know my sire for certain."

"Do you know how far along the chain you are?" Trish asked.

Frost preened at that, clearly having been waiting for someone to ask. He flashed them a grin and three sets of fangs flashed down over his regular teeth.

"I am the fourth in our line, sired by December Snow herself." He purred, clearly extremely proud of his pedigree, "When December decided to brave the Great Sleep, she left me as heir to our bloodline, small though we may be now. Until such a time as I cannot continue or Marcine returns to us from wherever she was lost to."

Xinghua blinked, surprised but impressed by that. She'd known Frost was powerful and important, but to her surprise he had *wildly* undersold it.

"That sounds like a lot, honey. Aren't you also heir apparent to your coven too?" Ziggy asked.

Frost tucked his fangs back into his gums.

"Having a limited bloodline helps a bit. Most are in the same coven as I am, so it's really the same thing." Frost chuckled.

"Is that the one you kept trying to get me to join? Also, what do you mean *the Great Sleep?*"

"But of course, dear. And I was referring to the process by which a vampire decides to cut contact with the world for a while and sleep. December, of course, found herself a place where she would still feel the snow pile up around her."

It was that simple, one moment she was sitting listening to Frost tell her more about vampires, the next she was freezing to death, crumpled and unable to move as the world slowly went dark.

Her eyes were freezing over, she knew they were, she had seen the ice blossom across her vision and now it was getting so dark.

She couldn't feel the tree behind her that she'd slid down, only the ache in her lungs as they continued to be bullied by the cold, harsh air.

She'd been walking for so long, she'd thought when she finally stopped, her muscles would start to feel better. But they hadn't, too cold to unclench, making the cramping feel even more pronounced. It had gone away eventually, but the numbness was worse.

Numb meant nerve endings dying. Even as young as she was, she knew that pain was bad, but it meant her body was still working. But this tired, numb, wrung out pile of frozen flesh she'd become was barely anything anymore, never mind working. She was *so tired.*

She would have been scared, but she didn't have the energy to spare. It felt like a Herculean feat just to have her heart still beating.

She was going to die. She didn't *want* to, but she was going to. She knew that in the calm, distant way she knew the sun would still rise after she did. She would have cried, but she was sure her tear ducts had frozen over already too. She wouldn't have had the moisture left for it anyway, she hadn't had a drink since the day before yesterday.

Part of her wondered if it wasn't better this way. Mom was dead, Grandma was dead, and Dad would have killed her too if she'd stayed. She might be dying regardless, but at least this way her Father wasn't the one to end her. That was a small comfort.

She blinked slowly over eyes that could no longer see the world around them.

It wouldn't be long now.

She should just let go, let herself drift off to it like a waking dream.

"...and then he-- *Tom.*" Came a soft voice.

"Hm? *Oh.*" Said another.

Xinghua couldn't tell if the voices were real or something she had imagined to keep herself company. Honestly the break in the silence was appreciated, imagined or not.

"Listen." The first voice said, "...Tom, I think she's still alive."

"No for very much longer, the poor thing." The second one nearly cooed, "Frost bite already set in, looks fairly extensive. She must have been out here quite a while."

"Jesus." The first one whispered with horrified sympathy, "She's just a kid. How did a kid even get this far out here alone?"

Something shuffled closer to her. Reflexively she blinked as something touched her.

"Oh!" The first voice gasped, "She blinked! Shit, do you think she can hear us?"

"One way to find out. Child, blink once if you can hear us." She blinked.

"Oh shit, oh, oh!" The first one exclaimed, "Oh that's horrible! You poor thing! We have to help her!"

"And what is it you think we can do for her? I'm a doctor, not a miracle worker." The second replied back.

"I know you've been working on something new since the last one, don't give me that. You *absolutely* could save her."

"Fletcher--"

"I swear I won't make you take care of her. Her recovery, once she's stabilized, will be entirely on me. I swear it on Father's grave."

"You never liked Father."

"Thomas!"

"Fine. Pick her up and let's go then. If she dies before we make it home I won't have you bemoaning our lack of haste."

"Thank you!"

Xinghua felt the sense of being moved, and of vague pressure, but little else. That, in its way, was also probably a small mercy if what they'd said about the frostbite was true.

"It's alright little one," The first voice, *Fletcher* her mind supplied, murmured to her, "We're going to take you some place warm and safe. We'll help get you better, you needn't worry about a thing."

Xinghua had never been the trusting type, growing up in the rough side of town, on the wrong side of the law will teach a kid that if nothing else. Don't ask for help because it won't be given, and anything given isn't given for free, always look for the catch. She didn't like the lulling way the stranger spoke to her, but there was little she could do about it. She couldn't move, couldn't speak, couldn't even see him.

She was just along for the ride, waiting patiently for Death's shadow to finish settling over her.

"Here we are," The other voice, Tom she thought he'd been called, said calmly, "Set her on the couch by the stove. I need to check the extent of the nerve damage we're dealing with."

Xinghua felt confused, with what sliver of her mind that wasn't actively crying out at the rush of heat from an opened door. She hadn't seen a house anywhere nearby, and they hadn't traveled very long. Had she *really* been just minutes away from salvation?

Vaguely she felt herself being laid down, heard the sound of someone riffling around nearby.

"You're really that worried?" Fletcher asked, "I thought this 'virus' of yours is a cure all. I mean, look what it did for *us*."

"Our cases were infinitely less complex. It's far easier to mend a flesh wound, however fatal, than it is to rebuild nerve endings and it's certainly easier to cure a fever than to re-generate dead tissue. The virus may be miraculous, but this child has suffered far more damage than either of us did. As well, she is a *child*. Her body may not be able to withstand the strain of the virus itself, or did you forget it nearly killed you too, dear brother?"

There was a pause.

"No. I didn't. You know how I get. Continue, please."

"Yes, your optimism and propensity for hope counterbal-ance my fatalism and practicality as well as ever." Tom's voice drew a little closer, "If nothing else, the results of this will be fascinating."

"If I didn't know you better, I would accuse you of using altruism as a smoke screen for scientific curiosity."

"Well then it is a very good thing you know me better now isn't it?"

Xinghua felt the vague hint of pressure against her fingertips. Or at least she thought she did, though the sensation was fleeting enough that she couldn't tell. She couldn't look to confirm either way.

After some few minutes of quiet working, she assumed, Fletcher spoke up again.

"How's she looking?"

Tom sighed, "The damage is extensive, though not quite as bad as I first surmised. If we'd caught her yesterday, I would have been certain we could save her. As it is, the little dear is just barely clinging to life."

"Can't we at least try?"

"Oh I didn't say anything about not trying anyway."

"You have that tone. What are you thinking?"

"Are you ready to be a father?"

"Me?" There came a low chuckle and the sound of something being slapped, though the hit wasn't loud enough to be much more than reactionary, "Thomas, were it possible your choice of words would one day be the death of me."

"Don't let yourself get caught in the minutia of it, I know you've longed for a child, dear brother. Two birds with one stone, yes?"

"I...suppose. But wouldn't you be the better candidate?"

"Ordinarily yes. But I think your gift, should it take, would actually be beneficial to her. Look here, you can see the ice has well and truly made a home in her."

Fletcher hummed, taking a moment before he answered.

"I'll do it."

"See, brother mine, how could I ever want for altruism when you are its very definition?"

"Hush up and tell me what to do."

"I can only do one."

"The second then Thomas."

She heard snickering before Tom evidently decided to put himself back on track.

"That part is relatively simple. Bite her wrists, neck, and ankles. The damage is most severe at her extremities, and the neck will get the virus circulating much faster. The rest, you can leave in my capable hands."

"Right. While I have the utmost faith in your abilities as a scientist, I'm not sure I've ever seen you display the skills of a capable caretaker."

"Fletcher, on occasion when you speak I am sorely tempted to believe father's grand assertion of mother's infidelity on the matter of your conception." Tom retorted coolly.

"And when *you* speak, I am similarly inclined to believe mother's claim that it was an ass who carried you to term rather than herself."

"Touche."

"So, wrists, neck, and ankles?"

"Yes."

There came more shuffling and a pause between their banter and the next words spoken to *her.*

"I apologize for any discomfort, little one."

Xinghua felt a dull press against her neck, the skin too numb to feel much more than that. Then a few seconds later the same at her wrists and then again at her ankles. While Xinghua couldn't make sense of how biting a person was supposed to heal them, she quickly put the thought aside in favor of the sheer *rapture* she felt as warmth began to creep back into her veins.

"There." Fletcher said somewhere past the euphoria, "Your turn."

"One moment. I need to see how her body reacts to your venom before I proceed."

The warmth had engulfed her whole body. She would have liked to relax into it, but the pain of the muscle tension had begun to make itself known again now that she was warming up. No, that wasn't quite it. Her muscles had begun to *burn*, but she couldn't feel them loosening, like the warmth was only in her mind, like the burn of the shots she'd taken with the little gang she ran with back home. Her body was still frozen.

"As I thought." Tom sighed, "The damage will take quite a lot to mend. I'm afraid most of the virus may burn itself away doing that kind of work, or it will kill her trying. I will need blood, a half pint of yours will do just fine for the time being, and we'll have to keep her well fed throughout. The key will be in finding a balance between filtering out the old blood as she burns through it, transfusing new blood into her, and making certain to retain a baseline of the virus in her system until it has finished its work. If I can do that, then we should be in the clear. Though if that is the case I may yet be able to-"

"Thomas."

"What?"

"You're doing it again."

"Fetch me my syringe, Fletcher." Tom said flatly.

Xinghua floated in the warmth and the silence, the only ripple coming in the form of another light pinch, once again at her neck.

Xinghua listened, but neither said anything further, leaving her to luxuriate in the false warmth within her. That was fine, Xinghua didn't really want to listen much more anyway, little to none of it made sense to her anyway. She could just float forever, maybe she might even sleep. She wasn't sure what they had done, but she hoped it lasted long enough for her to die peacefully.

But the longer she laid there, the less pleasant the warmth became. It felt less and less like the burn of alcohol and more like the heat of a wound healing. Her skin had begun to feel too tight and an itch was settling underneath it. She wanted more than anything to scratch herself but she knew she couldn't move. She tried, somewhat surprised that she felt a single muscle in her forearm twitch.

"See there?" Tom's voice finally spoke up, excitement readily apparent, "That muscle contraction? Your venom is quite potent to be working so well so quickly. It will be focusing on the most severe injuries first, so at this rate I think we'll be needing to administer a third dose by this evening at the latest. Hmm, I wonder how the rapid metabolic rate of the virus will work paired with that of a child."

"Three doses in a single day? Won't that be more harmful than beneficial?"

"Ordinarily, yes. But the injection that I gave her is a much more mild form of the virus that I've been working with for quite some time now. I'll of course need to synthesize a strain made with your incarnation of it instead of my own, but one or two doses won't be too much of an issue."

"To make certain I'm still following you, this milder virus, it's still potent enough to continue to mend her?"

"Mmm, yes and no. That is why we started with your venom straight from the tap. It will take care of the most urgent repairs. It will be easier on her as well, to use a more gradual method of infection. It may even lessen the chances of her body rejecting it as well. Hmm, I'll have to look into that later."

Xinghua heard the scratching of a pen on paper.

"Your eyebrows are set as though you have other questions." Tom muttered.

"You aren't even looking at me."

"I can *feel* them, Fletcher. You've quite a heavy stare."

"Will she...if this succeeds she will stay as she is for eternity?" It wasn't a question, even though his voice pitched it as if it were.

The sound of a pen being set down greeted her ears.

"Were I anyone else, more than likely yes."

"But you *aren't* anyone else."

"Indeed I am not. I have made several modifications to the original virus to be able to call mine more mild. Among those changes is restructuring parts of its DNA to only begin replication in response to a certain level of hormone present in the blood."

"In English, or Deutsch please."

"I built a timer into it."

"*Oh!* .....did you plan for this?"

"Not this specifically, the girl has been a surprise."

"You are *unbelievable*. Is this to do with that coven who came to speak with us last week?"

"In part."

"Thomas!"

"Oh don't *"ThOMaS"* me, Fletcher! You were willing to throw all of those rules to the wind fifteen minutes ago over this girl. At worst I provided a better way that may not result in us being drawn and quartered."

"....I suppose you're right."

"I'm the eldest, I'm always right. Now be a dear and fetch me another notebook. It's hardly a true experiment if we fail to record the data properly."

*   *   *   *

Xinghua came to on the floor without any memory of how she got there.

Within seconds of being conscious she became aware of a pit in her stomach. A looming sense of *loss* that had her feeling flayed open and hollow.

"H--" She hiccuped, *"How did I--?* He made me. Had to make me. I wouldn't have...*I couldn't have*...no no no, I wouldn't--"

"Easy there Li." Came Ransom's basso rumble, followed by his arms wrapping around her to prop her up against his chest, "I know you probably don't need air, but how about you focus on breathing with me for a second?"

Ransom made a show of taking a big, heavy breath in, and Xinghua forced herself to follow along with it. It didn't calm her down quite the same way it did when she was human, but it did give her something physical to focus on. She could still feel the air in her lungs, still taste the scents on it, all familiar and safe and *not back there.*

"There we go. In and out, easy does it." Ransom said, taking another deep breath with her.

Xinghua gradually began to calm down, noticing the others sitting close by, looking concerned. When she made eye contact with Frost he reached out and rubbed her arm.

"Are you alright Xi-Xi?"

She nodded, but then thought better of it and shook her head.

"He made me forget him, Lee." She whispered, "He made me forget my *Sire.*"

She watched Frost's eyes flicker blue for a moment as his jaw clenched against whatever he was fighting himself not to say.

"Did you recover a memory, just now?" His voice was eerily calm, though Xinghua knew him well enough to know he was anything but.

She nodded, "The day they found me and turned me. You were right, Tom didn't Sire me, his brother did. I didn't remember he even *had* a brother!"

She pressed the heels of her hands against her eyes and focused on breathing again before Ransom could remind her.

"I had a suspicion that might have been the case."

Her head snapped up, *"You knew?"*

"Not for certain but I-"

"It sure sounds like you've had a *lot* of suspicions you've never bothered to share with the class." She snarled.

Frost's expression dropped in an instant and he made eye contact with the tiling, exhaling slowly.

"Be honest, would you really have listened if I'd told you sooner?"

"...No." She deflated.

"Mmm," Frost's shoulders relaxed a little, "That being said, I still apologize for not having said something. Though I'm surprised he kept you in the dark about something like that."

Xinghua let herself sag back into Ransom's chest, tired and worn out despite being physically fine.

"I don't get it either." She groaned, "I mean I don't *remember.* All I saw was the day they found me, and technically not even *that* since my *eyes* were *frozen.*"

Ransom's hands found her shoulders and began to knead out a little of the tension in them.

"Don't go down that rabbit hole, Li. You just got back."

"For what it's worth, he's right." Frost added in.

Xinghua couldn't argue with the idea of leaving that particular memory alone for a while. Especially not with a warm pair of hands squeezing the tension out of her. She hadn't realized how cold she felt.

A shiver passed through her as she registered the frost that had begun to gather at the tips of her fingers, her elbows. Fear lurched against her heart like a bucking horse, and in a bid to keep it from wrapping around her still heart, she tucked herself up against Ransom's warm side.

The effect was almost immediate. He was still too hot to be totally comfortable for her to touch, but right this moment that was perfect.

"So uh, can I ask what triggered that? Cause you sorta fell out, like out of nowhere." Trish chirped up after the silence had gone stale.

Xinghua sighed, "The thing about sleeping in the snow. I....don't really talk about it. Mostly cause I couldn't remember much but being afraid and cold until *just now*, but uh... I froze to death. That's how Tom and F-Fletcher found me. I...really don't like ice or snow and I *hate* being cold. Not that I can *feel* it anymore, but just seeing it freaks me the fuck out. Or, apparently just thinking too hard about it will do the trick too."

"Oh." Trish said in a tiny voice.

Ransom's hand rubbed down her back and Xinghua couldn't help but be grateful to the man. It occurred to her that she'd gotten more physical affection in the last couple days than she was used to getting over a period of months. It was a little overwhelming, but it was also keeping her sane. As Ransom settled in a little more comfortably, she allowed herself to really relax.

"Do you mind me chillin' here for a bit, Rich?" She asked.

"I was going to insist. You're still shaking."

She hadn't even noticed.

"Actually," Frost said, smiling between the two of them, "It's far past Xinghua's bedtime, perhaps a certain werewolf wouldn't mind carrying her to bed?"

Xinghua threw him a look, while Ransom made a noise that sounded somewhere in the neighborhood of agreement. Before she could tell him Frost was more than likely joking, Ransom was getting to his feet, hoisting her up like she weighed next to nothing.

"Fine, but this isn't happening twice. No more fainting."

"Technically that wasn't a faint, it was more like.... a slow release PTSD episode."

"No more fainting."

Xinghua let herself tuck closer into Ransom and he didn't argue about it.

"Fine, *Dad.*"

Xinghua couldn't remember having been so tired in all her life. Her body felt so heavy, especially around her chest and eyes. It was as if she'd been trying to sleep off a cold which had only gotten worse as she'd slept. Her mouth tasted about like that too.

"Thomas!" A vaguely familiar voice called out, "She's moving, Tom come here!"

Xinghua made the effort to crack open her eyes, finding that while they were blurry, she could actually see again.

In front of her was another person, which would have been shocking enough considering the last thing she fully remembered was dying alone in the snow without a soul in sight. The concern in their voice also had her startled.

"Hello," The man-shaped silhouette continued, presumably now to her, "Are you able to speak, little one?"

She opened her mouth to try, finding her throat to be dry and sore and incapable of making a noise any louder than a kitten mewling.

"Don't worry yourself over-much," He replied when it was obvious she wouldn't be able to, "You've all the time in the world to recover your strength. Thomas! Bring tea, would you?"

"Yes, my dear, pushy brother!" Came the shouted reply from across the house. Xinghua thought she heard the figure in front of her chuckle.

Xinghua squinted hard, trying to make her eyes focus well enough to make out more of the person in front of her. There were patches of darkness in her vision, almost like a burnt out TV, making it hard to really get a good look at him. If she tilted her head just right, though, she could just see him between the damaged spots.

He had to be the prettiest white boy she'd ever seen. She was used to the pretty, painted faces of some of the boys back home and they were beautiful in a way that seemed almost unreal, which in her experience just wasn't a look white guys could pull off. Their features were too angular, too bold to hold beauty that way. But apparently this guy had not gotten that memo. His features were soft and delicate in a way that age had yet to take from him, and his hair, thick and blond, fell in long waves around his neck and shoulders. She couldn't see his eyes well, but she noted they looked faintly purple though she suspected that might just have been her vision.

"How are you feeling? Or rather, are you? Able to feel, that is."

It took a moment for her to manage it, but she clenched her hand, rubbing the tips of her fingers against the sheets of the bed she was laid in. The sensation was muted, but it was there.

"Yes." She managed in a stripped out whisper.

The man lit up in a smile, somehow making his already pretty face even prettier.

"Good! That's very good!" He slid his hands forward and took hers gently, "We were very worried for you, to have found you in such a state, good heavens! When you're in a better way, I should like to know how you came to be in such dire straits."

The faintest flicker of a memory ghosted through her mind, causing her to flinch away from it.

"Or not," He amended, "Forgive my prying, it's not my place."

Before she could figure out a way to respond to that with the limited vocals available to her the door creaked open.

"My apologies for the delay, I thought our guest may also be hungry."

Another man entered the room then with what smelled like a bowl of soup in hand. Xinghua thought he was brunette, but couldn't really be bothered to pay much more attention than that. Not with how her stomach had begun screaming exactly how hungry she actually was.

She couldn't remember the last time she'd eaten. Days ago?

The man brought the food over and she realized one incredibly large problem even as he did. Try as she might, no matter how hard she fought, she couldn't raise her arms to take the bowl.

Frustration akin to rage swept through her, making fat tears flood her eyes.

"Here," The new man said, lifting the spoon to her mouth, "Allow me to help."

Normally mistrustful and flighty by nature, Xinghua hesitated just long enough for the hunger to meet her once again. She then sucked down the broth as quickly as she could, the taste so sublime after days without food that she whined a little in the back of her throat for more.

"Easy," The man said with a smile in his voice as he helped her to drink down more, "There's plenty, no need to rush."

She would have argued that there very much was a need to rush, but she slowed down if for no other reason than that he did. It allowed her a chance to appreciate the rich saltiness of the broth. She had no idea what it was, couldn't see well enough to make out what it was other than that it was darkly colored. It tasted almost like the bone broth her mother would make her when she felt sick.

The memory had the tender edges of her heart aching.

"Thank you." She eventually replied when she'd sipped down as much of the broth as she could. Her voice was stronger, though not by much.

"Of course," The blond replied, "We worked so hard to save you from the cold, it wouldn't do to lose you to hunger."

The brunette pressed two fingers to the inside of her wrist, looking at his watch for a long moment before he took his hand away. He then pressed the back of the other hand to her forehead, startling her with how cool his skin was to the touch.

A jolt of adrenaline caused her heart to race, chasing the dizzy feeling in her head as she jerked away from his hand.

"Are you alright?" He asked with the immediate clinical seriousness of a doctor, "Was that a muscle spasm?"

"No," She trembled, "Don' like c-cold."

Even with her limited vision, she could see the two men exchange rueful glances.

"No, I would imagine you don't. My apologies, miss. My bedside manner has been remarked upon many a time."

"My name is Xinghua. Li Xinghua. Are you a doctor?"

"What a lovely name," The blond replied at the same time as the brunette said, "In a manner."

"Sorta isn't a thing for doctors. Either you went to med school or you didn't."

The blond laughed so suddenly it was more of a snort, pitching over to laugh into the brunette's shoulder.

"Well, you're quite the spitfire, aren't you?"

"Oh dear Thomas, that's exactly the kind of counterbalance you need!"

Xinghua narrowed her eyes while she waited for her answer.

"Yes, I have been to medical school. It's just that I attended some hundred and ten years ago." The brunette explained with a sigh.

Xinghua laughed, rough and unrecognizable as the noise was, though she was the only one to do so.

"Oh... you're serious."

"Very." He crossed his legs primly at the knee, "Before our conversation derailed, I had been about to ask you how you were feeling. The version of the vampyric virus we used to heal you is quite a bit different to the version present in us. As such, I'll be studying how it presents itself in you, both to keep track of your recovery and as a sort of payment for having saved your life."

Xinghua felt as though she'd just ridden a roller coaster in the span of that speech.

"Okay, no, **what?**" She squinted so hard at him her eyes nearly closed, "Do you **seriously** expect me to just believe you're vampires? I'm eight, not stupid."

The blond chuckled a little though at least he had the good sense to look contrite when she stared him down.

"No, I don't think either of us think you're stupid, Miss Li." He replied, sounding fond already.

"Do speak for yourself, Fletcher dear." Tom muttered.

Fletcher smacked him without hesitation, rolling his eyes and his head away from his brother.

"No wonder people bitch about your bedside manner." Xinghua retorted.

"I'll remind you I did recently save your life. You'd do well to be more grateful."

She took a breath to launch another barb back, but Fletcher interrupted.

"She's right, but you aren't exactly wrong either Thomas. However, there are quite a few things more urgent than arguing at the moment, hm?"

Tom looked as though he wanted to argue about that as well but deflated, gesturing Fletcher forward.

"Go on then."

Fletcher shook his head, turning to Xinghua with a look that conveyed the exasperation every sibling has felt.

"Since my brother has evidently elected to pout, I apologize for any inaccuracies in the information I give you."

Xinghua snickered a little as Tom sent him a glare, getting to his feet and leaving without another word.

"He always like that?"

"Oh no, he's normally much worse. He was using his "people manners" since you're new." Fletcher replied, smiling conspiratorially at her.

She couldn't help laughing again, though the noise sounded about like a sandpaper conveyor belt moving gravel chunks.

"But seriously...vampires? Should I be worried about him?"

Fletcher cocked his head, "That bit, regrettably, is actually quite true. I could explain more, but I think it would be most expedient to simply show you my fangs."

The words rattled around in her head for a long moment before she could parse what they meant, taken together.

"Uh... I think you're gonna have to, 'cause I'm calling bs."

Fletcher smiled, lifting up his upper lip delicately. As she watched, three sets of long, needle-like teeth of varying sizes descended from his gum line. He lowered his lip back down, though he didn't retract his fangs.

Xinghua could almost feel her brain fight what it was seeing. It felt like a wasp nest had replaced her brain, all she could hear was buzzing.

It didn't make any sense, and her eyes were still more blurry than not, so it would be easy to tell herself she was seeing things wrong. The last thing she remembered was dying in a forest, there was every chance that she was just dead right now. There was **no way** 'mysterious vampire virus cure' was the actual thing that was going on.

"Miss Li, you do still need to breathe, I suspect."

"If you're secretly Death trying to get me to cross over, you've got to be straight up with me about it. I'll totally go with you, like that's not even a thing, I've got nothing to live for. You don't have to do this whole, crazy, whatever it is you're doing right now."

Fletcher looked at her like she'd punched him square in the nose for a moment, which nearly made Xinghua laugh again, though the urge felt quite a bit more manic this time.

"Oh my dear girl, no. You are **not** dead, quite the opposite really, and I am no reaper." He said gently, "Everything we've told you is the truth, I swear it."

The buzzing sensation that had been growing at the base of her skull since she'd seen Fletcher's fangs only grew stronger as she tried to digest those words.

"Oh." She said in a tiny voice, "That's... **bitchin'.**"

"Excuse me?"

"Well when you were first explaining, I kinda was thinking super shady government agents, or like escaped nazi scientists but vampires are waaaaaay cooler."

"Well that's... unexpected. I'm sorry, how old did you say you are?"

"Eight."

"Ah." Fletcher nodded, though he frowned shortly thereafter, "You're far too young to be swearing like that."

"Hey, I think I earned a couple after the week I've had."

"That is also very true. While we're getting to know one another better, I should introduce myself. I'm called Fletcher, and the other man was my brother Thomas. What would you like me to call you, young lady?"

"My name is Xinghua," She replied.

"While that's true, you're beginning a whole new life. You could choose to be anyone you want, you could call yourself anything you'd like."

She thought it over for a few moments, "I think I like my name."

"Then it is very nice to meet you, Miss Xinghua." He smiled, his pronunciation startlingly perfect, "Welcome to the family."

*　　　　　*　　　　　*　　　　　*

The very first thing Xinghua managed to do in the morning was cry her eyes out. Though, *managed* was the wrong word for the way she curled in on herself while grating sobs tore out of her shaking body.

Memories that had been so well hidden she'd entirely forgotten they were ever there in the first place were now digging their claws into her. Each time she fell asleep it seemed like a new piece of her that she dug up came screaming back to the surface. Parts so long buried in the darkness they'd become as photosensitive as Xinghua herself.

She could still barely believe that Tom would *do* something like this to her. It was undeniable that he had, but what she couldn't understand was *why.* She wanted to believe it was to spare her pain, to keep memories from her that would only cause her pain. Fletcher wasn't around so maybe he'd left and she couldn't take it so she'd asked him to..? Tom was a little cold, but he'd never been *cruel.*

Had he..?

Just last week she would have said she knew practically everything there was to know about him, but now she felt like she barely knew him at all. If he'd managed to keep something this big from her for **years**, *how could she possibly think she knew him?*

Sure she would drive herself in maddening circles if she didn't, Xinghua pulled herself out of bed.

She went through all the motions of making it, something she almost never did, picking up the couple articles of clothing she'd already scattered around the room, and collecting the other miscellaneous bits of trash littered here and there.

Once she'd run out of reasons to delay, she forced herself into the shower and washed top to bottom more thoroughly than she had in recent memory. She took care going through her usual hair routine, grumbling when she realized she'd not grabbed any of her makeup, because of *course* she hadn't. Now out of things to distract herself, Xinghua couldn't justify hiding out anymore.

She stared herself down in the mirror, glaring at the faded silver ring she could still see in her eyes.

"Don't be a little bitch." She said firmly, "Go out there and make a plan to deal with this bullshit. When it's all done you can have that pity party, but not a damn second before."

With one last useless deep breath, she left her room to face the night.

The others were already out in the bar area, which wasn't a huge surprise, it was pretty late in the evening. The surprise was in how empty the club was, with just Trish and Ziggy sitting together at one table, with Ransom and Frost at another. From the looks of it, Ziggy was trying to teach Trish more about magic. They had a book between them with pages that glowed a variety of colors, and Trish looked far more focused than Xinghua was used to seeing her.

Ransom and Frost's own table was strewn with paper and pens balled up pieces of what looked like notes. She was surprised to note Frost pressed right up against Ransom's entire left side.

None of them looked up when Xinghua walked in so for a moment she just let herself watch them all.

Eventually, however, she cleared her throat.

The focus of both groups shifted to her immediately and just as quickly, Ransom was putting distance between himself and Frost.

"Xing! You feeling better? Or at least less shitty?" Trish chirped, diverting her attention.

"Yeah, all good. No more fainting, promise."

"You're just in time, Xi-Xi!" Frost called with a smile, "We were *just* tossing around ideas, weren't we, Dick~?"

Ransom heaved a long suffering sigh, *"Don't call me Dick."*

"Sorry, we were just tossing around ideas, weren't we *puppy?"*

The look Ransom gave him would have killed lesser men.

Xinghua took a bit of pity on him, "That's a lot of shit you're talking there, *Yijeong."*

Frost looked so betrayed for a moment she nearly took it back but before he could pitch a fit, Ransom loudly segued over them.

"From yesterday, we already know we have a way in through Ziggy, but how well do any of us know the building?"

"Oh you are *no fun at all."* Frost huffed his complaints under his breath before he raised his voice to address the rest of the room, "Xinghua, have you ever been there?"

Xing dropped herself down onto the nearest booth, "Bunch of times. Sometimes Tom wouldn't actually fuckin' leave and I'd have to go drag him home."

"Can you tell us anything about the layout?" Ransom jumped in.

"I can tell you where Tom's at."

"Perfect~!" Frost clapped his hands together once, "You tell Ziggy where to go, they trapeze in there and collect the info we need and jet."

"Uh, about that." Xing spoke up as Ransom opened his mouth to do the same.

Frost narrowed his eyes at Xinghua and she had the unnerving feeling that he knew exactly what she was going to say before she said it. She continued regardless.

"There's a security desk, gotta pass a check to get in there and they're pretty strict about who they let in." She explained, "If you don't have a pass or they don't know you, they're not going to let you in."

Ziggy frowned, pressing their fist up under their chin.

"I could change into you, but that'd be a little weird." Ziggy shrugged.

"Not to mention pointless, really," Frost cut in, "If you're mentioning it, you want to go don't you?"

"Li--" Ransom started.

"Yeah, I do."

"I feel like I'm talking to myself today." Ransom grumbled, rubbing at his eyes, "Li, I know what you're thinking, and I get it, but that's a terrible idea."

"Oh yeah? And what am I thinking Rich?" She retorted back, knowing even as she snapped the words out at him that she was being an ass.

"You want to confront him." Frost tagged in, "Obviously."

Bingo.

"I just want to-"

"It's a terrible idea."

"-talk to him. It's *not,* I'm not going to *tell* him anything!"

"How do you know that?" Frost examined his perfectly veneered black nails, sounding casual despite the tension in his neck, "He's already rewritten your mind before. What will you do to stop him from doing it again? What do you plan on telling him about where you've been the last three days?"

"I can tell him I was on a binge. Wouldn't be the first time I've wandered off and forgotten to call." She shrugged, "And he's not going to try anything in a place that public. He's not stupid."

"No, he isn't. He's incredibly manipulative and he knows you inside and out." Ransom narrowed his eyes at her, "Which is much worse."

"I'm afraid I'm going to have to side with Detective Buzzkill on this one." Frost added before Xinghua could argue, "Thomas is dangerous under any circumstances, but most of all to you."

Warm, sharp energy roiled violently below the surface of her skin, like a trapped thing waiting to get out, pacing and growling in front of the bars of its cage. The effort it took to keep herself from shouting had her fingertips trembling.

"So I'm just not getting a choice in this, then? Is that what you're telling me?"

She knew it was a low blow, she could see it had just the effect she'd wanted by the way Ransom flinched ever so slightly. But then his expression locked down and she suddenly remembered he'd been a father at one point.

"If that's what you're going to take away from this, then that's exactly what I'm saying." He folded his arms in the universal signal of a Dad ending a conversation.

She resisted the urge to stomp her feet because she *was not* a child, she *wasn't.* Instead she clenched her teeth and leaned back in her seat, folding her arms right back at Ransom.

"*Fine.* But I'm at least setting up a call so I can listen in."

Frost raised his eyebrows in a look of surprise that Xinghua studiously ignored while Ransom looked quietly relieved which she *also* ignored.

"That's more than fair. Can you get it to record too?"

"You bet your age defyingly shapely ass I can."

Frost barked a laugh and she heard Trish gargling a little as she choked on her drink.

"*Great.*"

*   *   *   *

Three hours later saw them with a fully flushed out plan, ready to implement it.

Ziggy re-entered the room dressed in one of the long white dresses Xinghua had left there on one of her many "overnight excursions". It was one of the ones she'd bought specifically to get Tom's attention since she knew he had a soft spot for the classics. It hadn't worked on *him* but everyone else had seemed to have appreciated it.

"How do I look?" Ziggy twirled, showing off the dress as well as their perfect replication of Xinghua's form wearing it, "I miss any bits or bobs?"

It would have been unsettling if Xinghua had been settled in the first place.

"Nope, I think you nailed it Zig." She gave them a thumbs up.

They smiled at her and reached out their hands for hers.

"Then let's get this party going. So what you're gonna wanna do is take my hands and imagine a hole opening up to the building. I'll do the rest, I just need you to *reeeeeallly* focus baby girl."

"I'll do my best."

Xing laced her hands together with theirs, closing her eyes to focus on the image of Tom's building in her mind's eye. She hadn't been the best with magic, all two other times she'd used it, but Ziggy's felt almost intuitive as it fizzled through her veins. Without the strain she'd gotten accustomed to when helping with magic, a portal opened right in front of them.

"Huh." She mused as Ziggy dropped her hands, which, hindsight being 20/20 they absolutely shouldn't have.

Xinghua was through the portal before anyone had the chance to realize what she'd done. She waved back at them just as it closed, the look of shock on their faces nearly worth the tongue lashing she knew she'd be in for after this.

Her phone rang.

She muted it.

"Alright, Xing you've got like ten, fifteen minutes tops before they figure out they can just google this place and roll up on you. Make it count." She muttered to herself as she jogged up the stairs and up to the revolving doors.

She trotted over to the secretary, Amanda or Amy or Ashley.... something with an A she thought, smiling as sweetly as she could.

"Hi, I'm here to see Thomas Airius."

"Name?" She asked like Xing hadn't been here at least fifteen times.

"Xinghua Li."

"He left a request for you to meet him in his office, Miss Li."

That wasn't uncommon. Usually when she'd been gone like this, the first thing he wanted to do when he saw her again was to have her on his lap. He was only ever needy like that when she wasn't around, she'd never given much thought to it before but now couldn't see it in the same light.

She tried not to wince as she thanked Alice and walked to the elevator.

Tom's office was on the eighth floor, and it was also, as she now remembered, incredibly private.

She was beginning to regret not having listened...

Ignorant to her inner existential crisis the elevator dinged open after far too short a time.

She should walk right over to the stairs and leave. Aline would tell Tom that she'd been here, but that was fine. He wouldn't know where she'd gone. Sure it would mess up the plan a little, but not as much as--

"Xinghua!" Tom's cheery voice sounded from the doorway of his office as his head popped out to meet her, "There you are! Did you have fun on your blood binge, darling?"

He was in her field of view seconds before he finished talking, looking for all the world like an adoring boyfriend and not a manipulative *monst*--

She smiled.

"I did~ You want the deets or do you want a reenactment~?"

His eyes raked up and down her and his lips twitched into a pleased smile.

"I'll take both~"

She tried not to visibly startle and she thought she succeeded since his expression didn't change. He only held his hand out to her.

She didn't want to touch him.

She took his hand.

"How many did you manage to wrangle this time? Or did you just flit from donor to donor like a little butterfly?" He led her towards his office by her hand, not pulling or anything, like he was certain she'd just follow him.

"Uh, the second one. I started off bar hopping, pretty much. Fell in with this group of sorority girls and they were *fun.*"

He chuckled, sitting himself down on his office chair. If the ridiculously large thing could even be *called* a chair anymore. He gently tugged on the corner of her shirt-sleeve twice, indicating he wanted her in his lap. She went, working to make her muscles stay loose as he nuzzled up against the base of her neck.

"And when did you bump into our detective friend?"

Xinghua froze and cursed herself for doing so. *Of course* he knew she'd been with Ransom, he could smell him. He already knew she was lying, he probably had since the moment he'd seen her.

Fuck.

"I, uh, he--"

Tom leaned back, his expression betraying nothing. He looked just the same as he always did when he was listening to her work something out before she could relay it to him. The only difference was the hands that had been holding hers were now more like loose manacles around her wrists.

"He arrested some of the girls I was drinking with. They were underage."

He smiled at her, the indulgent one he gave her when she did something that amused him.

"You've always been quick on your feet, Xinghua. I've come to appreciate that about you." He tilted his head again, "But why are you lying to me?"

"I'm not--"

"Ransom is a homicide detective, dear. There's no reason he'd be arresting a bunch of sorority girls, especially if it were outside of his precinct, which by the smell of salt and soot on you, you were nowhere near. I can also smell your two friends on you, so I very much doubt you were with anyone else given that I can't smell a single other human on you. Now, would you like to try again?"

Xinghua couldn't remember the last time she'd been so nervous.

"Okay, okay you caught me." She took a deep breath, trying to exhale as much of her anxiety as she could, "I was at Wreckquiem with Trish and Zig, drinking our asses off because Trish might kind of be dying due to this whole crazy ass Witch *thing* that happened a couple days ago and when I finally went to head home I deadass ran into Ransom. I didn't tell you because I freaked out because he got bitten by a werewolf of all fucking things and it ended up being this whole crazy *thing* and I might have brought him to our place cause I didn't know what else to do with him and I didn't want him to like die alone because that's *sad as fuck*, even for that dude. I didn't tell you because I didn't want you to be mad at me."

She put on her best puppy eyes, hoping the mish-mash of truth bent at creative angles would be enough to fool him.

She watched each piece of information she'd just dropped click into place, watched him process each one before he spoke.

"I will say, that certainly explains a few things. But why did you think I would be angry with you?" His hands slid away from her wrists and up her arms, one cupping her face ever so gently, as if she were made of porcelain.

"I brought Ransom home without prepping, and I'm pretty sure the bathroom looks like a murder scene."

"It did, yes. That was what had me most alarmed. I'll admit I thought you had simply gotten tired of his hound dogging and killed the man. I was going to offer to help dispose of him." He grinned conspiratorially.

Despite herself, Xinghua laughed. Maybe it was the absurdity of the situation or possibly the relief that got to her, because she couldn't seem to *stop* laughing.

"*No.* I didn't kill him. I did think he was going to die though, to be honest."

Tom nodded, his hands now petting up and down her arms in a way that would have been soothing if it wasn't making her skin crawl.

"I'm quite surprised he survived as well. He didn't strike me as the 'burning will to live' type, though admittedly I've only met him once."

She swallowed the defense of Ransom's character that wanted to crawl up out of her throat and nodded instead.

"How did you get him out of the building? Werewolves are quite large, if I recall correctly."

She grinned, "Well, the superintendent is probably a little traumatized, but right out the front door."

"You *didn't.*"

"*I did~*"

Tom's bark of laughter was interrupted by a soft thud in the back of the office.

Xinghua had a moment of panic, thinking one of the others had arrived before Tom rolled his eyes.

"It's one of the testing rats. It's developed an unfortunate tic that causes it to kick its enclosure every so often. Pay Dmitri no mind." He dismissively waved the sound off, "Though that does remind me, are you thirsty? It seems you may have been the one to be too busy to eat for once."

She nodded, eager to send him out of the room for even a few moments.

"Yeah, actually that would be great."

Tom gave her a smile that was so genuinely affectionate for a moment, just a moment, her heart stuttered.

"Then I'll be right back."

He shifted her from his lap onto the edge of the desk, giving her cheek a kiss as he stood.

"Thanks Tom."

"Of course dear, back in a tic."

He dropped another kiss on her forehead and then swept gracefully from the room. She waited until she couldn't hear his footsteps anymore to bolt up and start looking for anything she could find. She also immediately dialed Ransom.

The phone only rang once.

"Listen I'm sor--"

"Save it. I'm outside, keep the call going. If you need me, work the word blueberry into a sentence and I'll be up there in forty-five seconds."

She swallowed hard at the sharp, barely contained anger in his voice, nodding before she remembered he couldn't see her.

"Got it."

"Have you found anything?"

"No, he just left to grab dinner. He'll be back soon, but I'm looking right now."

A grunt was his only answer.

Xinghua reminded herself she *knew* he'd be angry, that there was no use in being upset about it since it was her own damn fault. She pulled open one of the large drawers in the back of the room and nearly dropped her phone out of shock, barely managing to whip a hand over her mouth to catch her scream.

"There's a--! Oh fff--, there's a *guy in a drawer.*"

"Explain."

He was alive, she could tell that much, able to hear his heart beating slowly now that she'd opened the door. But he looked to be unconscious.

"Uh, black guy, late thirties I think. *Super* naked. Drugged, probably, because he's not waking up, like, at all. The drawer is like one of those ones in a morgue. I.. oh my fucking God I didn't even *hear* him, how long has he--"

"Li, I'm going to need you to get your shit together really quickly. Airius cannot find out that you know that man is there. Can you keep him distracted until I can extract you?"

"How are you gonna--"

"Answer the question Li."

"I-- *fuck,* yeah, yes, I can."

"Good. I'll get the others ready. Close that drawer and get back into position, phone beside you."

"Got it."

Xinghua hustled to obey what Ransom had told her and a good thing too, as Tom came back into the room about two seconds after she'd sat down, a thermos in either hand.

He smiled and handed her the pink one, and she struggled to smile back.

"So, uh, what did- what did *you* do while I was gone?" She asked, wanting to kick herself for the stutter.

"Hmm? Oh you know, this and that. There's always work to do around here." He shrugged, "You know how I like to keep busy."

She sipped the blood in her thermos for something to focus on that wasn't the man in the drawer five feet from them. It tasted a little odd, but bagged blood always did.

Tom sighed and set his thermos down, crossing his arms.

"I'm disappointed, Xinghua."

She forced herself to finish drinking her next mouthful without doing a spit take, despite the cold fear running laps down her spine.

"Did an experiment go wrong?" She asked, proud of herself for not stuttering this time.

"Something like that." He pursed his lips, "Do you know why I agreed to take you in, when you first came to me?"

She glanced up at him, a little disoriented when the movement of her eyes made her vision sway a little.

"Huh?"

"Because I saw potential in you. Certainly, Fletcher did too, but not like I did."

Her surprise over Tom's sudden, explicit mentioning of a sibling she wasn't supposed to know about was overshadowed by the roaring in her ears, the heaviness in her body.

"I still see that potential, Xinghua, really I do. But perhaps I was mistaken in the application of it."

The world was spinning and Xinghua couldn't parse the meaning of a single word Tom was saying. She wanted to ask what was going on, but she couldn't remember where she'd left her mouth. She registered the world swirling before it all went black.

Richard couldn't seem to climb the stairs fast enough. He was taking them two at a time, but it was not fast enough. His instincts had been screaming since the moment Li had stepped through that stupid portal, but they were going absolutely ape shit now.

Perhaps I was mistaken in the application of it.

He didn't want to know what the hell Airius meant by that.

He took the stairs three at a time.

It only took him a few minutes to find the room, there was only one with the sound of movement but an absence of heartbeats, but those few minutes were agonizing.

He slammed his fist into the door, knocking with much less care than he normally would have.

"Catering!"

The door opened and Airius' smiling visage greeted him, making Ransom's blood boil.

"Ah, Detective Ransom. Decided to start harassing me at work as well, have you?"

"Where is she?" He asked tersely.

"Whoever do you mean?" He cocked his head, his tone and the slant of his eyebrows painting the perfect mask of confusion, "Has another girl gone missing?"

He tried his best to look around Airius, into the room to spot Xinghua. But she didn't have a scent or a heartbeat, if he couldn't see her he wouldn't be able to tell where she was.

"Detective?"

"You know damn well I'm talking about Xinghua." He practically snarled.

Tom's brow furrowed even more, and if Richard hadn't just been on the phone with Xinghua he might have been tempted to believe that he legitimately didn't know.

"I'm sorry, I haven't seen her in a few days. Sometimes she does that though, she'll find a group of pretty girls and bed herself down with them for a while. Did you two have business?"

Richard leaned in closer, his nose inches from Airius'.

"Cut the shit, I know she was just here. Where. Is. She?"

Tom's expression schooled itself into nervousness.

"I'm sorry but I can't help you. And if you continue to try to intimidate me, I'll have to have you escorted out by security. As it is, you're already trespassing so they'd have little choice but to hand you over to the police. Given your occupation I imagine that would be rather *embarrassing.*"

Richard wanted to push it. Everything in his body screamed at him to charge in, to fight tooth and nail to drag Xinghua out. But he knew that would only be playing right into Airius' hands.

So he clenched his jaw and stepped back.

"Have a nice day." He gritted out.

"And you too, detective." Airius sing-songed as he stepped back into his office and shut the door.

Richard stalked back to the elevator, thoughts of stealth abandoned in favor of calling the rest of the group.

"Where do you need us?"

"I don't know. He's got her, and I can't get in without getting arrested."

McKnight swore.

"Perfect, truly perfect. Ziggy, love, did you perchance have the foresight to put a tracking spell on her?"

Richard couldn't hear the response but he doubted it was good since McKnight swore again.

"Then we'll have to do this the old fashioned way."

Richard began to put together a list of what he'd need for a stakeout on short notice, only to be interrupted by his phone buzzing. Anxious that it might be Xinghua somehow, he opened the text message.

Now it was his turn to swear.

"What?"

"I've got to go." Richard said, the words feeling like acid on his tongue, "Urgent business."

"Pardon? What the fuck could possibly be more urgent that this?"

Richard smacked his forehead against the elevator wall, "I just got a message from my Captain that we received a lead on the other case I've been working. Serial killer focusing on young boys. They found his hideout."

The line was silent for a few moments and Richard wanted nothing more than to be *out* of this damn tiny metal box. Even his bones felt too small for him.

"We'll work on tracking Thomas and when we find Xinghua we will send for you. I'll consult my coven and inform them of what's happened."

"Thank you."

"Do hurry, Richard."

The elevator dinged open as the line went dead.

Richard allowed himself one long, deep breath to switch gears as he walked out of the elevator.

As upset as he was, focusing on anything other than the task he was going into would only put people at risk. And given what he'd learned about this monster over the years, there was already enough of that to go around.

He decided to review what he knew about this suspect as he left the lobby to flag down a cab back to the station.

They had taken to referring to him simply as "The Killer", given that his taste in victims was too painful to address directly, and no one wanted to give the bastard the satisfaction of a nickname. It also lined up with the 'TK' they found carved into the left heel of each victim.

He was meticulous in making sure no physical evidence stayed on the bodies, nearly as precise as Airi-- Richard forcefully turned the thought back around.

He was sadistic, the bodies they found always heavily injured, though none life threatening with the exception of the killing blow. He very much wanted his victims to suffer as much as possible without the risk of death, and his efficiency with it suggested he was either someone in the medical field or someone with a background in it.

However that criteria had turned them up almost *nothing* of use. And so it had been for years.

Richard had no idea how the Captain had caught wind of a lead promising enough to investigate, but if led to bringing this guy down, he was grateful.

It didn't take long to get from the Clinestra building to the station, though every second made him feel as though he was simply going to burst at his seams. He'd felt anxiety before, obviously, but this felt as though he were also now trying to cage the wolf that now lived in him in the meager prison of his skin.

He needed to move, needed to do *something*, so he jogged the stairs up to the station doors. He would have jogged all the way to the Captain's door, but she was waiting for him already.

She looked about as tired and half dead as he did, her button up a little wrinkled and the heavy bags under her dark eyes hinting that she'd been pulled out of bed for this her-self. Her normally pinned back curly black hair was tied up in a messy bun that was struggling to contain its volume, and she'd opted for flats rather than her usual professional kitten heels. Despite this, she still had every inch the presence she normally carried, filling the room with her quiet confidence. As ever, seeing her made Richard feel a little better moored.

"Sorry to call you in on your time off Ransom, but I figured you'd want in on this one."

"Thank you, Captain. Today has been a shit show, I could use a win."

She smiled at him and clapped him on the shoulder, "That's the spirit Rich. Come on, let me give you the rundown on the way to my office."

"Right. Uh, where's Terry?" He said, glancing around for his partner.

"He didn't call you?"

"Er, he might have. I've been tied up trying to help a friend... get away from her shitty ex."

"Oh, sorry to hear that. He called in for at least the next week. Broke his ankle hiking."

Richard frowned, "Since when does Terry hike?"

The Captain closed the door to her office behind them, shrugging.

"I can't recall, but you know he'll do anything to spend time with a pretty girl. Ten bucks says he was "appreciating the view" instead of watching where he was going."

Despite the heavy weight in his chest, Richard managed a smile at that. He could imagine that perfectly.

"Yeah, sounds about right. I'll be sure to call him back tonight and give him hell about it."

"If this tip pans out, you'll be able to tell him you caught The Killer too."

Richard's attention shifted back to the spread of papers scattered over the Captain's desk.

"So what do we have?"

"An address. Tip came in fifteen minutes ago. Someone saw a boy matching Johnny Rizzoli's description being taken out of a car. Kid put up a fight so the neighbor called us."

A thrill of nervous hope surged through him. That was recent, knowing The Killer's MO the kid was definitely still alive.

"That's great. Do we have any uni's down there?"

"No, we don't want to spook him. A guy like this sees the cops and he'll kill the kid then go out shooting. That's why I called you actually."

Richard bit his lip, his expression pinching as he looked up at his Captain.

"I'm the most cop looking cop we have."

"You're also the only guy on call who's dealt with somethin' like this before."

He winced.

"Look, I'm not trying to poke you in a sore spot, Rich, but you're the best I've got right now. If I send one of these greenhorns in there that kid is as good as dead, and if we wait, there's no telling if he'll still be there."

She crossed her arms, concern balancing out the severity on her face.

"I know." Richard sighed, understanding all too well how delicate something like this could be.

"I'll have everyone on standby if things start to go south. Two blocks away, that's it." She promised, "Can you do it?"

With what was on the line, there was only one answer.

"I can do it."

*   *   *   *

The house was nondescript. Richard wouldn't have looked twice at its white paint and light blue trim. Despite the weeds in the front yard it was neither too run down nor too well kept. Perfectly ordinary and according to the very groggy realtor, supposedly, perfectly empty.

Richard crept beside the garage, his gun drawn and his focus honed in on the house.

This was his first time back in the field since he'd been bitten, and honestly he immediately wished he'd been turned years ago.

He could hear two small, quiet heartbeats. Not well enough to tell where they were, not yet, but well enough to know they were alive and not in danger at the moment. But also, there were two victims in there and not just one.

Richard crept all the way to the door on the side of the house, trying it only to find it locked. Naturally.

He knelt down, taking a measured breath as he took hold of the knob again. This would be difficult to do quietly, but he had little choice.

As slowly as he could, Richard pressed against the door, taking advantage of his unnatural strength to force the door open. It took a bit of a shove, but it worked with minimal noise to his relief.

Now able to enter the house, Richard swept inside the garage, gun first. He didn't bother with a flashlight since he could see just fine in the dark. All a flashlight would do was give The Killer a heads up if he was still around.

He quickly cleared the garage and crept into the back room adjoined to it. Once inside the house proper he paused to listen, trying to hone in on those two little heartbeats.

It almost sounded like they were.... below him.

He was fairly sure the houses in this area didn't have cellars, which most likely meant there was a crawl space instead. But where?

Richard crept into the next room, clearing it as well as he began looking for anywhere a crawl space would fit.

He cleared three bedrooms and a bathroom before he found what he was looking for.

In the closet of the main room, there was a door on the floor, uncovered and dust free.

As badly as Richard wanted to rush down it, he needed to clear the rest of the house first. He couldn't hear any other heartbeats, but as he'd learned recently, that didn't mean there wasn't someone there.

He didn't find anyone else.

Richard rushed back to the door, and threw it open.

The space wasn't very big, even for children. One would be alright, but two was pushing it. And there *were* two.

One boy, Johnny Rizzoli, took one look at him, the badge on his hip, and flung himself up into Richard's arms, sobbing.

"It's okay, son, I've got you. You're safe now, it's okay." Richard tried to sooth him, gently rubbing his back as he radioed back to his backup, "House is clear and I've got him. There's a second boy here too. Send an ambulance."

The second boy was in *much* worse shape, and an ambulance was the very least he needed.

He looked like he'd been kept here much longer than The Killer's usual victims, he was older than the average as well, looking closer to a young teen than a child, though he was so skinny and small it was hard to tell for sure. He was also fully naked and covered in bruises and scars alike. From the blank way he stared at Richard from beneath overgrown, matted hair, he looked to have disassociated entirely.

Richard moved closer, reaching out to him, as slowly as he could to keep from frightening him. His heart broke, filling back up with rage and disgust as rather than shrinking away or even taking his hand, the boy let his legs fall open and bore his throat in an obvious display of submission.

Bile rose up in his throat, and he tried to put aside his horror to get through to the boy instead. But before he could think of the words to try to do that with, Johnny whispered to him.

"He's here."

Richard hadn't noticed the sound of another heartbeat, too focused on the long haired boy. He barely had the time to set Johnny down, a snarl meeting his ears as what felt like a bat met his ribs.

"I should have known it would be you."

Richard reeled from both the pain of the blow to his side and the horrible familiarity of that voice.

Disbelieving, he stared up into the face of his own partner.

"Terry?" He gasped.

A blow rained down against the side of his head, and somewhere in the back of his mind, Richard registered that there was no bat, but rather despite his relatively small stature, Terry could hit hard enough to feel like one.

"Honestly I'm disappointed that it took you this long to figure it out. I mean all the convenient absences, the unexplained scratches and bite marks, 'TK'? How many more bread crumbs could I have **dropped?**"

Terry sent another bone crushing kick to Richard's ribs. He was dimly aware of one of the kids screaming.

"Shut up you little shit or the next one is yours!" Terry growled back at him.

Richard used the momentary distraction to kick Terry's legs out from under him.

The man crashed to the floor with a shout, leaving Richard free to leap onto him. Immediately they descended into a full scale fight, trading blows and grappling for the better position.

There were alarm bells going off in Richard's head, but he couldn't focus long enough to address them.

"Just! Fucking! Go! Down! You stubborn *bastard!*" Terry roared, grabbing Richard by the hair to slam his head into the wall, "Why are you so goddamn *difficult!*"

That. That was exactly what Richard was wondering. He was a werewolf, this should be *much* easier.

Right, he was a *werewolf.*

Richard snarled, pushing back with much more strength than he was used to using, launching Terry across the room. He got back to his feet, placing himself between Terry and the kids. By rights he shouldn't be getting up from that, but he'd seen adrenaline do much more with people.

The shape of Terry stirred but all that looked up at Richard from the darkened corner were a pair of glowing yellow eyes.

"Is that right?" Terry growled, his words harder to make out for it, "Well I'll be damned. So *you're* the poor son of a bitch Arney mauled. Small world, *pup."*

There wasn't the time to wonder on a damn word of that, not with Terry leaping back at him, now more wolf than man.

His teeth gnashed centimeters from Richard's neck, his claws looping around Richard's hands and sinking into them. He couldn't focus on the pain, only pushing him back to keep him away from the kids.

As strong as Richard was, Terry was still stronger, and Richard was losing ground quickly.

Crack!

For a moment, Richard was worried that noise came from him, but quickly identified it as a gunshot instead.

His back up.

He didn't know how he missed them rushing in and announcing themselves but he was also hyper focused on not dying, in his defense.

The gunshot wasn't enough to put Terry down. If anything it just made him angry, by the way his eyes lost focus and his growls grew louder. His teeth snapped closer to Richard's throat, longer and more deadly than they were seconds before.

"Ransom, get your ass out of my shot!" Called one of the other officers.

"Hostages, nnng, behind me." Richard gritted out, losing another inch as Terry bit into his shoulder, *"Fuck!"*

He could feel the burn of something in the wound, be it saliva or more of whatever it is that makes werewolves create other werewolves. Terry shook his head, tearing at the wound and Richard cried out again.

Deep in the pit of his stomach he knew that if he fell, Terry would take out everyone else in the room. There was no way they'd be able to stop him, not if bullets couldn't even make him pause. Richard had to find a way to take him down or everyone here was going to die.

He couldn't be responsible for that, not again.

Glancing around, Richard noticed there was only one light bulb in the room, just above his head. This would be a hail Mary if ever he'd seen one.

Praying to Saint Michael, the same way he always did when he was about to do something bat shit insane, Richard pushed himself up to knock his head against the bulb.

Three things happened. The first being the hunk of flesh that had been in Terry's mouth was ripped from him, which nearly made his knees give out. The second was a short electrical current going through the top of Richard's head as the light bulb burst. The third was the room going blissfully dark.

The humans among them wouldn't be able to see, though Richard and Terry had no such impairments.

Richard used the half second of confusion to grow out his claws, about the only part of his wolf he'd gotten a solid handle on, and sent an uppercut directly into Terry's side.

His claws tore through the flesh, puncturing a lung in the process.

Terry grunted and took a step back, which Richard followed up with a kick to his knees, felling the man.

Seconds later there were twelve flashlights on, and twelve guns trained on Terry, who was slumping down the wall, more man than wolf again, clutching his injured side.

"Killian...?" The Captain's voice whispered from the gloom.

Terry smiled maliciously, blood dripping from his lips. The hand that wasn't on over his wound raised into the air.

"You're... The Killer?"

"I was hoping for another ten years, but I should have known Richie would catch me sooner than later." He shrugged and winced, "How about that ambulance?"

Richard's jaw clenched as he stared him down, knowing full well, even in that state he could easily escape custody.

Terry gave him a look back that seemed to say "I won't pull anything in front of the humans". He didn't believe him for a *second.*

"Can I go with him? I'd like to talk. And I need a patch up too." Richard asked, not looking away from Terry for a moment.

Terry pouted at him, just as he would have if they were on a patrol together and Richard told him to wait for back up. The action was so jarring Richard felt sick to his stomach.

"Yeah. Yeah, keep an eye on him, please." The Captain said, eyeing the two as she walked over to the two captive boys.

"It looks like I've got some 'splainin' to do." Terry sighed.

*　　　　*　　　　*　　　　*

"Why did you do it?" Richard snarled the moment the ambulance doors closed.

Terry was staring up at the roof of the vehicle, looking almost in a daze. Richard could hardly stand to look at him.

"Is that *really* what you want to know, Rich?" His head slumped over to direct his empty gaze at Richard, "Out of *everything?*"

"It's where we're starting."

He rolled his eyes, shrugging, "It's not complicated, I just *really* like hurting people and kids are easier to control and keep track of. You get 'em young enough and they don't even *think* about running, especially after you--"

"*Enough.*"

Terry's smile made Richard feel like there were bugs crawling beneath his skin.

"I was just answerin' the question~"

"No, you're trying to get under my skin." Richard shot back. "I've known you for *fifteen years, Killian.* I know when you're bullshitting me. This wasn't some random, wild hair up your ass, so what drove you to this? And why did you never *talk to me?*"

Terry paused, his disgusting smile wobbling around the edges like a candle trying not to be put out by the first drops of rain. Instead of being doused, it folded itself into a sneer.

"What do you want to hear, Rich? About how poor little Terry grew up in a strict 'Yes Ma'am, No Sir, better not talk back or Daddy'll get the belt' household? About how my perfect and pious Preacher Papa found me kissing my best friend one day and shipped me off to "camp"? Or maybe how that "camp" whooped my ass bloody for weeks every time I even *looked* at another boy? Oooh, or maybe you're askin' 'bout them fancy electro-whatever machines they used to try to put my brain right?" Terry's disgust tinted darker and darker with each word, his accent slurring them until they ran right into each other in a rage filled haze, the same one that clouded over his eyes.

Richard wiped his hand across his mouth, barely noticing the blood he dragged along with it, "Jesus Terry, you--."

"Oh spare me," Terry practically hissed, "That little bit of pain weren't nothin' next to what I did to them boys. I don't need your goddamned sympathy."

"Sympathy?" Richard near spat the word, "I don't-- You've killed *half a dozen* kids, I don't *feel bad* for you because your childhood sucked! I'm pissed off that you decided the best way to deal with that was to kill and *sexually assault* God knows how many minors!"

"Sexua-- ah, that's right you found Jackson. In my defense, he's the only one I've touched like that. The rest just had to watch."

The casual way Terry spoke about something so *horrific* lost Richard's battle with nausea for him. He just managed to grab a hold of the trash can beside him to catch the bile that rose up his throat.

"I still can't believe you've made it this long on the force with a stomach like that."

Richard had half a mind to dump the contents right into his lap, but the thought of some poor EMT having to deal with that kept him from it.

"How long?"

"You're gonna have to be a bit more specific Richie."

The continued use of the familiarity had his teeth grinding, *"How long have you had him?"*

"You mean Jackie?" Terry appeared to recover his good humor at the mention of the boy, "Mmm, he's my favorite I've had, I've got to say. I've had him for…. six years this May? Be careful with that one, he's got a little bite behind that bark, if you know what I mean."

Richard nearly snapped his neck with how quickly his attention jerked back to Terry.

"Did you--"

"I *did.* Not on purpose, mind you, honest. I'm still surprised the little bastard survived it. Made him a *lot* more *durable* though."

Richard was sure he was going to be sick again, bile climbing back up his throat. His own transformation had been traumatic enough in the company of someone he was relatively sure was going to help him through it. He couldn't imagine suffering through it in the company of someone like The Killer…

*"You are a **monster.**"* Richard's expression folded in on itself, horror shaking his voice to the core of it.

Terry's expression didn't change a meter, he simply shrugged.

"I made peace with that years ago, brother."

*   *   *   *

Once Terry was sedated -which to the doctor's horror, it took far more sedative than they would normally administer- and off to surgery Richard paused in the lobby of the hospital to look at his phone.

He had several missed calls and a slew of text messages, which he'd been more or less expecting. He thumbed through all of them, his shoulders slumping as each one of them informed him that they'd found next to nothing.

Richard leaned his forehead against the wall, letting out a long, slow breath.

The sound of a gurney distracted him, the faint scent of another wolf nearby immediately perking up his senses.

He glanced around, finding the gurney going by him held the tiny, battered body of Jackson. He watched the nurses wheel him into the room across the hall from him, a million scattered thoughts bouncing off each other like fireworks as he tried to think through them all at once.

He turned and walked toward the nurse's station.

"Excuse me," He greeted the nurse, "I was the officer who found the young boys that were just admitted."

She sat up a little straighter, her expression taking on a deeper seriousness.

"You won't be able to speak with him for quite a while. We ended up having to sedate him...for his own safety." She swallowed hard, her expression darkening.

Richard wasn't entirely surprised to hear that, but it still hurt a bit to know he couldn't recognize that he was safe now.

"If I leave you my phone number, could you call me when he wakes up? I have another case I need to follow a lead on, but I want to make sure the kid sees a friendly face, you know?"

His words seemed to soften her a bit, she took the card he handed to her without protest.

"That boy is lucky to have you watching out for him, officer."

The words made his chest feel warmer, though he didn't feel worthy of them necessarily. He didn't reply verbally, but she seemed to understand his expression well enough.

Richard tapped her counter, and headed toward the exit.

As horrible as this entire incident had been, it did give him an idea.

It wasn't hard finding his way back to Charlotte. The moment he got to the edge of the forest Xinghua had taken them to the last time, it was as though he could just...sense her.

He made it to the cave fort with no other guidance than that, faster than they'd gone the first time.

He shifted back into his human form away from the cave to avoid giving anyone an eyeful. He changed into the spare clothes he'd started keeping in a backpack he made sure he had with him.

When he rounded the corner to the mouth of the cave, Charlotte was already there waiting for him, her expression welcoming but concerned.

"Welcome back, Detective! You... smell like a wolf fight, is everything okay?"

He thought for a moment, before deciding that Charlotte absolutely knew more about this world than he did. Telling her about this would be nothing like telling a civie.

"No." He said with a heavy sigh, "No it's not. Tonight I had to arrest a werewolf for a serial string of kidnapped and murdered young boys."

Charlotte's hands flew to her mouth and her eyebrows creased together.

"That's *horrible.*"

To Ransom's surprise, Charlotte almost immediately came over to hug him. She was tiny, could only really reach his waist and her arms weren't long enough to encircle it, but he felt a rush of warmth hit him anyway.

Comfort.

"I feel like a fucking moron." He mumbled, letting himself hug her back, "I should have *known,* I should have--"

"Uh uh uh, none of that. We don't self-blame in this house." She pulled back only to lean onto her tiptoes and tap him on the nose.

He wrinkled his nose, pulling away from her with a startled blink.

"Did you just--"

"It's effective, I need you to pay attention to me."

He frowned but he focused his attention back down to her.

She put her hands on her hips, her brows furrowing down over her bright green eyes.

"You're going to live for a very long time, Ransom. Longer than you can imagine right now, I promise. And from what I've seen from you, just so far, you're probably going to keep helping people in whatever way you can. Which means, you *cannot* take on the weight of every sin committed around you, just because you happened to be there. It's not really feasible for a *human* to do either, but they'll eventually die and get to rest one way or the other. Without that luxury, you're gonna have to learn how to forgive yourself instead, or you won't make it very far in this life without losing your shit."

Richard wasn't entirely surprised by her speech, he'd been told more or less the same thing by several people over the years. He *knew* he should work on it, but he'd never thought of it as a *necessity.* Why did it matter if he took on those feelings? There wasn't anyone around to mind if he couldn't crawl out from under the weight of them, and he did his job just as effectively as he ever did. It never seemed to *matter.*

But looking down into those wide green eyes, recalling the equally concerned white ones in his memory.... Maybe it did matter, even if not to him.

Though, that brought to mind a much more important conversation.

"Thank you, I'll....work on that. In the future. But, uh, I actually came here for more than emotional support."

"Oh?" She perked back up, her eyes brightening again, "What's up?"

"Two things, actually." He started, "We got two of the kids back, but one of them was turned."

Charlotte looked like she wanted to say more, *far more,* but she held herself back.

"Right, okay, well ideally we'd love to take him in, but I'm guessing he's in no shape to be going anywhere."

"Physically, he's doing pretty bad, and emotionally I can't imagine he's going to be anywhere near alright for quite a while."

She nodded, swallowing hard, "That makes sense. I'll send one of the girls to keep an eye on the hospital if you'll tell me which one he's at."

"Thanks Lottie." He smiled a little at her. That was far more than he'd expected, and honestly it made him glad he'd come to her.

"Thank *you* Rich. But what was the second thing?"

"You remember my vampire friend, right?"

"Xinghua?"

"Yeah. She's in trouble, and given what I know about the man who has her, I think I'm going to need back up." He bit his lip, "I know that's a lot to ask back to back but--"

"Hold up, *has her?* Was she *kidnapped?*"

"Yes." Richard snarled the word more than said it.

"Jesus Christ! Did all this happen on the *same day?* No-- don't answer that you can tell me the story while we start a search party." She lifted her hand to her mouth and used it to whistle the loudest New York cab whistle he was sure he'd ever heard.

Richard heard footsteps head toward them, half a dozen or so barreling toward them at high speed.

"Start your sniffers boys, we've got a friend to find!"

When Xinghua came to, the first thing that occurred to her was the cold.

For a moment she was back in the forest, terror choking her even as her body failed to respond to it properly. Her heart didn't speed up, she was frozen, it *couldn't,* she was going to die all by herself out here, she was going--

"Psst." Came a soft whisper, "Are you awake?"

Xinghua blinked her eyes open, finding the task to be much harder than it should have been. She felt like she'd been on a two week long bender.

"Unng, y-yeah. Wha--" She nearly choked on her tongue, her mouth too dry and her head too hazy to make sense of words, " 'S goin'on?"

"We were moved. I don't know where. I didn't come to until about ten minutes ago." The unfamiliar voice scoffed,

"He still doesn't really get how to adjust the sedative for the mutations."

Xinghua squinted into the gloom in front of her. Normally her night vision was almost perfect, but everything was blurry around the edges like a smudged charcoal drawing.

She could just make out the dark form of a man, she was pretty sure. He was hanging from the ceiling by his hands, the same way that she could feel she was, his head slumped to the side. He looked vaguely familiar but her head was too stuffed full of cotton to be able to suss out why.

"Looks like you're still pretty well dosed up." He swore, his head tilting to let his eyes peek out from behind his long braids, "Can you tell me your name?"

"Shhhhhii…" She frowned as her lips refused to cooperate. *Could* she?

She tried again, "Shiiingwhaaa."

Close enough.

"Xinghua?" He repeated, much better than she herself had done, "As in Li Xinghua?"

"Mmmhmm." She nodded, "S'me."

He made a noise that Xinghua couldn't put an emotion to, then took a deep breath.

"Right. That's-- uh, thank you, I'm Seriah. It's okay, Xinghua, I'm going to try to get us out, but you've got to do something for me, okay?"

Xinghua had no idea what she could possibly do right now. She could barely feel her body, and what she could feel was cold and limp and heavy.

"Wha?" She asked anyway.

"I need you to freeze my chains."

Xinghua was well aware that her head was not at full capacity at the moment but she was pretty sure she hadn't heard him right.

"Huh?" She asked intelligently.

"Your tag. It says 'Ice' so if you can, I need you to freeze my chains."

None of that computed. Xinghua cast her gaze clumsy around until she found the tag the man, Seriah, was talking about. It was attached to her toe, and for a moment she could only wonder when she'd lost her shoes. But upon squinting at it, the tag did in fact say 'Ice'.

Her confusion must have shown on her face because Seriah began to explain.

"The others all have tags, and they all say things like that so I was figuring vampires plus labels equals powers."

Xinghua let that rattle around her head for a full minute before she could figure out where to start asking questions.

"Oth'rss?"

He frowned at her for the first time, "Look beside you."

She did.

To her great surprise there was another body there, hung like a piece of meat. Although the word 'body' was generous to use to describe the dried up looking husk that was hung beside her. With the lack of hair and the sunken in skin, it looked more like a mummy than a person. Had she been in her right mind she would have screamed. As it was she whimpered, causing the poor, apparently very much *alive* vampire to crack open their light lilac eyes and look at her.

They made eye contact before they shut their eyes again, looking once more like just a hanging corpse.

The fear was enough to sober her for a moment.

"Dunno know how to use my power, didn't even know I had it until a couple days ago." She rattled off anxiously, "'M sorry."

Seriah shook his head, "That's okay. I don't really know how to use mine either."

"You have powers?" The 's' in powers slurred a little as the drug slammed back into her.

"One. Kind of. I've only managed to do it once and it hurts like hell." He shuddered, "But if it's 'agonizing pain' or 'Tom's guinea pig for eternity' I know the choice I'm making."

She blinked one eye at a time as she tried to hold onto the thought sparking somewhere at the back of her head. There was something in there that needed talking about but the words were slipping right out of reach.

"Right, okay, totally going to live up to saying something that badass." He said under his breath, seeming to steel himself, "I'm sorry if I scream."

Xinghua tried to focus on replying to that, something about 'sorry' and something about pain but she dropped the words in short order once Seriah started screaming.

At first she couldn't tell why, he was hard to see in the dark given that he appeared to be dark skinned and her eyes just *couldn't* right now. But after a few seconds of looking him over, she noticed black fur where there should have been skin.

How many werewolves was she going to meet this week?

The thought made some other half-thought niggle at the back of her mind, but she wasn't fast enough to catch it.

Seriah continued to transform and scream until there was an entirely different shape in front of her. Though if she were honest, he didn't really look that much like a wolf. With his short muzzle and giant, *giant*, head, his rounded ears and short, sleek fur, he looked more like a really big cat.

She watched, distantly as the maybe-wolf maybe-cat version of Seriah tugged the chains that were securing him. They'd been built to hold a vampire, though so he didn't make much headway.

Rather than giving up, however, he started straining harder, giving his all to the cause.

The ceiling groaned.

Xinghua was surprised by that, and Seriah only seemed encouraged, yanking and twisting with his entire body.

The cuffs didn't break, but they did bend, which seemed like exactly the opening Seriah's leonine body needed. His muscles bunched, decreasing the size of his wrists as he slipped out of the cuffs like a house cat. When he landed on the ground, Xinghua noticed with muted surprise that he was, in fact, a very large black cat. A panther? Since when were were-panthers a thing?

Seriah's head whipped around, as if scanning for traps but when no blaring red lights went off and no alarms sounded he seemed to relax a bit. With a few dozen more horrifying snaps and pops that seemed to take much longer to end than they did the first time, he shifted back into his human form.

It took him a few more moments of panting and shuddering before he could pull himself to his feet and work on freeing Xinghua, but she found she didn't mind the wait. Time felt like liquid and she couldn't make any real sense of it at all.

She lost sight of him standing up, didn't recall he'd done it until she felt herself being lifted.

He laid her across the ground, swift hands working to disconnect the tubes and remove the needles from her arms. Her head didn't clear up immediately, but she didn't feel any worse so that was a boon.

She noticed his hands trembling.

"You...'kay?"

He glanced up at her like he was surprised to hear her voice, "Yeah, I'm fine. Just shifting that fast back to back like that is...not great."

"You a....a, uh, were-whate'er?"

A dark look came over his face.

"No. At least... I don't think so. I don't really know *what* I am now."

Seriah gave her another once over before helping push her into a sitting position, hauling her arm over his shoulders to do so. Her fingers brushed against something downy soft.

Blearily she squinted at him through the darkness, only just now noticing the silhouette of two large black wings folded up against his back. Her muzzy head whirled with questions but the only one she could manage felt like the most important.

"Di-diiiid.... Tommmm..." She gestured vaguely to him, "Do th's?"

His jaw clenched and he nodded, his stare locked on the floor.

She felt her stomach roll.

"Yous...yourss nname? Ser-i-ah? Not...ung, not on vac-c-caaation?"

"He's been telling people I-- of *course* he has." He grunted, getting them both up to their feet, "Yeah that's me."

Xinghua glanced at the wings anchored to his back and bobbed her head in a nod that she was sure looked more narcoleptic than not.

"Leeeeeave firs' thnnn, story timmmme."

Seriah gave a weary smile.

"Right, one thing at a time, yes." He nodded, glancing around only to frown, "Please tell me you can see in the dark."

"Yep." She squinted, "C'n't see s'good righ' now, buuuut."

She looked out into the warehouse, looking for anything that might be useful to getting out, or at the very least learning where they were. Things were still blurry, and if she glanced around too quickly the room still spun, but she did her best to ignore that.

There wasn't much, mostly just wooden crates, but she did notice a door on the far side of the room.

"Thatta way." She broadly gestured in the direction of the door, knocking Seriah in the face in the process, "Oop."

His feathers ruffled as he scooped her up into his arms.

She *really* wanted to ask if those worked.

"Not sure. I've never gotten the chance to try to use them." He glanced apprehensively at his back, "I have no idea how to fly."

Well apparently she'd just gone on ahead and asked without her own consent. What the *hell* had Tom dosed her with?

"Un'erstan'able," She blurbed, the word rattling out of her mouth like an old truck down a gravel drive.

When they reached the door, she wiggled until he set her down. She was still wobbly as the short leg on an old table, but she stubbornly stayed standing. She'd been blackout drunk *more* than enough times to know how to make her body work through a complete lack of balance and functionality.

She let herself lean forward into the door, throwing her weight against it so she was holding herself up with her forehead and shoulder.

The surface, unsurprisingly, was made of metal.

If she knew Tom, and she was positive she at *least* understood how paranoid he could be, it would be strong enough that it would take a vampire hours to tear it apart. Her cheek smooshed against the door as she tried pressing her finger against it with all the strength she could muster.

It was hardly enough to dent it.

"Naaaaaht that." She groaned and pushed herself back away from the door, flailing her arms to keep her balance, "'S gon'be'a *thingy.*"

"A thingy?"

She gestured out into the wider warehouse area, rambling about the door as she tried to find her way to the words she was actually looking for.

He stared at her, lip and brow furrowed in synchronized confusion, the barest hint of light reflecting off his cat-like eyes. It took her a long moment to realize whatever she'd just said, she'd said in Cantonese and he decidedly did not speak Cantonese at all.

"The openey-closey doory thingy."

"Oh! You mean the electric locking system?"

"Tha's the bitch!"

"Why the hell didn't I think of that?" He shook his head as he glanced around, trying to spot it.

"Not 'nough drrrrrrrggggsssss."

Seriah was gone before she could finish her sentence, faster than her addled eyes could track. Xinghua wondered if this was what it was like for humans to deal with the supernatural world.

The concern slipped out of her mind quickly and she turned her attention instead to scanning the room for a control room or a panel or something she could break to open that door.

The warehouse was enormous, and eerily silent. As far as Xinghua could see, there were no extra rooms, though it was hard to see through the veritable *forest* of bodies hanging from the ceiling. Xinghua shuddered at the thought of how close she'd come to being just another one of them.

"Xinghua!" Seriah called out, "I think I found something."

He jogged back over to her from the corner, scooping her back up with little warning.

"You're *buuuuuuuffffffff.*" She tried to smile, though it didn't feel like the expression succeeded.

He squinted down at her as they reached the far back wall.

"Uh, thanks... There's this big silver box right next to the door that I'm pretty sure is the control panel. I took a semester of an engineering class in college and I was an apprentice electrician before I got this job. I'm *reasonably* sure I can do something with that. I just need to get into it."

She pulled back her hand and smashed it right through the panel.

It brought her no small satisfaction to rip the wiring from the wall, tossing the handful of mechanical guts onto the floor.

"I guess that works too." Seriah muttered.

"Fasser." Xinghua's arm tingled, falling limp at her side, "Like brrreakin' hizzzz st'ff. Mmmmmakes m'h feel allllllllll warm'n'f'zzzzy 'nside."

Seriah's eyebrows were twitching like they couldn't quite bear to choose between making him look concerned or amused.

"Okey-dokey then, checks out."

She grinned back at him, the smile widening as she heard the electrical current cut off.

"Cliiiiick clic, got it!" She attempted to snap her fingers, managing nothing of the sort.

"Right. Now we've just got to open it manually. Cause that shouldn't be impossible or anything…"

"Ya got sssssssuper stren't?"

"Super strength? Uh, shit, I don't know." Seriah shook his head, "I don't *think* so, but I also have literally no idea."

"Pumme down."

"You're not gonna try to lift that on your own are you?"

"Imma biggurl." She assured him.

"You're *drugged as hell.*"

"Psssshhh, jus' means 'm gonna break the door. 'S fiiiiiine" She wiggled again until he set her down.

She held her arms out wide, making sure she didn't tip over or wobble. She did pretty well, she thought.

"For the record, this is a terrible idea." Seriah muttered, "I'm not a medic, if you crush yourself, I absolutely *cannot* help you."

"Shhhhssshhhshshshshshhshsshssssshhhhhhhhh." She held her finger up to her mouth, "No bad vibes."

Seriah held up his hands, though his expression didn't look in the least convinced.

Xinghua took a step toward the door, surprisingly stable for how many multiples of her foot she was seeing. She took another, though she overdid this one a bit, making her stride look a lot more giraffe-like than she intended. Didn't matter, the next one got her to the door.

Xinghua let herself crumple to her knees beside the door, which would have felt like defeat if the ground weren't so re-assuring. And also, if it weren't where she was intending to go, of course.

Seriah took a step toward her, like he was going to help her up, but she waved away his outstretched hand.

"Waaaaaai', wai', wai'." She all but demanded.

She scooted closer to the door and began inching her toes underneath the weather stripping of the door. It was already heavy on top of her feet and she was very very glad she'd chosen to do this with her legs instead of her arms.

"Gonna push'it'up, 'n yoooooooou're gonna rrrrroll. Got it?"

"Uh..."

"Good!"

Xinghua put every ounce of strength she could summon into pushing her legs upward. To her immense relief, the door did in fact lift up. But to her immense anguish, she felt like she was doing the world's most intense leg lift and she'd been skipping leg day for years. And because she couldn't seem to suffer in *one* dimension these days, it was also daylight.

"Gogogogogogogogogo!" She hissed, continuing to push the door until it was just high enough to let Seriah army crawl through the opening.

Thankfully, he didn't hesitate to do so.

Xinghua breathed through her teeth, trembling as her body fought against the leftover drugs in her system to be able to accomplish this frankly *cruel* task she'd asked of herself. The sun was turning her legs into boiling sacks of cottage cheese and it *hurt*. She wanted to shut her eyes to block all of that out, but she wouldn't be able to make sure Seriah made it if she did that.

Instead she just started listing off every swear word she could think of in every language she knew them in.

"I'm through!"

The relief nearly made her drop the damn thing.

"How are you go--?"

"SSSSHHHHSSHhHSHHS!" She hissed again, her focus wobbling with every word.

Seriah, bless him, shut right up.

She swallowed hard. This would be hard under *normal* circumstances given how heavy the damn door was, and the shit angle she had it at. But all that, plus how fucked her motor skills were at the moment? There was every chance she was losing an arm to this thing today. But like Seriah had said earlier, if the choice was between agonizing pain and being Tom's plaything, she knew what choice she'd be making.

Just as Xinghua was preparing to put as much force as she could into kicking the door upward, the weight of it on her legs lessened.

"Xinghua!"

Her attention snapped to her left where the all too familiar voice was.

"Ransom!"

He was holding the door from the bottom, his own teeth gritted as he and another person who rushed up to help began to hoist the thing up and off of her. She was pretty sure she'd never been so grateful to see him in her entire life, and she'd been *exceedingly* grateful to him all week.

"Move!" He growled.

Oh, right.

She rolled out from under the door, all limbs intact. Boiling and rapidly becoming indistinguishable from each other, but intact.

The door slammed shut behind her and within seconds, despite her dizziness, she was throwing herself into Ransom's chest. He wasn't prepared, at all, and she hit with enough force to stagger him, but she couldn't be bothered to mind. Someone threw a jacket over them, which she was thankful for.

"Are you hurt anywhere?" Ransom's big hands took her head between their palms, tilting it this way and that as he examined her, looking into her eyes critically, "Were you drugged?"

"Drugged? Ooooh yeah. Ther's liiiiiike...four? O' you? Also the sun."

Ransom glanced down at one of her swollen arms and winced.

"Uh, *who are you?*"

Xinghua had all but forgotten about Seriah, too caught up in the relief of seeing Ransom. She'd also managed to ignore all of the other people that had appeared around them.

"Th'ss Ransom! He'sa good boy! Ransommmm, th'ss Ser-i-ah."

Ransom looked a little pinker around the gills than usual, but held out his hand to Seriah.

"Detective Richard Ransom," He introduced himself, "Were you also taken hostage by Airius?"

"Seriah Nix, and yeah. That's a good place to start." Seriah glanced around at the rest of the group, "Are *all* of you cops?"

"Nope!" A jovial redhead peeked out from behind Ransom, smiling when Xinghua met her eyes, "We're his pack."

"Lottie!" Xinghua cheered, wiggling out of Ransom's lap to tumble gracelessly into the woman's arms, "You c'me ta save us toooo?"

Xinghua all but melted at the warm hands in her hair, "Of course I did. You're practically pack too, baby girl."

"I've got...just so many questions, but we should really get out of here. We kind of broke the door to break out of there, and who knows what kind of security Tom has hooked up to this place."

"Right." Ransom grunted, glancing around as if to make sure they weren't being surrounded, "We need to regroup with the rest of ours too. Do you have somewhere safe to go?"

"Uh...."

"I'm sure no one will mind you joining us."

"Normally I'm not a big group person, but right now I cannot think of anywhere I would like to be more than a highly populated room."

"Ya know. Yoooouuuuuu guys do tha'. 'M gonna go'a *schleep.*" Xinghua interrupted, and promptly did just that.

"This moss is good for binding wounds, meaning if someone is bleeding a lot from an open wound you can use this to pack into the wound to help stop the bleeding. It will help reduce the fever as well so the quicker you can apply it, the better." Fletcher explained, his hand brushing over the plant he'd been telling Xinghua about for the better part of twenty minutes now.

"But isn't it...bad? To just have plant stuff hanging out in an open wound like that?" She wrinkled her nose at the thought.

"It is! That's why you turn the plant into a salve first if you can. But if you're desperate, the raw form works too, you just have to be careful to keep the wound clean too."

"Humans are so delicate." She pouted up her nose.

"You're still mostly human yourself Xinghua," He tapped the tip of her nose gently, "You may be becoming a vampire, but you shouldn't work so hard to put distance between yourself and humans."

"Why not? They suck." She quipped a brow, daring Fletcher to argue her bold stance.

"Some do, though the same could be said of vampires." He shoved at her lightly when she started to laugh at the unintentional joke, "But here's something I've noticed about the vampires that suck. They let themselves forget what it's like to be other than they are. They remove themselves from the world and act as though that makes them better, when all it really does is make them lonely."

She folded her arms over her chest, "I won't get lonely, I've got you."

He smiled, "You do, forever. But I'm very old, someday talking to me is going to feel like trying to talk to your grandfather. Do you want to get stuck with just boring old me forever?"

She slumped over, hugging onto his arm as she aimed her big, kitten-like eyes up at him, "Yes."

He rolled his eyes even though he was smiling. She was sure he would have continued to lightheartedly argue with her if not for the call of his name that pierced through the air.

He was alert in less than a millisecond, that had been Tom's voice.

"You stay here, **Xiǎo biānfú .**" He slid his arm out of her gasp and threw himself to his feet, "I'll be back."

She nodded, though she knew she had little intention of staying put.

He flashed a smile down at her, ruffling his hand through her hair, then he peeled out of the room, headed toward the sound of Tom's cries.

Xinghua gave it a good ten count before she slipped out of the garden and after him.

By now she'd recovered more than enough to get around on her own. Actually, if anything she had an easier time than before. She took longer to run out of breath, she almost never tripped over her feet, and she actually knew where the hell she was going in the forest now. She'd gone on plenty of hunting trips with Fletcher, and he'd been meticulous about making sure she didn't get lost again. As scared as she'd been the first time, she appreciated it now.

Though she hardly needed the expertise, she could hear the brothers shouting just fine.

What she didn't recognize were the snarling noises ripping through the air between shouts. Though she wasn't kept in suspense for long.

Xinghua saw it before she saw Tom or Fletcher.

A giant, silver beast with claws like filet knives and enormous white shovel sized teeth gleaming in the moonlight. It looked like a dog, though she knew no dog could possibly be that colossal. She froze in shock as the scent of blood met her nose.

"Duck!" Fletcher's voice shouted, a spire of ice erupting from the ground after his cry.

The ice tore through the giant creature, sending it reeling back with a noise that sounded far too similar to a hurt dog for Xinghua's comfort. Tom grunted, drawing her attention to him.

Which meant she saw what Fletcher didn't.

"Thank you, brother." Tom smiled, stabbing a needle into Fletcher's side, pressing the plunger into him.

"Augh! What was...wha...?"

Fletcher collapsed to his hands and knees, though he immediately tried to push himself back up to his feet. He glanced nervously between Tom and the giant creature, which to Xinghua's confusion melted away like so much snow.

"It's much easier if you don't fight it. You can't really, it's dead man's blood." Tom said mildly, as if he were talking about the weather, "In a couple minutes you're going to be unconscious regardless of if you choose to struggle or not."

"Wh-wh-why...?"

"Well, recently I've found out I can do something **quite** unique." Tom said blithely, "When I ingest the blood of another vampire, I can borrow their abilities for a time. So I've elected to start a collection for myself. And you, my dearest brother, are to be the first in it. It's only fitting."

Fletcher continued to try to crawl away but he wasn't making much progress, and Xinghua couldn't watch any longer. She refused to stand by a second time as someone she loved was hurt.

"GET AWAY FROM HIM!" She shouted, running to put herself between Tom and Fletcher.

She held her arms out defensively, locking her knees as they started to tremble. Her heartbeat was racing as much as it could and she felt sick to her stomach, but she growled at Tom anyway.

"Ah yes, what **lovely** timing you have."

"Xing...hua... ru...n." Fletcher croaked.

"No, I'm not letting him hurt you!" She shook her head.

Neither got a chance to argue as Tom snatched her up into his arms in the next instant.

To her credit, she struggled with everything she had. She bit, she kicked, she scratched and growled like a feral cat. Unfortunately Tom hardly seemed bothered at all, he only tightened his grip.

"Shhh, shhh, shhh, it's just me, Xinghua." He said in a soothing tone she knew he didn't come by naturally, "It's alright, it's just me."

"LET ME GO!! FLETCHER! FLETCHER HELP!"

She glanced down at him, only to find him unconscious, his hand outstretched toward them.

"Don't worry, little one. I'll make sure you don't remember any of this, I promise."

She whipped her head toward him, but that had been what he was waiting for. His free hand caught her by the chin, forcing her to look him in the eyes. Once they made contact she couldn't look away. How come she'd never noticed how beautiful his eyes were...?

"That's it," His voice intoned hypnotically, "Let me in."

She felt each of her muscles relax without her permission, though she couldn't really recall why she'd wanted to be tense in the first place. Her head felt full, and fuzzy and hollow all at once. She felt herself slump into Tom's palm.

"That's my sweet girl."

Something about that felt odd for a moment, just a moment before she figured it must be the good kind of odd that came with butterflies in her belly. After all, she was in Tom's arms, she knew he'd never let anything bad happen to her.

*   *   *   *

Xinghua sat slumped across Frost's bar, trying not to pick at the bandaging on her arms. They'd scraped her sun-cysts, which was an experience she would gladly never repeat, and now with the excess tissue gone they'd begun to heal. They itched, she couldn't scratch them, and everything sucked.

She couldn't stop replaying that last dream in her head.

She hadn't been looking for that piece of her history back, but now that she had it, she felt complete again. Depressed as fuck, and violated as all hell? For sure. Enraged and disgusted? Also a yes. But at least now she had the full story. Or, as much of it as she'd been personally around for. She hadn't seen what happened to Fletcher after that, but she had a terrible suspicion she now knew the answer.

She despondently watched Ransom bid his pack goodbye at the door. Evidently she'd missed more than she thought as they talked about something important sounding in hushed voices. She couldn't make her brain wrap itself around what they were talking about, and frankly it hurt to try.

"Here." Frost's voice captured her attention as a warm mug was pressed into her hands, "The girls are off for the morning, but lucky for *you* I had a blood pack left."

Xinghua lifted her head off of her arms and stared at the mug for a moment before her thoughts aligned with the appealing smell coming from it. She grabbed it with fumbling fingers and drained it down faster than she could remember having done since she was a newborn.

Frost dropped himself down onto the seat next to her, petting her hair gently and rhythmically as the un-life began to creep back into her.

"Uuuuunnnnggghhh." She groaned, "Thanks Lee."

"Mmmhmm. It's been quite a long time since I've seen someone *actually* get dosed with dead man's blood. It's old fashioned, but I'm not surprised Thomas knows the trick." He said, "It'll take a couple hours to finish working itself out of your system, but you ought to start feeling better soon."

She nodded, wanting to mention her memory-dream, but dreading the idea of actually putting it all into words.

Though Seriah beat her to the punch.

"Dead man's blood did all that?"

"*Hello*, I don't think I caught your name in all the commotion." Frost turned his best smile on him, "I'm Leeland McKnight, but you may call me Frost if you'd like."

"Uh, thanks, Mr. Frost. I'm Seriah Nix. Sorry, for the inquisition, occupational hazard."

Xinghua let herself lean into Frost, deciding her mini revelation could wait until the talk they were doubtlessly going to have to have. She still felt achy and tired anyhow, she could use the comfort.

"Mister? Oh that's too *cute!*" Frost smiled wider, his broad palm rubbing Xinghua's back soothingly, "But in answer to your question, yes, it very much did. Blood taken from a host who was already dead when it was harvested doesn't have the nutrients that our bodies require and it very quickly gums up our systems. It's not dissimilar to heroin, truth be told. Though prolonged dosing won't *kill* us, I've seen it wreck a vampire or two in my time."

Ransom joined the group once again, having finished whatever chat he and Charlotte were having. He sat himself down on Xinghua's other side and the girl found herself relaxing that little bit more.

"Where are the other two?" Ransom asked with a head tilt.

"Trish I sent to bed, poor thing stayed up all night and she was running on fumes. Ziggy needed to refuel as well, though I believe they're currently on the other side of The Veil doing so. Neither would go until we'd had word that Xinghua was recovered however. You've got good friends, Xi-xi."

Xinghua wanted to cry a little at that, and resolved to tell them as much when she saw them next. Or, she could do the millennial thing and send them a damn text message to let them know how she was too.

Shit, did she even still have her phone?

To her surprise, when she reached into her pocket, her phone was right there along with what felt like a neatly folded bill.

She pulled both from her pocket, finding a crisp hundred dollar bill that she knew she hadn't had on her earlier. Her hand trembled as she stared at it for a moment before pressing the button to wake up her phone.

It was fully charged. She had one message.

She tapped it, her heart in her throat as she read.

'I've never liked to punish you, Xinghua. I hope you've learned your lesson. This ought to be plenty to cover bus fare should you need it.'

Xinghua nearly threw her phone, disgust roiling through her stomach with fear chasing after it like ouroboros swallowing its own tail.

"What's wrong?" Frost asked, glancing over her shoulder.

"I'm going to kill him." She whispered, the lump in her throat not allowing for any more volume.

She crushed the bill in her hand, tears gathering at the edges of her vision.

"I'm going to peel his skin from his body with my fucking teeth."

Frost read the message and she felt him go tense beneath her. She handed her phone to Ransom next, more to keep herself from crushing it than anything.

"I'm afraid we may have a bit of a queue, Xinghua." Frost gave her a squeeze.

"He's trying to bait you into doing something impulsive." Ransom said, though the words came from between his teeth.

"Yeah." She muttered, because anything else felt like it would lead to doing exactly that.

"Which you know better than to rise to, right?"

She glanced over to the officer and their eyes met. She could see the genuine concern there, and it soothed some of the ache in her chest. She nodded.

"Yeah." She let herself unfurl from around Frost a little, "Actually. I kind of had an idea."

"What kind of idea..?" Ransom narrowed his eyes a little.

She smiled, "The good kind. Now that my head isn't filled with Tom's bimbo juice, it's a lot easier to do that. Feel like I should reintroduce myself since this's gotta be the first time you've met *me*. Later though, plan first."

"What is this plan of yours, darling?"

"So you're investigating Tom for murder, right Rich?"

"Yes..."

"And murdering donors is still illegal within covens too, right Lee?"

"It is." Frost replied with interest.

"Well you've got a star witness who's very *very* willing to testify about how many people he's killed." She smiled, "I'd say it's time to pay a visit to the council."

"Oooooh." Frost grinned back at her, "I *like* this version of you, that's a *very* good idea. I've been keeping them up to date as much as possible of goings-on, but I haven't had a chance to give them the latest update."

"Uh, not to keep being *that guy,* but I'm lost again. I'm guessing y'all don't mean the city council do you?" Seriah cut in, reminding Xinghua he was there.

"I was just about to ask." Ransom agreed.

"Vampire government, or what passes for it, we're not terribly strict about many things." Frost explained, "The Council is a group of five of the eldest vampires in a particular area. Think about a couple counties worth of land. Even those who do not belong to a coven still fall within our jurisdiction to oversee, and Thomas has been skirting around us for *years*. I've known he was up to *something* and yet until recently I've not had enough proof to make a move."

"I know that feeling exactly." Ransom patted Frost's shoulder in a surprising show of comradery.

"Yes, well, with Xinghua willing to testify, that changes quite a lot for us," Frost leaned into Ransom's touch, as though he too needed the comfort, "There are at least two others on the council who are eager to see Thomas get his comeuppance. With their sanction, we should be able to take him into custody fairly easily."

"Normally I would insist on the proper legal channels, but I can't imagine a human jail being able to hold a vampire. Even if it could, that would lead to a lot of questions we're not going to be able to answer." Ransom sighed, "Trying to figure out what to do with Terry has been enough of a pain."

"With who?" Xinghua asked.

"I'll tell you later."

"Oh you've got plenty of time. It's 9am, we're not going anywhere until sundown, I don't really feel like giving Xinghua's sunbathing experience an encore." Frost cut in, "After this whole adventure, I know I could use my beauty sleep. Seriah, you're welcome to stay in any of the empty rooms in the back, help yourself to any food you might find, or order something. The bar has an ongoing tab with most of the restaurants around this area. Drop my name and they'll take care of you."

Frost gently slid Xinghua from his lap onto Ransom's instead and stood to stretch. Xinghua didn't hesitate to snuggle up to Ransom, who, despite seeming surprised, held her close without hesitation.

"Same goes for you, Mr. Ransom." Frost said with a wink and a smile, turning to head to the back rooms himself, "Good morning everyone!"

Frost sauntered away, taking most of the energy in the room with him.

"I cannot tell if that man is hitting on me or not." Ransom grumbled.

"Oh he is." Xinghua let her eyes close, smiling a little at how tense Ransom got, "Don't get your panties in a twist, he doesn't mean anything by it. That's just how he is."

"Right."

"You know, I *actually* haven't eaten anything in like…. I think three months? I'm taking him up on that offer." Seriah got to his feet, immediately locking onto the takeout menus stuffed behind the bar, "Thai sound good to anyone else?"

*   *   *   *

"Okay, it's officially later." Xinghua said from her cross legged position beside Ransom. "What's the tea on this Terry dude? You were making the kicked puppy face."

"I don't have one of those."

"Yeah, okay." She leveled a look at him over the mouthful of noodles she was preparing to slurp down.

"I've only known you for a couple hours, but you definitely do." Seriah chimed in.

Seriah had gotten relatively comfortable, having changed into a loose t-shirt and night pants he'd found in one of the spare rooms. He'd swept his braids up into a bun when he'd started eating, and with it out of the way Xinghua had caught a glimpse of his eyes, which to her surprise were a deep, rich blue.

Now that she wasn't high as a kite, Xinghua realized she'd missed so much about the man the first time she'd seen him. The wings being the largest oversight. Sure, she'd *seen* them, but they'd seemed more like smudges of shadow than the moving, *living* things they were. They rose when he breathed, they ruffled when they touched the bar or the floor, and he had to adjust their positioning pretty regularly, just like with any other limb. Xinghua had been trying valiantly not to stare, but it was like having an angel beside her. Their dark coloring did nothing to sway the illusion.

Ransom sighed, bringing her attention back to him as he set down his food.

"He's my partner." He explained, "Or he *was* until earlier this evening. This evening? No, the sun is up, that makes it yesterday night. *Jesus H Christ on a cracker.*"

"Did you not sleep yet?" She narrowed her eyes at him.

"No. After Airius snatched you, I got a call from the Chief about another case I've been working." His eyebrows slid down his face to settle grimly over his eyes, "Long story short, there was a series of kidnappings, I found two of the victims alive, and the piece of work responsible turned out to be my partner."

Xinghua choked on her food and Seriah set his down with a look of concern and surprise so loud she could hear his tone before he spoke a word.

"Hang the fuck on--"

"This *just* happened? Shouldn't you be talking to, like, a councilor or something?"

"Did you fucking just casually deal with that and then come to save us?"

In their panic, they spoke over each other and Xinghua could see Ransom trying to untangle the statements from each other.

"There were a few hours between that and finding you. And I went for backup, so I didn't just ride in while emotionally compromised."

"That is in *no* way what I'm concerned about you crazy old bastard, but that's even more impressive." Xinghua set aside her food as well and hugged Ransom instead, "*What the fuck Richard?* Are *you* okay?"

"Okay? No. Probably not for a while. But, I'm reminding my-self that there are two little boys who survived today, because of me. We got a dangerous man off the streets. You're not in harm's way anymore. There are plenty of wins there."

He frowned then continued, "Although, Terry isn't a *man*, exactly. Turns out, he's a werewolf. His, uh, friend? Packmate? Something. According to him, they were the one who bit *me.*"

Xinghua stared at him, unable to think of a satisfactory response to that.

He pinched his eyes closed and shook his head, "It's been a long fucking night."

"Cheers to that." Seriah raised his beer.

"Rich, buddy, once this is over, we're taking you to a spa or something."

"I won't even fight you about that." Ransom's eyes slid closed and he let out a puff of laughter, "It's been a long time since I've had a week like this one."

"You've had another week where you were turned into a werewolf, made privy to the supernatural world, betrayed by a partner, and caught up in a Machiavellian plot to start an interspecies class war all within like 72 hrs of each other before?"

"I've served two tours overseas, so, nearly." Ransom shrugged. "And I've been on the NYPD for twenty years."

Xinghua could only imagine the look on her face, based on the feeling of sheer horror that welled up from the bottom of her soul. He cracked open an eye, his lips twitching up into the slightest of smiles.

"Rich, don't take this the wrong way, but you are *fucking worrying* some times."

"I think so too from time to time." He closed his eye and folded his hands over his stomach, "Regardless, this week has been a little much, even for a crazy old bastard like me."

"I feel you on that, at least." Seriah picked his food back up.

"I would imagine you do. Do you...want to talk about it?"

"Kinda. I've more or less been keeping myself sane for a while by imagining getting to talk about it." Seriah poked around at his food, "I imagined it a little less Columbo and a little more Dateline though, no offense."

"None taken, I'm no Barbara Walters."

Seriah smiled a little at the joke before taking a deep, slow breath.

"So, as best I can tell, he had me for three months." He began, "Back in August he called me after hours to ask me something about the plant we were studying, I don't even remember what it was now. It sounded like he had an accident while we were talking, and me being an idiot, I went to go check on him instead of just calling an ambulance or something. It was a trap, of course. When I got there he was nowhere to be seen, the lab was perfect like it always was. I stood there and *looked for him* for a full minute before he got me. Sedative straight to the thigh, I was out cold before I even saw him.

"I didn't actually know it *was* him for a while. I wasn't really left unmedicated for long in the early days. I'd be in and out of consciousness for what felt like days at a time. It wasn't until these," He fluttered his wings, "Started growing in that that stopped."

"So they *grew* in?" Ransom frowned.

"Mmmhmm, yep." Seriah nibbled his lip, "My entire torso had to rebuild itself to be able to carry them. Hurt like *hell.*"

"Not... uh, to be insensitive, but do you know how that happened?" Xinghua winced, "The wings growing in, I mean."

"No, it's okay. This... isn't something you see every day." Seriah sat up a little straighter, "I have a pretty good guess, based on what we were working on last."

He paused to take a big bite of his dinner.

"*Technically* I'm just an intern, and *normally* we work on commercial stuff. Vaccines, gene sequencing, hell during grant season we even help out with those family DNA test packets. Easy stuff. But there's this...pet project he's been working on for a few years now."

"It wouldn't happen to be called HSV1, would it?" Xinghua asked softly.

"How... do you know that name?" Seriah's eyes widened.

"I found a file about it on Tom's desk the day before yesterday." Xinghua explained, "That's why I found you, we were looking for more information about it."

"Well, you found it." Seriah sighed, deflating, "I... sort of helped him research it."

Ransom met her eyes for a moment before putting his hand over Seriah's arm.

"I didn't think he'd... when we tested it on the rats it-- it wasn't ready for human trials *at all."* Seriah shivered, "The effects were wildly unpredictable, and the virus itself is so *aggressive* it killed more than half of its hosts, and the rest developed symptoms similar to rabies. Some of the ones that died *came back,* and those ones were *never* the same."

"Sooooo, they were basically vampires?" Xinghua raised her brows in Seriah's direction.

"How di--?! Oh, right. Uh, yeah. That's... yeah they were, *sort of.* But like with the rabid ones they showed very little if any sentience. The first few batches all had one of those three. But eventually Tom started pulling more late nights...and we started getting...*other* side effects" Seriah glanced back at his wings, "I genuinely am at a fucking loss as to how a virus could do something like this, but there's always been a factor to this thing that's outside of the variables that we can account for."

"That'd be the magic." Xinghua weighed in.

"Magic?? Of course! *Why not?!"* He fidgeted with his pant leg as his voice hitched higher, "There's always been a wild card factor to this thing. In the rat trials, we had rats double in size, become nearly invisible like chameleons, grow additional limbs, all *kinds* of shit. And in me, *this* happened."

"I'm pretty sure you got magic whammied too." Xinghua held up a hand, trying to focus for a moment, "I was tripping balls earlier, but I could have *sworn* I saw you turn into a panther."

"No, that happened." Seriah bit his lip again when Ransom turned a look towards him, "I don't know how or why it works, and I can't really do it all that often because it fucks me up and I get stuck one way or the other for longer and longer, but I can, uh, shapeshift now? I know that sounds crazy to have come out of a freaking *virus* but--"

"I'm a recently turned werewolf, remember, I can't even *begin* to tell you you're crazy." Ransom patted his shoulder then took his hand back, "We're in similar boats there. Crazy virus, almost died, now I can turn into a giant wolf. Weird ass week."

Seriah looked like he was going to ask something but held himself back.

"Yeah, *weird ass week*, man."

"So if these are all the... hiccups of HSV1, what's he *trying* to do with it?" Xinghua asked, "I could barely make heads or tails of that file, to be honest. Tom's handwriting is shit, and half of it's in German and then the other half is in medical-ese."

"Induce immortality." Seriah muttered, like he couldn't quite bear to say it any louder.

"Excuse me?" Ransom frowned.

"He fucking what? Why?!"

Seriah winced and set his food back down again, "On paper, he's trying to use it to cure diseases that have no other cure, but the way he's trying to get it to *do* that is by inducing immortality in humans."

Xinghua couldn't tack down one single thought, her mind racing from idea to idea before she could properly suss out even one of them.

"Well *shit.*" Ransom breathed.

"But it doesn't really *do* that, does it? If you take it you're more likely to just die." She frowned, "Why would he say he's close to done with it, if it's still that volatile?"

Seriah shrugged, "Beats me. You know almost as much as I do now, sans the incredibly boring virology details."

Xinghua frowned into her bite of curry, the question of why chasing itself around in circles around her head. She was sure she had to be missing something, something big, and it was going to eat at her until she found it.

Vega-Polvo arrived back an hour or so before Arcana woke up, and Arcana woke up about two hours before McKnight did. By the time the blonde crawled out of his rooms, the entire group had gotten acquainted.

"So, this council thing," Arcana edged as McKnight poured himself a cup of coffee, "I'm gonna guess this is a no humans allowed kind of deal?"

"Mmm, you guess right. Even magical humans such as yourself. The only humans permitted are donors and Gliders, though that's obligatory."

"Gliders?"

"Tell you when you're older, sweetie." McKnight patted her chubby cheek affectionately, "Anyway it shouldn't take me long. Just a quick sesh' to appraise them of the situation and see what they would like to do about it."

"You're going on your *own?*" Xinghua shot him a disbelieving look, "That's a *terrible* idea, we're going with you."

McKnight raised his eyebrows, earning himself an eye roll in exchange.

"If he wasn't before, he's definitely watching us now." She elaborated, "He knew exactly what I was up to back at his office, and I'm sure he either followed us here or planted a tracker on me, or *something*. I *know* he went through my phone, he deleted every contact but himself. None of us should go *anywhere* alone."

McKnight looked less than pleased, but she had a point and he didn't argue.

"Alright, *fine,* group field trip it is."

* * * *

Richard didn't know what he'd been expecting, but the stereotypical enormous mansion with monogrammed gates probably should have been on that list. He'd thought that perhaps, given that this was the modern age a vampire coven wouldn't seem quite so much like...well a vampire coven. If he'd seen this place without context he still would have idly thought there were vampires living here.

It was almost funny.

"Before we go in, ground rules." McKnight began, "Vampires are not terribly fond of werewolves, so Rich if you would avoid drawing as much attention to yourself as possible, that would be lovely. Xinghua, as much as I love you my dear and *I* value your personality, do try to keep the sass to a minimum. The council is very old fashioned and your... mannerisms might cause more harm than good."

Xinghua folded her arms peevishly and Ransom sighed. Somehow he'd thought this might be the case.

"I'll be as good as I can be, but I draw the line at taking shit from crusty ass old dudes." She informed him, "And if they're mean to Rich I'm gonna say something."

Ransom put a hand on the top of her head to gentle her, "I appreciate that, but there's no need. I'm a big boy, Xinghua, I can handle it."

She turned her glare up at him, *"Nuh uh.* I know that's code for 'suffering in silence.' You've been nothing but amazing and I'm not gonna let you get shit on for *existing* just because some self important assholes think they're hot shit. Either they act civil or they're setting served a big bowl of 'Fuck Off' flakes."

Her expression was pulled into something more forceful than he was sure he'd seen on her. The sharpness of her features made much more sense drawn together with that kind of ferocity. It was like he was seeing the person that face truly belonged to for the first time, and she was *vicious.*

He caught McKnight's shoulders tensing just a fraction.

"Let's just hope everyone is in a better mood than we are, hm?"

With that he turned on his heel and headed toward the mansion.

Richard followed with Xinghua striding like a rolling wildfire at his side.

He was glad they had a guide, as the mansion was even larger than it looked from the outside. There seemed to be endless staircases and rooms with twisting hallways that never led to any common areas. Richard definitely would have gotten lost if he'd had to try to navigate, but McKnight seemed to know just where he was going.

He led them to a room which was debatably one of the smaller ones the mansion boasted. Like a.... parlor! *That's* what those kinds of small meeting rooms were called.

Inside there were already several other figures, none of which Richard recognized of course.

One was a tall man with skin as dark as the night sky and eyes to match. Unlike Xinghua and Frost, he wasn't translucent. If anything he seemed *more* solid than the rest of the room around him, like moving obsidian. He only turned his head to look over at them but the movement was so achingly graceful Ransom would have known he wasn't human just at a glance. His features were sharp but bold, handsome in a way that belonged in paintings or on a runway.

Beside him was a significantly smaller man, or rather, boy, as he didn't look to be much older than his late teens or early twenties. Of course that was probably inaccurate given that this was a vampire coven. But his eyes glittered with amusement and fascination in equal measures, lending him a more youthful air. Richard noted that he seemed to have heterochromia, one eye being bright green while the other was an odd shade of yellow. His skin was pale as death, and like his companion his movements were unnaturally graceful.

Then there was the stately woman sitting in the chair across from the door, staring them down from over a pair of oval glasses. She looked at ease, as though she owned the entire room. She reminded Richard of a big cat, unconcerned and deadly. Her wavy hair was left down, falling like a black waterfall around her uncovered shoulders. She was wearing an evening gown, dripping with valuable gems and jewels, a big blue stone nestled at the hollow of her throat, making her skin seem that much more pale. She smiled at him when they made eye contact, but there was nothing warm or inviting about the expression.

She was the first to move.

"Hello, Leland, my dear, it's so good to see you." She addressed McKnight, swaying over to him to kiss each of his cheeks in turn, "It's a shame it always seems to be under these circumstances."

"Indeed, Maria." McKnight responded with a fang filled smile that made Richard tense ever so slightly, "We really should do brunch one of these days instead."

The woman, Maria, laughed delicately as another person slipped quietly into the room. To Ransom's surprise, she looked relatively ordinary. If not for the vampire grace, he probably wouldn't have spared her a second look. She was dressed plainly in a gray long sleeve shirt and jeans, her short blonde hair styled away from her soft face. She took a seat at the back of the room without a word to any of them. The only one to acknowledge her was the tall vampire and she seemed nervous to even be nodded to.

The young looking boy hopped to his feet, drawing Ransom's attention back to him.

"Well, I for one, am *ecstatic.*" He chirped in a voice that sounded like it had just barely finished dropping, "We've been waiting for this for, what, fifty years now?"

The taller man rolled his dark eyes and sent the boy a withering look.

The boy stuck his tongue out at the other and Richard felt Xinghua snicker beneath his hands, drawing his attention their way.

"You must be Xinghua." The boy said with all the enthusiasm of the young man he appeared to be, "I've wanted to meet you *forever.* Were you really turned as a *kid?"*

Xinghua opened her mouth and before her words could even begin, he was standing in front of her, practically vibrating on his toes. To her credit, she hardly flinched.

"I was." She said a little shortly.

He looked her over faster than Richard could really follow, taking one of her hands into his and looking it over for...something.

"Vexx." McKnight scolded, "Manners. She is a *guest* here, *not* a curio."

The vampire pursed his lips but didn't drop Xinghua's hand.

"Would you please tell me about how that happened?"

Xinghua narrowed her eyes in a look Ransom now recognized meant he should expect a snarky quip.

"I think there's more pressing matters currently at hand." She said instead, surprising Richard and McKnight as well if his brief expression was any indication.

Vexx smiled at her like a chastised kid, "Right."

"An excellent point." Maria interceded, "You brought us here over the girl's sire, yes?"

"Yes," McKnight nodded, looking grateful to be back on task, "Earlier today, Xinghua was taken captive by him. By her description he has broken one of our most sacred laws. He is keeping vampires captive and draining their blood for his own purposes."

"Oh? That is quite the serious accusation." Maria's expression shifted to become even more predatory, "What proof do you offer beyond her word?"

Xinghua made eye contact with McKnight.

"I don't have any. He wiped my phone of the conversation I had recorded on it." Xinghua said softly, "But I can offer my own memories to you as proof."

Maria asked, "Memories can be altered."

"I'm well aware," Xinghua's posture stiffened, "But that ability leaves a trace in the iris of its victim. You're free to check me over for it."

Maria tilted her head, her own eyes narrowing at Xinghua, "That power and its wielder were lost to us quite some time ago. How did you come to know of it?"

"Tom has used it on me in the past." She admitted, "I'm sure he's got the vampire that gift belongs to somewhere in that warehouse of his. Which would be why none of you have seen her in a while"

The tallest vampire glanced at the other two in well concealed alarm.

"Warehouse?" He asked in a low voice like velveteen chocolate, a light accent Ransom didn't recognize tinting his words.

Xinghua nodded, "The place he was keeping me in was a warehouse. And it was *full* of other vampires."

Maria stood once again and crossed the room to stand in front of Xinghua. Richard couldn't quite resist the urge to pull her closer to his chest. The woman was dangerous and every single instinct he had shouted to keep Xinghua away from her.

Maria's gaze flicked over to him, regarding him as though he were little more than a gnat.

"Tell your pet to relax, I'm not going to harm you."

Xinghua's body tensed and Richard could *feel* the retort working its way up through her. He gently squeezed her again, trying to convey that it was alright. He'd been called far worse over the years.

"He's not my *emotional support werewolf* or some shit, thank you very much." She said anyway, "And I'm not going to *tell him* shit. He's right in front of you, if you've got that much of a problem, you can talk to him yourself."

Richard wanted to shake her sometimes.

"Oh?" Maria's deep, dark eyes flashed, "Aren't you a *bold* little creature."

She sounded equal parts amused and annoyed, her expression conveying much the same.

"Its been a long fucking week and I don't really want to stand here and listen to someone disrespect my best friend." She replied, meeting Maria's gaze head on. *"Ma'am."*

"Hmm." The woman reached her hand out for Xinghua, clearly expecting Xinghua to give her her own hand, "Don't lose that fire, it will serve you well over the years. Though I would caution you to be more selective with its application."

Xinghua presented her hand to the woman and Richard had to fight himself to keep from pulling her back again.

"I'll keep that in mind."

Maria nearly smiled at that, Richard could see the sides of her lips twitching upwards. But rather than responding, she bit into the meat of Xinghua's hand.

Xinghua's hand flew up to cover her mouth, but not quite in time to muffle the little noise she made. Richard immediately opted to pretend he hadn't heard that.

Maria didn't spend long drawing blood from Xinghua, pulling back scant seconds after she started. The wound closed before she opened her eyes. Richard noticed with mild surprise that they were white now, rather than the deep brown they'd been.

"Oh." She breathed, taking a step back.

Instantly the tallest vampire was there beside her, supporting her. Vexx and McKnight were watching with equal but opposite types of tension, anxious and anticipatory in kind. The blonde in the corner Richard had mostly forgotten about finally moved, taking Vexx's hand in her own. The boy gave her a reassuring smile that she did not return.

"The memory has not been tampered with." Maria confirmed, closing her eyes, "And it is quite damning. But the girl was generous in her supposition that he was breaking only *one* law."

"Oooooh?" Vexx smiled, "What has our naughty mister Airius been up to?"

"There is another in this memory, someone called 'Seriah'. It would seem Thomas has been conducting experiments with our venom, and what was once human is no longer. Nor is he one of our kind. Something *new.*"

When Maria opened her eyes they were brown once again.

"When we are finished dealing with Thomas, I would like to meet this Seriah."

"Are you going to try to fuck with him?" Xinghua bristled.

"That depends entirely on him." Maria turned to the tall vampire at her shoulder, "Xerxes, gather your Sanguinists. We will need to strike quickly, the longer we wait the longer he has to move his captives."

The tall vampire, Xerxes, nodded and ceded the room. Richard couldn't help but wonder if Xerxes was a name sake or if he was actually looking at an ancient Persian king.

"Vexx, darling, you will take point at his other location. Take whomever you think will be best suited to the task."

Vexx lit up, letting go of the blonde's hand to clap his hands eagerly, "Oooh I can't wait! I hope he's where I'm at, I want to rip his spine out through his nose~!"

The boy rushed from the room, practically skipping. Good riddance, he gave Richard the creeps.

"Angela, be a dear and make sure he actually does as he's told." Maria turned ever so slightly to the blonde, "You know how he is when he's excited about something. The last thing we need is a repeat of the Inquisition."

Angela nodded and left without a word.

"Leland," Maria turned next to McKnight, "You know him better than we do. Where would you place yourself?"

"I think it's unlikely he'll be at the warehouse." McKnight mused, "He thinks he's untouchable, therefore he'll be in the most open place possible."

"His office."

"His office." McKnight nodded, "I've waited for *years* for this, if you don't mind I'd like to watch him receive his dues."

Maria patted his shoulder, "Of course. And you?"

She directed a glance at Xinghua.

Richard felt her shiver, her shoulders bunching up towards her ears. He ran a soothing hand over her back, watching as she made the effort to calm down.

"To tell you the truth I don't want to be anywhere near him. He's been...he's been doing some really fucked up shit to me for a while. But I don't think I'm going to be able to accept that it's over if I'm not there to see him get brought down." She threaded her fingers through Richard's. They were so very small compared to his own.

"That is understandable." Maria nodded, "Then if you'll follow me, I have something to give you."

Xinghua frowned but ultimately nodded and Maria turned and left the room without a glance back, expecting to be followed.

"She gives *wonderful* gifts, don't be nervous." McKnight encouraged.

"Right, then I'll be right back." Xinghua patted Richard's arm, jogging after Maria.

He wanted to follow her, his instincts raged at him to, but he hadn't been asked so with great difficulty he stayed put.

"She'll be fine." McKnight strode over to massage Richard's tense shoulders, "I'd trust Maria with my life at this point. Actually I believe I *have.* Why, there was a time during the Cold War..."

*   *   *   *

To Xinghua's surprise, Maria had waited for her outside the door.

She'd only known her for a few minutes but already the older woman didn't seem the type to wait for much of anything. Actually, she seemed like the kind of cutthroat bitch that kept lesser bitches on their toes with the business end of a whip. There was just something in the way she walked that said she would snap a man in half as soon as look at one.

Normally Xinghua would be *into* that, but her nerves were frayed at best and if anything it just put her even more on edge.

Maria didn't say a word as she led them through the labyrinth that was the mansion, and for once Xinghua wasn't overly eager to break the silence either. Actually, since her mind had become her own again, she didn't feel the need to fill silences the way she had before. That craving for attention and validation hadn't gone *away* per se, but it had become a lot less all consuming.

"Here we are." Maria stated, stopping in front of a tall, surprisingly ornate iron door.

She pushed it open, revealing a floor to ceiling armory inside. It was filled with everything from swords and bows to guns and shields. She was surprised they *had* such a room, much less that Maria had taken her to it.

Maria strode into the armory without waiting for Xinghua to get her shit together.

"Choose anything you'd like and it's yours. But choose wisely, I have a very distinct feeling your Thomas won't be coming quietly."

"Uh, thanks?" She stepped into the armory after her, "But can I ask why..?"

Maria ran a hand over one of the spears secured to the wall.

"There isn't a woman alive or undead who doesn't know the anger that you're feeling right now." Maria began, "Or the feeling of helplessness it stems from."

Xinghua froze with her hand outstretched towards a flail.

"I think," She continued, "That one of the best cures for that feeling is personal agency. And one of the best methods to gain *that* is to know you can defend yourself should it come down to it."

She took a matte black gladius from the wall in front of her and spun it over her hand deftly.

"It's no substitute for true emotional healing, of course, but it is a great first step." She held the sword out to Xinghua, hilt first.

Xinghua took the blade without a word, surprised to find how comfortably it fit in her hand.

"You are *not* helpless, and you are *not* a plaything." Maria said the words with such conviction even the critical voice that lived in the back of Xinghua's head had nothing to say, "What you *are* is your own decision to make and no one else's."

There was no pity in her tone, no sympathy either. She wasn't trying to make Xinghua feel better, she was saying this because she saw it as fact.

Xinghua clenched the hilt of the sword tighter in her hand, swallowing back the swell of emotion rising in the back of her throat.

"Thanks." She said with gravity, forcing her voice to stay steady, "I think I needed to hear that."

When she looked up at Maria, she was smiling. She still looked like she not only could, but *would* bite the throat out of anyone who crossed her, but Xinghua could see the resolve behind the expression. She could feel its twin growing in her own belly.

"Hurry and choose your weapon, we still have a raid to run."

"I like this one." She held up the small sword, flicking her wrist to slash through the air with ease, "We match."

Maria inclined her head, imperiousness spreading across her features like a well worn ensemble.

"That you do."

*   *   *   *

If Xinghua had had a pulse, she was sure she would have been able to feel it through every inch of her body. She couldn't rightly tell if she was excited or terrified as the shape of Clinestra Pharmaceuticals came into view.

She was definitely far beyond nervous, pushed into a level of hyper-awareness she couldn't explain and could barely stomach. It was only Ransom's presence by her side that kept her from vibrating out of her own skin.

While they'd been driving, Xinghua had messaged Trish and Ziggy, letting them know what the plan was. They'd agreed to shadow the warehouse team and let her know how it went. In the event of an emergency, Ziggy's portaling ability might just make the difference. She didn't like not being beside them, but the idea of them anywhere near Tom was worse.

When they arrived, Xinghua's nerves kicked into high gear at finding the lobby all but abandoned. It was never *busy* this late at night, but there was usually at least the night guard at the front desk. But the only soul to be seen was Seriah who looked to have arrived just before them.

"Where is everyone?" Xinghua asked as the group approached him.

"Dunno." Seriah replied, his expression pinched, "There was no one there when I got here."

Vexx held up a hand, a surprisingly serious expression etched into his cherubic features.

"Listen." He whispered.

Xinghua froze in place, shutting her eyes and forcing herself to push her senses out into the room.

She didn't hear anything at first, not so much as a single heartbeat on their floor. But the harder she focused, the more she was able to hear... *something.* It sounded like scratching and clicking, insect legs scratching against plastic..

"What is that?" She hissed.

Vexx's eyes glowed, and Xinghua briefly noticed that the ring he wore on his left hand also began to glow faintly. His eyes grew wide.

"We shou--"

Behind them security doors slammed down in front of the rotating glass doors they'd come in through, as well as over every window, sealing off any possible exits. Xinghua didn't have to check to know they were made of the same metal Tom has used at his warehouse.

"Hello, esteemed intruders." Came Tom's voice over the building's PA system, *"I would ask what brings you here today, but I think we're quite past beating around the bush."*

"Then you know we're here to take you in." Ransom sneered.

*"I know you're here to **try.**"* Tom's voice purred back at him, *"But I can assure you, that won't be happening."*

The noise Xinghua had been hearing grew louder. Now it sounded more like a racoon caught in someone's attic. She drew her sword from its sheath on her hip.

"You see, today is a very special day for me. In time I think everyone will agree with that sentiment, actually. I'm afraid I simply can't allow you to spoil my fun." Tom's tone was far more jovial than Xinghua was used to hearing it, almost like it was on the rare occasion he actually managed to get drunk.

The scratching noises sounded as if they were directly on top of them, and Xinghua found herself dearly wishing not to find out what was making them.

"Do give my regards to Zero when you see her."

Vexx shouted something that Xinghua couldn't make out over the sound of the ceiling caving in.

Without thinking she threw herself at Ransom, pushing him to one of the outer edges of the room, to safety. She only had half a moment to feel relieved before something fell on her instead.

It wasn't enough to crush her, though it had knocked her legs out from under her. Her vision swam a little and she could have sworn the chuck of ceiling that had fallen on her was… *writhing.*

She only caught a glimpse of graying, warped skin before whatever it was was ripped from her by a pale hand covered in ice.

"On your feet, Xinghua." Frost's voice growled, his figure sliding in front of her.

She obeyed without a second thought, her head whipping around to assess the room. There were chunks of plaster all over the ground, and dozens upon dozens of *creatures* climbing out of the wreckage. They were humanoid, but their skin was gray and leathery, their round, glassy eyes glowing a misty white. Their hands flexed, and a few of them had odd… auras surrounding them.

"Damn him." Frost snarled under his breath.

"Formation Alpha!" Vexx's voice cried out, catching her attention.

The boy had a cut bleeding from his forehead into his eye, and a snarl on his mouth. He seemed much less like the jovial kid she'd met and much more like the bloodthirsty immortal he truly was.

The group of vampires he'd brought closed in on him, forming a wall of claws and snarling fangs. From within their formation Xinghua saw black tendrils lashing up into the air, like some sort of ink monster had spawned from within the ring.

"Come and get me!" Vexx's voice rang out, though there was an oddness to it, like there were two of him speaking at once.

Xinghua didn't have time to watch the result, as several of the creatures ran at she and Frost.

She didn't hesitate to strike out with her sword, grateful that she'd chosen a weapon that had a relatively low learning curve. She cut down the first creature to reach her with relative ease, but two more took its place without pause. She deflected one set claws by the grace of sheer reactionary instinct, missing the second set which tore into her forearm. She hissed, trying to put some space between herself and the creatures, but they were surrounding her on all sides.

Ice crept up her hands, over her cut up forearms and to her shoulders. Instinctive panic seized her chest hard enough that she didn't dodge the next creature that plowed into her. She went down with a yelp, flailing as she tried to push away both the creature and the ice on her limbs.

It was alarming how strong they were, much more than their emaciated bodies would suggest they should be. The one that had attacked her, much to Xinghua's horror, was also crackling with enough electricity to make her drop her sword.

The fear pounding through her only seemed to make more and more ice spill out from her fingertips until to her surprise, the creature she was grappling with was frozen solid by it. She shoved it once again and it fractured into glittering pieces.

"Oh. *Fuck.*" She breathed, shaking her hands to try to clear both the ice and the chunky bits of creature caught between her fingers.

She felt around for her sword frantically, rolling to her feet just in time to miss another creature leaping onto the spot she'd just been. Another lash of ice leapt from her hands to pierce the creature's chest before it could double back on her.

Blind panic was *not* making this any easier. Despite the dread nestled bone deep in her, she forced herself not to flinch away from the ice creeping up her neck. Reminding herself that it was her own power did nothing to calm her, but it did give her something to cling to at the very least.

She heard a snarl from behind her and whirled around, hands thrust forward.

An arc of ice leapt forward from her open palms, piercing through the creature behind her, slamming it up against the far wall.

"There you go!" Frost's voice growled triumphantly from beside her, followed by a muffled snapping sound.

She didn't have time to focus on the commendation as another three creatures rushed her from all sides.

Jesus tap-dancing Christ, where had Tom *gotten* all of these damn things?

Xinghua dove between their legs, toward where her sword had fallen. This time she actually managed to grab the thing, spinning on her knees to slice it through the creature's legs. She didn't expect for the move to work given that she'd pulled it straight from a movie, and it didn't. She only managed to put shallow cuts in their hides, given that she was too far away for the short range of her weapon.

She saw a fluttering of feathers out of the corner of her eye that she briefly hoped was Seriah before a wall of fur and muscle blocked her view.

"Ransom!" She jumped to her feet, happy to see him in all his lupine glory, "Mind if I hitch a ride?"

He struck, biting one of the creatures in half with his powerful jaw. It gave Xinghua an opening to climb on his back, which she did without hesitation. It was tricky to do while fending off the other two creatures and also not accidentally freezing him. She killed one by accident as it tripped over the corpse of another, impaling itself on her sword.

"Can you get us upstairs?" She asked, swinging her now iced over sword at the third creature. She missed the first time and the second time as well, resorting to kicking it when it got close enough.

Ransom huffed, tossing his head as if to say something sassy. Or maybe just 'Hold on' as he bolted for the stairwell seconds later. She had to bury her fingers in his fur to keep from flying off. It took all of her concentration to keep upright and keep the ice restrained to her hands.

Later on, if they made it out of this, she was going to tease Ransom for being such a pain in the ass to ride.

Ransom made it up the first flight of stairs with little trouble, Xinghua was not at all surprised to find that the floor above them was filled with yet more of the creatures. There were *dozens* of them flooding the halls. As fast as Ransom was they still clutched at his fur, attempting to pull him down into their snarling pit.

Xinghua kicked and slashed at the clingers in an attempt to dislodge them. She wasn't sure enough of herself to try to ice the ones already on Ransom, but wished she could summon spires of ice to pin the creatures ahead of them. To her shock, icy stalagmites shot out of the ground to do exactly that.

"Ha!" She crowed, "Get *rekt* scrub! Anxiety ice ftw!"

Ransom made a snorting sort of sound and if he hadn't bounced off a wall she would have been tempted to flick his ear. As it was the best she could do was hold on for dear life.

"You remember where his office is?"

He stomped down on a creature and shook his head.

"Top floor, second door on the left!" She cut down a pair of creatures coming at them from behind, "He's got a lead, but if he's trying to run we should still be able to cut him off!"

Ransom didn't need any more prompting than that. He raced for the next staircase, hardly pausing to deal with the creatures rushing toward them.

Xinghua focused on crowd control, doing her best to use the ice to keep the creatures as far away from them as possible. It felt like trying to paint the Mona Lisa while blindfolded, and she was glad she had her sword for closer calls.

To her surprise there were less and less of them the further they got up the building, until, on the top floor, there were seemingly none.

Xinghua didn't relax for a moment. She kept her hands outstretched, her eyes flickering around nervously as she kept an eye out for threats.

The only thing she saw was the open door to Tom's office.

"I don't like this." She muttered under her breath.

Ransom growled back, cautiously padding over to the door.

"Come in." Tom's voice called from within.

The sinking feeling in her stomach from earlier returned in full force.

Xinghua slid from Ransom's back and walked beside him instead, wanting to have full mobility for whatever it was Tom was planning. She crept into the room with her sword clutched tightly in one hand, the other ready to freeze anything that got too close.

Tom was sitting at his desk, his feet propped up on it, with a glass of wine in one hand, seemingly unbothered by the veritable war going on below them. He greeted them with an amiable smile, gesturing them forward.

"I'm not surprised that you're the ones to have made it up here. Although I did think Seriah would be with you." He said conversationally.

"Cut the shit," She snarled back, "Put your hands on your head and stand up from the desk."

"Ooh, you *have* been spending a considerable amount of time with the Detective. I'm assuming that's who your fuzzy companion here is?" Tom sipped his drink, making no move to stand.

"I'm not gonna ask you again."

Tom arched an eyebrow at her, his smirk twisting up ever so slightly more.

"And if I refuse? What will you do, Xinghua?" He set his glass down and folded his hands over his lap, "I'm nearly a century your senior, you know you can't *force* me to do anything."

"Maybe I can't, but there's a whole coven of vampires down there out for your blood." She shrugged, "You're not getting out of this building under your own power, so why not make it easy?"

He laughed, one of his rare genuine laughs and Xinghua wanted to pretend it didn't make her gut twist into knots. He reached for a remote she hadn't noticed on his desk and pressed a button, turning on the TV mounted into the wall behind him. She nearly collapsed at what she saw.

The lobby looked like a slaughterhouse. There were arms, legs and various other *chunks* strewn across nearly every inch of the floor, like some sort of grotesque carpeting. She recognized the heads of several of the coven's vampires. In fact the longer she looked, the more of them she saw. There were only two bodies still upright and fighting.

Seriah and Frost.

One of Seriah's wings was hanging at an awkward angle and Frost was missing a hand. They were losing ground and it seemed like there were still just as many creatures as they'd started with. They'd be overwhelmed in minutes at this rate.

"Would you care to rethink that?" He asked smugly.

She forced the shock and fear down deep into her belly, "There are others."

"The ones you sent to my warehouse? I'm afraid they will have met a similar fate." Tom shrugged, "Those that manage to survive will be rather occupied soon anyhow."

Xinghua clenched her hand around her sword and took up a fighting stance, "Then I guess this is just going to be us then. I'll be honest, I was kind of hoping for this."

Tom stared at her for a moment, and Xinghua felt as though his amaranthine eyes were picking her apart, breaking her down to her individual elements.

"If you're sure. But first, I have to know, what exactly *are* you doing this for, Xinghua? I've been nothing but good to you."

The sincerity in his voice was like a slap in the face. She was so flabbergasted she nearly dropped her fighting stance. Not that it mattered too much, he still had yet to move so much as an inch.

"Good to-- you *lied to me!* For *years!*" She shouted, "You've been fucking with my memories, and killing girls who look like me, and you *took* my *Sire!* That's not even touching this whole virus bullshit!"

Tom's expression pinched.

"I don't relish what I did to my brother." He said, his eyebrows pulling together, "But it had to be done. And if I hadn't wiped your memories they only would have hurt you. I was trying to *take care of you,* Xinghua. You were too young, too new to this life to be alone. I thought perhaps you might not want to experience orphanhood a *second* time.”

She felt the words almost as if a blow directly to her chest.

“As for my virus, I’m afraid you’re already far too late.”

Her eyes widened and she caught the corner of his mouth lift again.

“Did you not know?” The amusement had chased the melancholy from his voice again, “Oh dear you don’t.”

“Know what?”

Tom reached for his remote again and changed the channel from gore on the CCTVs to a standard channel which appeared to be running an advertisement.

It boasted a new miracle serum which could reverse and suspend the effects of aging.

As she watched, the woman pedaling the product called an audience member up from the crowd. A hobbled little old man came forth, his gait slow and painful. He didn’t hurry, though he did seem excited.

Xinghua watched with dawning horror as the woman explained the effects of this miracle drug that she already knew entirely too well. The old man sat down eagerly and a nurse came forward to administer the injection as the woman continued to talk the thing up to the crowd.

Seconds after the injection was given, the woman stepped out of the way as the little old man gasped. He jerked, making a noise not of pain but of relief as his knobby joints filled back in with cartilage and supple flesh. The audience murmured among themselves as the clock visibly rolled back on the man, erasing every trace of aging but for his gray hair.

The woman selling the product seemed quite surprised as well as the now young man stood up to his full height and began to weep.

The screen flashed a number to call, a price that was too cheap for the miracle the drug promised, and offered a deal for a second dose with purchase of the first for....

Xinghua had stopped listening.

"The preorders arrived earlier this evening." Tom clicked off the TV, "Today is the *official* launch day, and already we've sold out. Selling immortality for twenty dollars a vial is quite the offer. Even skeptics will be tempted to try it for that price."

"You..." Her lips felt numb.

"Do you remember last week, the night I took you out? I *told* you we were celebrating." Tom took another sip of his wine, grinning into the glass, "You see Xinghua, there was never any risk of you pulling off this little coup d'état. As fun as it's been to watch you struggle and chase your tail, it was over before it started."

She felt cold, numb and so very horrified.

"Soon we'll be living through the collapse of human society as we know it." Tom said with distinct relish in his voice, "And from it's ashes I will rebuild a new world to my liking."

Xinghua couldn't stop herself from leaping at Tom, she'd heard enough. She might not be able to stop him, she might not be able to kill him, but she could shut him up at the very least.

Tom caught her by the throat.

He looked disappointed though she didn't have long to consider the expression as in the next instant Ransom was attacking as well.

Tom dodged him as easily as one might dodge an open cabinet door. With brutal efficiency he brought up one leg and kicked Ransom's side hard enough to send him flying.

Straight out the wall of windows.

Xinghua wanted to scream as the werewolf crashed through the glass and out of the highrise, though her throat was still being obstructed by Tom's hand. He sighed as if mildly inconvenienced.

"Hmm, I suppose I'll have to switch offices. Too bad, I enjoyed the view from here."

Xinghua swung her sword, aiming straight at his neck. He blocked it with his forearm, the flesh rippling with what looked like... scales?

"I wanted to share this with you, you know." Tom continued as if she weren't trying to dig her weapon into his skin, "You may not be who I want *most*, but I *do* care for you. Before all this... mutinous-ness I was going to keep you beside me while I brought about my new age."

She hoped she could convey her hatred through eye contact alone.

"But, I suppose indulging in an old fantasy is just as good."

His hand on her neck tightened until she could feel the bones shifting and moving apart. She stabbed her sword at him, to no avail. She tried to wiggle as much as she could, willing ice to stab at him but Tom's grip remained unyielding, his skin unblemished by her efforts.

"Mmm, yes, this is *much* better than any substitute." He purred, "The others didn't fight nearly hard enough. Do you know I've dreamed of this since shortly after Fletcher brought you home? While tormenting you has been entertaining, there's nothing like a little carnal violence don't you think?"

He squeezed tighter and she could feel her skin stretching, her bones moving apart like his grip might just pop her head right off her shoulders. Her eyes bulged in their sockets, her arms felt heavy but she raised her sword regardless of the futility of it.

"Hey fucko!" Trish's voice called out.

A burst of bright energy entirely too similar to sunlight flew at Tom, rupturing on contact with his skin. The places it touched her began to swell and Xinghua hissed as soon as Tom released her throat, instinctively grabbing at his now misshapen flesh.

Xinghua couldn't see the hands dragging her away from Tom, but she'd spent enough time being manhandled by them to know Ziggy's touch when she felt it.

"Hold your breath baby girl." They whispered to her, pulling her further backwards.

Xinghua did as she was told and seconds later she was tumbling through a portal. The last sound she heard before it closed was Tom's frustrated shout.

"Xing? Xing!" Trish's voice greeted her next, adding to the vertigo of changing circumstances so quickly, "Oh my God your neck..."

"Ransom." Xinghua croaked out, "He-- is he...?"

She turned back toward Ziggy, desperate for information.

"I saw him fall right when I was getting Seriah out. I grabbed him but he's...he's not in great shape."

It was then that Xinghua looked around and noticed their surroundings. It wasn't Wreckquiem, and it wasn't any of their homes either. In fact, it looked like... a shipping container?

"Where is he? Where are *we?*"

Ziggy winced, and pointed to the far left corner "He's over there. And we are at the *docks*. After the attack I couldn't waste too much power getting us across the city so I grabbed as many people as I could and opened a portal into this thing. It's a miracle it's plastic, really."

She'd be asking questions about that later, but right then all she wanted to do was check on Ransom.

Ziggy let go of her hand and nodded.

"We can swap stories later" Trish echoed her own thoughts.

She nodded to her as she crawled over to Ransom.

She almost wished she hadn't.

He looked *broken.* His entire form was a bruise, his breathing was labored and shallow, with a watery wheeze at the end of each breath. He was covered in blood, all of it his, from what she could smell. He looked a few minutes from Death's door.

"Fuck." She whispered, "No, no, you don't get to die like this, you son of a bitch. You can't-- you can't just *leave me.*"

She took his hand in hers as gently as she possibly could, feeling tears rolling down her cheeks as he drew in a particularly wet and wobbly breath.

"You said you'd be here if I needed you and *I still need you.* So you can't go yet, okay? You *can't.*" The pleading edge that her voice had taken on hadn't escaped her notice, *"Not yet..."*

She barely noticed Trish sink down beside her, though the presence of her hands hovering above Ransom's chest shook Xinghua out of it a little.

"I'm not the best medical mage in the world, but I've learned some new tricks this week and I think I can help." She said gently, one of her hands beginning to glow a light green, the other pressed against the bottom of the container.

As Xinghua watched, the plastic beneath Trish's hand dissolved, and a sweat broke out across her brow. Her glowing hand shook a little, but the light of it didn't so much as flicker.

Ziggy dropped down on Ransom's other side, their own hands lighting up very faintly as they passed them over him.

"Bless y'all and your healing factor bullshit," Ziggy assessed after a long moment, "His body has already started healing the life threatening damage. With a little help and some rest, he oughta pull through."

Xinghua sagged with relief.

"Thank you." She said with gravity. "Both of you."

"Of course." Trish's hand stopped glowing, and she slumped back against the wall of the container "He's group Dad now."

Which reminded her.

"Where's Frost, did he make it out too?"

Trish winced, "He… might have. But he's not with us. He…wasn't in the room when Zig and I got there."

Xinghua felt her heart sink to the bottom of her feet. She nodded to herself, her fingertips going numb as she struggled not to spiral.

"Right." The word came out as a choked whisper rather than the assertion she'd meant for it to be.

"I'm sor--"

"Don't." The iron she'd been looking for braced the word "Don't, we don't know that he didn't. Vampires are-- we're hard to k-- he's *not*--"

She bit her lip, trying to stem the sobs that wanted to bubble up. This wasn't the time to have a breakdown, there was still more she could do, she was sure.

"I'm going to go back to the coven." She declared, jumping to her feet, "Maria needs to know what happened, we need to figure out our next move."

Before anyone could reply, she was streaking across the container to the door, prying it open with more strength than she really needed to. She nearly ripped the door from its hinges, might have if the sound of sirens hadn't caused her to freeze.

It wasn't an ambulance or even a few cop cars, no, it sounded like a *storm siren*, loud and close by. The longer she listened, the more she realized the sound wasn't one single siren but *hundreds* all shrieking at once.

She darted out from behind the door, glancing around to try to find what could possibly be making a noise like that.

She quickly found her answer.

People were running through the streets like ants in a flood, fleeing without thought or direction, being picked off like fish in a barrel. There were so many *people* that for a moment Xinghua didn't realize that the humans were the aggressors as well as the victims.

A thud slammed into the door of the shipping container, hard enough to nearly wrench it from Xinghua's hands.

Alarmingly quickly, she found herself being clawed at by what appeared to be a human. She tried to shove them off, but the human was far *far* stronger than they should have been. Their eyes were rolling into the back of their head and frothy spit was foaming out from the sides of their mouth as they snapped their teeth at her.

"Jesus!"

Xinghua brought up the hilt of her sword, semi-stunned that she'd managed to keep hold of the thing this entire time, and smacked the human between the eyes hard enough to knock them out cold. She shoved the now unconscious body off of her and slammed the door shut.

Milliseconds later another thud slammed against the container, accompanied by dozens of frenzied screams that sounded anything but human.

"What the hell was that?" Trish's voice called out, tinged with fear.

"The end of the world." Seriah answered morosely, drawing the attention of everyone in the container.

"Explain." A vampire she didn't recognize demanded.

Seriah was staring blankly into the middle distance, looking far older than his years, "He did it. He released HSV1."

Xinghua slumped against the wall of the container. The reality of just how screwed they were was finally settling in.

They were down most of a coven, Ransom was unconscious, Ziggy was all but tapped out, Trish too more than likely, there were a bunch of 'roided up humans everywhere, and Frost was... gone.

They were out of tricks, out of luck, out of *everything*. The only thing left was... her.

*You are **not** helpless.*

"Well," Her voice was thick with emotion and it hurt to speak, she trembled as she pushed herself up to her feet but she did it nonetheless, "Then I guess we're going to need a plan."